SPQR

THE
TRIBUNE'S
CURSE

SPQR

Senatus PopulusQue Romanus

The Senate and People of Rome

Also by
JOHN MADDOX ROBERTS

SPQR Series

The Gabe Treloar Series

SPQR VII

THE TRIBUNE'S CURSE

JOHN MADDOX ROBERTS

THOMAS DUNNE BOOKS
ST. MARTIN'S MINOTAUR
NEW YORK

THOMAS DUNNE BOOKS.
An imprint of St. Martin's Press.

www.minotaurbooks.com

Library of Congress Cataloging-in-Publication Data

Roberts, John Maddox.
    the Tribune's curse: SPQR VII / John Maddox Roberts.—1st. ed.
      p. cm.
  ISBN 0-312-30488-9 (hc)
  ISBN 0-312-30489-7 (pbk)
   1. Metellus, Decius Caecilius (Fictitious character)—Fiction.
  2. Rome—History—Republic, 265–30 B.C.—Fiction. 3. Private investi-
gators—Rome—Fiction. I. Title: SPQR 7. II. Title: Tribune's curse.
III. Title.

PS3568.O23874 S68 2003
813'.54—dc21   2002032509

First St. Martin's Griffin Edition: April 2004

10 9 8 7 6 5 4 3 2 1

For Susan Shortt
For years of friendship and good conversation

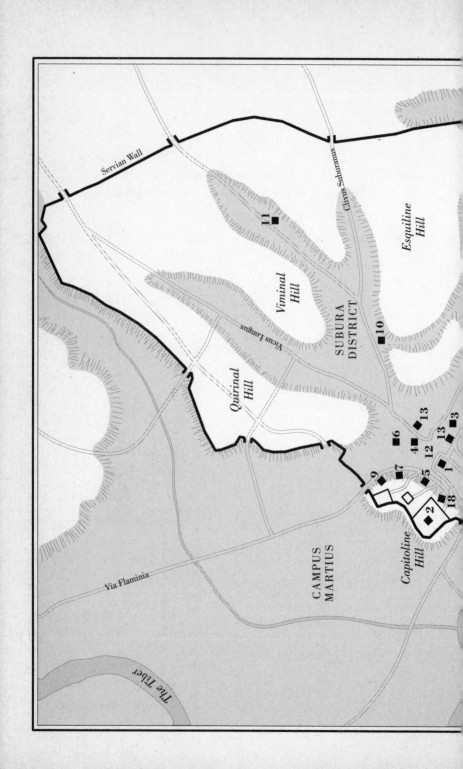

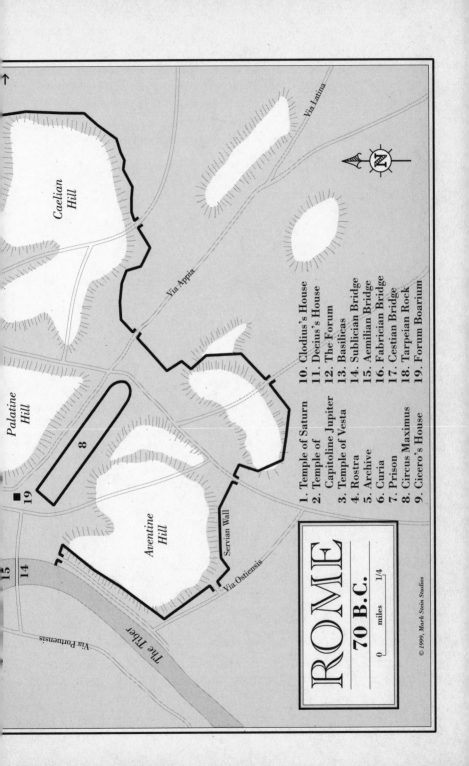

ROME

70 B.C.

0   miles   1/4

© 1999, Mark Stein Studios

1. Temple of Saturn
2. Temple of
   Capitoline Jupiter
3. Temple of Vesta
4. Rostra
5. Archive
6. Curia
7. Prison
8. Circus Maximus
9. Cicero's House
10. Clodius's House
11. Decius's House
12. The Forum
13. Basilicas
14. Sublician Bridge
15. Aemilian Bridge
16. Fabrician Bridge
17. Cestian Bridge
18. Tarpeian Rock
19. Forum Boarium

Caelian Hill

Palatine Hill

Aventine Hill

The Tiber

Via Latina

Via Appia

Via Ostiensis

Via Portuensis

Servian Wall

N

1

I WAS HAPPIER THAN ANY MERE
mortal has a right to be, and I should have known better. The
entire body of received mythology and every last Greek tragedy
ever written have made one inescapable truth utterly clear: If you
are supremely happy, the gods have it in for you. They don't like
mortals to be happy, and they will make you pay.

The reason for my happiness was that I wasn't in Gaul. Nor
was I in Parthia, Greece, Iberia, Africa, or Egypt. Instead, I was
at the center of the world. I was in Rome, and for a Roman there
can be no greater joy than to be at home, where all roads famously
lead. Well, if you can't be in Rome, Alexandria isn't a bad second
choice, but it just isn't Rome.

Not only was I in Rome, but I was in the Forum, where all
those roads converge near the Golden Milestone. It really isn't
golden, just touched up with a bit of gilding, but I'll take it over
any gaudy barbarian monument any day. And it was a beautiful
day, which always helps. And I was standing for office, which I

was going to win. I knew I was going to win because, when we men of the *gens* Caecilia Metella demanded high office, we got it.

There was one tiny, minute flaw in my perfect happiness. The office I was standing for was aedile. Now, constitutionally, the aedileship was not strictly on the *cursus honorum*, that ladder of public office one had to ascend one rung at a time to reach the highest offices of praetor and consul, where the greatest honor was, and their subsequent propraetorial and proconsular commands, where all the loot was to be had.

The aediles were loaded with responsibilities concerning the conduct and welfare of the City. They had charge of the markets, of upkeep of the streets and public buildings, enforcement of the building codes, the supervision of public morals (that was always good for a laugh), and all the other duties nobody else could be persuaded to perform.

The aediles were also in charge of the public Games, and the state provided only a ridiculously small allotment for those necessary but horrendously expensive spectacles. Which meant, if you wanted to put on really spectacular Games, you had to pay for them out of your own purse. That meant, if you weren't tremendously rich, you borrowed and ended up in debt for years.

So why, you might ask, would anybody want this onerous office if it wasn't constitutionally required? For the simple reason that the electorate had become accustomed to receiving fine spectacles from their aediles, and if your Games weren't suitably splendid, they would not elect you to the praetorship.

This unpleasant necessity of public life had been turned to unexpected advantage by Caesar, who, as aedile, incurred such tremendous debts that everyone assumed he had foolishly ruined himself in order to win favor with the mob. Then, much to their astonishment, some of the most important men in Rome woke up to discover that, if they were to have any hope of recovering their loans, they had to push Caesar into higher office so he could get rich. It worked neatly for Caesar, but it meant that the voters were now accustomed to an even more lavish standard in Games: more days of races, more comedies and dramas, more public feasts, and, most important, more and better gladiators. Where once a showing of twenty pairs from the local schools had been considered a good show, people now expected four or five hundred pairs of the best Campanian swordsmen tricked out in plumes and gilded armor. None of this was cheap.

But all such dismal prospects were far from my mind as I stood in the Forum on a perfect day in early fall when Rome and all of Italy are at their most lovely. The sky was cloudless; the smoke from the altars ascended straight toward the heavens; there were flowers blooming everywhere. The oppressive heat of summer was past, and the rains, clouds, and chill of winter were still far away. With the other office seekers I wore a specially whitened toga, the *candidus*, so everyone would know who we were, just standing there like fools and saying nothing.

By ancient law, a candidate was forbidden to canvass for votes. He had to stand in one spot and wait for someone to come up and speak to him, at which time he could wheedle for all he was worth. Of course, each candidate was accompanied by his clients, who acted as a sort of cheering section, always gazing admiringly at him, accosting passersby, and telling them all about what a fine fellow their patron was.

I suppose it all looked rather ludicrous to foreigners, but it was an agreeable way to spend your time when the weather was good, especially if you had just escaped Gaul and Caesar's huge and bloody war there. Caesar had granted me leave of absence so that I could come home to stand for office, with the agreement that I would return as soon as I had served my year. Well, we would see about that. Caesar could be dead before then, the war a disaster. This was the result for which his enemies prayed and sacrificed daily to Jupiter Best and Greatest.

But the war was far away, the weather was fine, I was fulfilling my Caecilian heritage by standing for office, it would be months before I had to present my feasts, my *ludi* and my *munera,* and all was right with the world. I was relatively safe from the mobs of my old enemy, Clodius, because he was Caesar's flunky and I was newly married to Caesar's niece, Julia. I should have seen the trouble coming—not that it would have made much difference if I had. And the day started out rather well, too.

The first man to approach me was my distinguished but tediously named kinsman, Quintus Caecilius Metellus Pius Scipio Nasica. With that much name you would have expected a bigger man, but he was rather slight, and a Caecilian by adoption, not that this meant much. All our great families were so intermarried that we all bore much the same degree of consanguinity, whatever name we happened to bear.

"Good morning, Scipio," I said as he walked up to me. "Are you on support duty today?" It was understood that, since I was standing for office, the most distinguished men of the family would show themselves in my company from time to time. Scipio was one of that year's praetors, but he was not accompanied by his lictors. He was also a *pontifex,* and that morning he wore his pontifical insignia, so I knew he was on his way to a formal religious event.

"A meeting of the Pontifical College has been called," he said. "I thought I would stop by and lend you an aura of much-needed respectability." My reputation in the family did not stand high.

"Will a ruling by the *Pontifex Maximus* be required? He's out of town, you know." The holder of that ancient office was, of course, Caesar himself, and he was off on his extraordinary five-year command in Gaul.

"I certainly hope not. It's a difficult question under discussion. We may have to call a conclave of all the priestly colleges in Rome." He didn't look as if he were looking forward to it.

"The *flamines,* the Arval Brotherhood, the *quinquidecemviri,* and the Vestals and all the rest? But that's only been done in times of grave emergency. Has something happened the rest of us haven't heard about yet? Have Caesar and his legions been annihilated, and are the Gauls marching on Rome?"

"Keep your voice down, or you'll start rumors," he cautioned. "No, it's nothing like that. A matter of religious practice, and I'm not permitted to talk about it."

Throughout this we grinned at one another like apes, so that anyone watching would see in what high esteem the distinguished *pontifex* held the lowly but dutiful and conscientious candidate who, in the best tradition of the Republic, sought to assume the heavy burdens of office. This was being repeated, with variations, all over the end of the Forum where the office seekers congregated.

"Well, I must be going, Decius. Good luck." He clapped me on the shoulder, raising a cloud of the fine chalk with which my toga had been whitened. It settled all over him, making him sneeze.

"Careful, there, Scipio," I said. "People might think you're standing for office, too." He went off to his meeting, snorting and brushing at his clothes. This put me in an even more cheerful mood. Then I caught sight of a man I was far happier to see.

"Greetings, Decius Caecilius Metellus the Younger!" he shouted, striding toward me with a great mob of hard-looking clients behind him. His voice carried clear across the Forum, and people parted before him like water before the ram of a warship. Unlike Scipio he was accompanied by his lictors. By custom they were supposed to precede him and clear his way with their *fasces,* but it took a fleet-footed man to stay ahead of this particular magistrate.

"Greetings, *Praetor Urbanus!*" I hailed. Titus Annius Milo and I were old friends, but here in public only his formal title would do. Starting as a street thug newly arrived from Ostia, he had somehow leapt ahead of me on the *cursus honorum*, and I never understood exactly how he did it. Whatever the means, nobody ever deserved the honor more. He was living proof that all you needed was citizenship to make something of yourself in Rome. It helped that he had energy to match his ambition, was awesomely capable, inhumanly strong, handsome as a god, and utterly ruthless.

He embraced me expertly, never actually touching me and thus saving himself from a chalking. His crowd of toughs made a ludicrous attempt at looking dignified and respectable. At least he kept them reined in out of respect for his office. He was the deadly enemy of Clodius, and everyone knew that in the next year, when neither of them held office, it would be open warfare in the streets of Rome.

"On your way to court?" I asked him.

"A full day's schedule, I'm afraid," he said ruefully. If there was one thing Milo hated, it was sitting still, even when he was doing something important. On the other hand, he had a trick of making everybody involved in a suit extremely uneasy with the way that, at intervals, he rose from his curule chair and paced back and forth across the width of the praetor's platform, glaring at them all the while. It was just his way of working off his abundance of nervous energy, but he looked exactly like a Hyrcanian tiger pacing up and down in its cage before being turned loose on some poor wretch who got on the wrong side of the law.

"How are the renovations coming along?" I asked him.

"Almost finished," he said, looking pained. He was married to Fausta, the daughter of Sulla's old age and possibly the most willful, extravagant woman of her generation. For years Milo had lived in a minor fortress in the middle of his territory, and Fausta had made it her first order of marital business to transform it into a setting worthy of a lordly Cornelian and daughter of a Dictator.

"If you'd like to admire them," he said, brightening, "we want you and Julia to come to dinner this evening."

"I'd be delighted!" Not only did I enjoy his company, but Julia and Fausta were good friends as well. Plus, I was in no position to turn down a free meal. My share of the loot from Caesar's early conquests in Gaul had made me comfortably well-off for the first time in my adult life, but that wealth would vanish without a trace in the next year, inevitably.

"Good, good. Caius Cassius will be there, and young Antonius, if he bothers to show up. He's been with Gabinius in Syria, but there's been a lull in the fighting, and he got bored and came home. He never stays still for long."

He was referring, of course, to Marcus Antonius, one day to be notorious but back then known mainly as a leading light of Rome's gilded youth, an uproarious, intemperate young man who was nonetheless intensely likable.

"It's always fun when Antonius is there," I said. "Who else?"

He waved a hand airily. "Whoever strikes my fancy today, and Fausta never consults me, so it could be anybody." Milo never kept to the stuffy formality of exactly nine persons at dinner. Often as not, there were twenty or more around his table. He politicked tirelessly and was liable to invite anybody who might be of use to him. At least his was one house where I knew I would never run into Clodius.

"As long as it's not Cato or anyone boring like that."

Milo went off to his court, and I went back to my meeting-and-greeting routine. About noon things livened up when two Tribunes of the People ascended the *rostra* and began haranguing the crowd. Strictly speaking they were not supposed to do this except at a lawfully convened meeting of the Plebeian Assembly, but feelings were running high just then, and at such times the tribunes ignored proper form. Since they were sacrosanct, there was nothing anyone could do except yell back at them.

I was too far away to make out what they were saying, but I already knew the gist of it. Marcus Licinius Crassus, *triumvir* and by reputation the richest man in the world, was preparing to go to war against Parthia, and a number of the tribunes were very put out about the whole project. One reason was that the Parthians had done nothing to provoke such a war—not that being inoffensive had ever kept anyone safe from us before. Another was that Crassus was unthinkably rich, and a victorious war would make him even richer, and therefore more dangerous. But a lot of people just hated Crassus, and that was the best reason of all. The tribunes Gallus and Ateius were especially vehement in their denunciations of Crassus, and it was these two who bawled at the crowd in the Forum that day.

All their yowling was to no avail, naturally, because Crassus intended to pay for hiring, arming, and equipping his legions out of his own purse. He would make no demands on the Treasury, and there was nothing in Roman law to prevent a man from doing that, if he had the money, which Crassus did. So Crassus was going to get his war.

That was all right with me, as long as I didn't have to go with him. Nobody objected, because they actually thought he might be defeated. In those days we thought little of the Parthians as fighting men. To us they were just more effete Orientals. Their ambassadors wore their hair long and scented; their faces were heavily rouged and their eyebrows painted on. As if that weren't enough, they wore long sleeves. What more evidence did we need that they were a pack of effeminate degenerates?

The proposed war was so unpopular that recruiters were sometimes mobbed. Not that there was great recruiting activity in Rome. The citizenry by that time had grown woefully unwilling to serve in the legions. The smaller towns of Italy supplied more and more of our soldiers.

Caesar's war in Gaul made no more sense, but it was immensely popular. His dispatches, which I had helped him write, were widely published and added luster to his name, and the plebs took his victories as their own. People liked Caesar, and they didn't like Crassus. It was that simple.

The City was full of Crassi that year. Marcus Licinius Crassus Dives was, for the second time, holding the consulship with Pompey. His elder son, the younger Marcus, was standing for the quaestorship. So it was a great year for Crassus, despite the unpopularity of his proposed war. He and Pompey were being amazingly amicable for two men who hated each other so much. Crassus was insanely envious of Pompey's military glory, and Pompey was similarly envious of Crassus's legendary wealth.

Friction had been mounting between the members of the Big Three, but, the year before, Caesar, Pompey, and Crassus had met at Luca to iron out their differences, and all had been cooperation since. Crassus and Pompey agreed to extend Caesar's command in Gaul beyond the already extraordinary five years, were raising more legions for him, and had given him permission to appoint ten legates of his own choosing. In return, Caesar's people in the Senate and, more important, the Popular Assemblies would give Crassus his war and Pompey the proconsulship of Spain when he left office. Spain had become a rich money cow, peaceful enough in those years that Pompey wouldn't actually have to go there but could let his legates handle the place and send him the money.

Roman political life had grown uncommonly complicated of late. The reason Pompey was getting the virtual sinecure of Spain was that, besides being a sitting consul, he also held an extraordinary proconsular oversight of the grain supply for the whole Empire, and this was his third year in that office. Inefficiency, corruption, and rapacious speculators had made a catastrophic mess of grain distribution in Roman territory. There was famine in some places even when grain was abundant. When people are hungry, they get rebellious and don't pay their taxes. We Romans regard the supervision of the grain supply to be fully as important as the command of armies, and Spain was Pompey's reward for straightening the situation out, which he did with his usual remorseless efficiency. He was given the power to appoint fifteen legates to assist him, and he chose incorruptible, efficient, ruthless men.

Cnaeus Pompeius Magnus was probably the most overrated general Rome ever had, but even his enemies, among whom I numbered myself, never doubted his administrative genius. If he had not allowed himself to be seduced by the dream of becoming the new Alexander, his reputation would shine today like those of Cincinnatus, Fabius, and the Scipios. Instead, he chased military glory and perished miserably at the hands of an Oriental tyrant, as did Crassus, who deserved that fate much more.

But these gloomy prospects, too, were far in the future on that day. My appetite told me that it was nearly noon, and I strolled over to the great sundial to check the time. This was the old one, brought as loot from Sicily two hundred years before. Since it was calibrated for Catania, it wasn't very accurate, but it was the first municipal sundial ever installed in Rome, and we were still proud of it. It revealed that it was around noon, give or take an hour. So much for politics. It was time for lunch, then a leisurely afternoon at the baths, where I would of course talk more politics with my peers, then dinner at Milo's. What a perfect day.

"Master!" It was my slave boy, Hermes. He was running toward me across the Forum, disrespectful as always of rank, age, and dignity. He jostled all with fine impartiality. Actually, he was about twenty-four years of age that year, but it was difficult for me to think of him as anything but a boy. Of course, I, too, was legally a boy, since my father was still alive. A man of my lineage and habits had to be grateful to reach his thirties alive and had no cause to quibble about being a legal minor.

"What is it?"

"Julia wants to know if you will be coming home for lunch."
In the subtle code of married couples, this meant she didn't care
greatly whether I did or not. Had she really wanted me home, the
question would have been worded differently: when might she expect me to appear for lunch? or something like that. Hermes was
sensitive to these nuances.

"Closeted with her cronies, is she?" I asked him.

"Aurelia has come to visit."

I winced. "I shall sacrifice a cock to Jupiter in gratitude for
this forewarning." Julia's grandmother was a gorgon no man dared
look upon save with trembling. On three separate occasions she
had demanded that her son, Caius Julius Caesar, have me executed. Usually indulgent of her whims, he had fortunately de-
murred.

"I'd recommend lunch elsewhere," Hermes concurred. He
had grown into a handsome young man, fit and strong as any legionary. He had spent almost three years with me in Caesar's
Gallic camps being trained by army instructors, and on our return
I had enrolled him in the gladiatorial school of Statilius Taurus
for further sword training. Of course, I had no intention of making
him fight professionally, but any man who was going to stay at my
back in those unsettled days had to be able to take care of himself.
He was forbidden to bear arms anywhere in Italy, and elsewhere
in Roman territory only if he accompanied me, but by that time
he was expert with all weapons and could do more damage with
a wooden stick than most men could with a sword.

"I'll find something at the booths here. Tell Julia that we are
dining this evening at the home of the *praetor urbanus* and the
lady Fausta. That'll put her in a good mood."

Hermes grinned. "Milo's place?"

"I knew you'd like that, you young criminal. When you've
delivered your message, bring my bath things to the new Aemilian
Baths. Off with you, now." He ran homeward as if he'd borrowed

11

the winged boots of his namesake. Hermes was a criminal by inclination, and he loved to hobnob with Milo's thugs whenever we dined there, which was often.

I sought out a stall owned by a peasant woman named Nonnia, whose specialty was a pale bread baked with olives, hardboiled eggs, and chopped pork sausage. Sprinkled with fennel and laced with *garum*, a small loaf of it would keep you marching all day in full legionary gear. With just such a loaf and a beaker of coarse Campanian wine, I went to sit on the steps of the rostra and refresh myself after the strenuous morning. One of my clients, an old farmer named Memmius, took charge of my *candidus* lest I get grease or wine on the hideously expensive garment.

"Here comes trouble," said another client, an even older soldier named Burrus. I had saved his son from a murder charge in Gaul, and the bloodthirsty old veteran was eager to slaughter all my enemies for me. I glanced up to see my least favorite Roman coming toward me.

"It's just Clodius," I said. "We're observing a truce these days. If you're carrying weapons, keep them out of sight."

"Truce or no truce," Burrus said grimly, "don't turn your back on him."

"I never have, and I never will," I assured him. I was not as certain of our safety as I pretended. Clodius was subject to the odd bout of homicidal insanity. Surreptitiously, I checked to make sure that my dagger and my *caestus* were tucked away beneath my tunic where I could reach them handily, just in case.

"Good day, Decius Caecilius!" Clodius called, all smiles and joviality. As usual when not in office, he wore crude sandals and a workingman's tunic, the sort that leaves one arm and shoulder bare. He was accompanied by a rabble of thugs as disreputable as those in Milo's train, but those closest to Clodius tended to be better-born. The noble youth of Rome in those days were much addicted to thuggery. After all, we couldn't all get involved in

12

politics. His gang looked like the younger brothers of the lot that had followed Catilina in his foolish coup attempt eight years before. Most of those had died in that ugly affair, but a new crop of young fools comes along every few years to fill the depleted ranks.

"Join me, Publius," I said, wiping my hands on my tunic. It is unwise to have greasy fingers if you have to go for your dagger. "There's more here than I can eat."

"Gladly." He sat by me and took a handful of the fragrant bread and bit into it. "Ah, Nonnia's. I was just by her booth, but she was sold out. Your cup looks dry." He snapped his fingers, and one of his lackeys hustled forward with a skin to fill my beaker.

I took a gulp and winced. It was crude Vatican from the third-rate vineyards right across the river.

"Publius, you can afford to bathe in Caecuban. Why do you drink this foul stuff? My slaves complain when I bring it home."

He sneered. "Frivolous trappings of *nobilitas*. I have no use for such things, Decius. It's all outdated, anyway. This whole nonsense of patrician and plebeian would have been swept away long ago if it hadn't been for Sulla. We're embarking on a new age, my friend."

"I don't see what that has to do with drinking decent wine," I protested, drinking the foul stuff anyway. "Besides, when you took up the cause of the common man, you didn't renounce your wealth, I notice."

He smiled conspiratorially. "What could be more common and vulgar than wealth?"

"I wouldn't know. Such vulgarity as I've achieved has been in spite of my poverty."

He laughed heartily, a real feat for a man with no sense of humor. "But money is very necessary. We must have money if the Republic is to live. We need money to buy votes in the Assemblies and to bribe the juries in our lawsuits. You're embarked upon a tenure of the most costly of offices. And you have a new, patrician wife. You'll find that they have expensive tastes."

I took another swallow of his wine, which was tasting better as I drank. Everything he'd said was damnably true. "I get the impression that you're leading up to something, Publius."

"Just that there is no need for you to suffer unduly for your service to the State. I think it's disgraceful that citizens should be enslaved to moneylenders."

"You'll never lose votes by flogging the moneylenders," I said. "But I don't see how that affects my case."

"Don't be dense, Decius. Wouldn't you rather owe one man who will never come dunning you for payment than be beholden to fifty little bankers? I know some of the men in your family are willing to ease the burden, but relatives are worse than usurers when it comes to lending money."

"I know you aren't speaking on your own behalf, Publius. You aren't that rich. In fact, there is only one man in Rome who has both the money and the interest to assume my debts so casually."

"I knew you were only pretending to be dense."

I sighed. "You weren't always a friend to Crassus."

"Nor am I now. But Caesar, Pompey, and Crassus have an agreement. Caesar, your new uncle by marriage, wants me to give Crassus every assistance in getting his Parthian war under way. That means smoothing his relations with the Senate, the tribunes, and the Assemblies."

It was beginning to make sense. "And a large bloc of the Senate and the Assemblies would cease to give him trouble if the Caecilian clan were to drop their opposition."

He beamed. "There you are!"

"Does Crassus fully understand in what minuscule esteem my family holds me? Does he really believe that I can sway them?"

"The prospect of not having to help pay for your Games could improve their disposition immensely." He refilled my cup. "I hear that you will be celebrating the *munera* for Metellus Celer. He was a great man. People must expect a celebration commensurate with his prominence."

The very thought could still make me gasp. "Publius, you are ruining what began as an extraordinarily splendid day."

"It could be the most important day of your life, Decius. Just come over to Crassus's side and clear all your debts. He'll give you liberal terms."

"He'll want far more than you are saying for that much aid I'll be his lackey for life."

"And what of that? He's old, Decius; he can't live much longer. Even if his war is successful, he'll probably keel over and croak during his triumph from the sheer excitement."

"But," I said, growing more and more exasperated because the prospect was so tempting, "I abhor the whole idea of this war, as does my family!"

"Be realistic, Decius! There is nothing you can do about it. Crassus has his war. The Senate has given him permission to make war on Parthia, he already has his own army, and the Assemblies aren't stopping him. Only some die-hard tribunes and recalcitrant senators are making a fuss. He would much rather not be embarrassed by this opposition, and he doesn't want people here working against him while he is out of the City. Give him your support. You lose nothing by it, and you gain everything."

"I must consider it," I said, stalling. "I will confer with my family." I had no intention of supporting Crassus, but I had enough political experience to know that a flat no would be unwise. A conditional no was always better.

He nodded. "Do that. And avoid those fools, Gallus and Ateius. They are beginning to stir up serious trouble. They should be arrested as a menace to public order." Hearing Clodius say something like that was worth putting up with his company. With a hearty, hypocritical clap on my shoulder, Clodius took his leave and went off to find someone he could bully and intimidate.

I refused to let him cast a shadow over my excellent day. With the wine buzzing pleasantly in my head, I repaired to the Aemilian Baths. This was a very imposing establishment, built upon a block of ground near the Forum that had been conveniently cleared by a catastrophic fire two years previously. It was completed and dedicated the year before by the praetor Marcus Aemilius Scaurus to the glory of his ancestors. It was the first of the really huge baths to be built in Rome, and included exercise yards, lecture halls, a small library, and a gallery for paintings and sculpture, all of it surrounding a main hot pool big enough for a battle between triremes. I pitied Sardinia, which Scaurus had been sent to govern, if he was using the opportunity to recoup his expenses on the place.

I was just dozing off on the massage table when a vaguely familiar man flopped onto the one next to mine. The Nubian assigned to that table commenced his ministrations, but the familiar slap of cupped palms was in this case somewhat muffled because the man was as furry as a bear. He had a wide, coarse-featured face that was just then smiling at me, showing big, yellow teeth through broad lips.

"Good day, Senator," he said. "I don't believe we have met. I am Caius Sallustius Crispus."

"Decius Caecilius Metellus the Younger," I said, extending a hand. "I've seen your name on the roll of the magistrates. One of the year's quaestors, aren't you?"

"That is correct. I'm assigned to the Grain Office." I saw now that he was perhaps in his late twenties. His crude visage and hirsuteness had given the impression of an older man.

"I've missed the last few elections," I admitted. "I've been with Caesar in Gaul."

"I know. I've been following your career."

"Oh? Why is that? It hasn't been very distinguished so far." In fact, I wasn't much interested. I didn't like the look of the man. I've always found ugliness to be an excellent reason for disliking someone.

"I am of a literary turn of mind," he explained. "I intend to write a comprehensive history of our times."

"My part in the affairs of Rome has been modest beyond words," I assured him. "I can't imagine what you'd find to write about me."

"But you were involved in Catilina's failed coup," he said, still smiling. "On both sides, I'm given to understand. That calls for a rare political dexterity."

I didn't like the insinuating tone that he disguised with disingenuous friendliness. And I disliked discussing that ugly incident that had killed so many, ruined careers, and destroyed reputations and that still caused hard feelings after eight years.

"I was, as always, on the side of the Senate and People," I told him. "And too much is made of the disgraceful business as it is."

"But I hear Cicero is writing his own history of the rebellion."

"As is his right. He was the central figure, and his actions preserved the Republic at the cost of his reputation and his career." Cicero had been exiled for the execution without trial of the chief conspirators. Even at that time he was not truly safe in Rome despite the protection of Milo's thugs. Much as it pains me to say anything good about Cato, his exertions on Cicero's behalf had been heroic and made him even more unpopular than he had been, which is saying something.

"But he will naturally slant the facts in his own favor," Sallustius said. "A more balanced account will be needed."

"You are welcome to try your hand at it," I said, sure that, like the scribblings of most amateur historians, his would not out-last his own lifetime.

"These are such lively times," he mused, apparently deter-mined to cheat me of my nap. "Caesar's war in Gaul, Gabinius campaigning in Syria and Egypt, Crassus's upcoming war against the Parthians—it seems almost a shame to stay here in Rome with all that going on."

"You can have it all," I told him. "Barbarians and Eastern despots hold no interest for me. If it were up to me, I would stay right here for the rest of my days and putter around in the gov-ernment offices and doze off during Senate debates."

"That doesn't sound like a Metellus to me," he said. "Your family is famed for its devotion to high office, not to mention the high-handed wielding of power." His tone was chaffing, but I de-tected a griping undertone of envy. It was not the first time I'd heard it. This was another nobody from an undistinguished family who begrudged my family connections and the all-but-unquestioned access they gave me to the pursuit of higher office.

"I don't claim to be a typical member of the *gens*. I have no desire to conquer foreigners or give Rome more desert and forest to garrison."

"I can understand that it's a daunting tradition to live up to. Why, within the memory of living Romans the *gens* Caecilia has added Numidia and Crete to the Empire."

"Wonderful. The Numidians are rebellious savages, and the Cretans are the most notoriously shiftless pack of lying, conniving pseudo-Greeks the world has to offer." I wasn't truly so contemp-tuous of my family's accomplishments, but something in me wanted to contradict everything the man said.

"Do you think we shouldn't add Parthia to the lot?"

Everybody wants to talk about Crassus today, I thought. Well, nobody was talking about much else that year.

"Everybody has had a try at taking that part of the world,"

I said. "Nobody's had much satisfaction out of it. It's mostly plains and grassland, a natural land for horsemen, not foot-slogging legionaries. You know as well as I that we Romans are wretched cavalry."

"I hear that Caesar is giving Crassus several wings of Gallic cavalry he does not need at the moment."

I groaned. This was the first I'd heard of it. I thought of the splendid young Gallic horsemen I'd commanded in the Northern war, their lives to be expended foolishly in some unspeakable Asiatic desert so that Marcus Licinius Crassus could have glory to match Pompey's.

"Is something wrong?" Sallustius asked.

"Nothing," I said, sitting up. "They're just more barbarians." I walked toward the *frigidarium*, feeling the need of cold water to wake me up and clear my head. Then I turned back. "But no army ever knew anything but disaster when a foolish old man was in charge. Good day to you."

I left him there and plunged into the cold pool, a jolting torment that I usually dread but that came as a relief after talking with Sallustius Crispus. When I climbed out, Hermes helped me dry off and dress. The cold water had cleared the wine fumes and sleepiness from my head. Thinking clearly, I wondered whether I might not have made a serious mistake in calling Crassus a foolish old man in front of that hairy little weasel.

2

"DINNER AT FAUSTA'S!" JULIA SAID, still delighted with the prospect. "You haven't wasted your day entirely if you've arranged that!" She sat at her vanity table while her handmaid, a sly, devious girl named Cypria, applied her cosmetics.

"We were invited by Milo," I reminded her, nettled as always that she barely tolerated my old friend, who had been a humble galley rower, while Fausta was a patrician of the Cornelians, the equal of the Julians. "And he's the most important man in Rome." The consuls that year were busy with their other projects, leaving the *praetor urbanus* the man with the real power.

"For this year only," she said, reminding me that a magistracy is for a year, while noble birth is forever.

"You're being uncommonly snobbish today," I said.

She swiveled on her stool, and Cypria began arranging her hair. "Only because I think this friendship between you and Milo will lead to disaster. He may be a successful politician, but he is a criminal and a thug no better than Clodius, and he will get you killed, disgraced, or exiled someday."

"He has saved my life many times," I protested.

"After putting it in danger most of those times. He's a jumped-up nobody and a danger to everyone who has anything to do with him, and I don't know why Fausta ever married him. I admit he's handsome, and he can be charming enough when he has a use for you, but that is purely in service of his ambitions."

"As opposed to your glorious uncle, who has nearly got me killed at least twenty times in the last two years alone?"

She admired herself in her silver mirror. "The dangers of war are honorable, and Caesar wars on behalf of Rome." Like everybody else, she had taken to calling him by his *cognomen* alone, as if he were a god or something.

"We'll discuss this later," I said, stalking out. I loved Julia dearly, but she worshiped her uncle and wouldn't recognize his self-seeking, dictatorial ambitions. Also, like most patricians, she talked in front of her slaves as if they weren't there.

Cato and Cassandra, my own aged slaves, stood in the atrium clucking. I went to investigate. They weren't much use anymore, but I'd known them all my life. They stood in the door looking out into the street, shaking their heads.

"What is it?" I asked them.

"Look what she's hired," Cassandra said.

I peered out over their shoulders and grunted as if I'd been punched in the stomach. Just outside the gate was a litter draped in pale green silk covered with Scythian embroidery done in gold thread. Squatting by its polished ebony poles were four black Nubians, a matched set, wearing Egyptian kilts and headdresses.

"Have they arrived?" Julia said from behind me.

"They have," I said, not wanting my slaves to hear me upbraiding her, although they knew perfectly well what was going through my head. "You look lovely, my dear."

And indeed she did. Julia had great natural beauty, and she knew how to enhance it. Besides that, she had the patrician bearing that makes its possessor seem taller and more stately, and her gown was made of the infamous Coan cloth, although it was multilayered to avoid the transparency that outraged the Censors.

We went outside and climbed into the litter, which was furnished with plump cushions stuffed with goose down and fragrant herbs. The bearers lifted the poles to their brawny shoulders and bore us off so smoothly that it was like floating. Hermes and Cypria walked behind us. Once in a while I could hear them trading barbed remarks in the slang used by slaves. They didn't get along well.

"Julia," I said, "with the expenses of the aedileship facing us, why did you hire this pretentious conveyance? It must cost more than our regular household expenses for a week."

"That is a vulgar consideration, Decius," she said. "I hired it because we are calling on Fausta." She shot me a sidelong glance. "And on the *praetor urbanus*, of course. We would be doing our distinguished hosts little credit if we were to arrive in some rickety old litter covered with patched linen and carried by spavined, mismatched slaves. You must live up to the dignity of the office you seek, my dear."

"As you say, my love," I said, conceding defeat. With Julia, winning an argument was usually far more painful than losing.

The Nubians deposited us in the narrow street before the massive door of Milo's house. The moment I stepped from the litter, I saw the effect of Fausta's renovations. The entire block of apartments facing that side of the house was gone. Instead, the other side of the street featured a beautifully landscaped park, complete with fountains and pools in which swans paddled contentedly.

"What happened here?" I said, gasping. "Was there a fire?"

"Nothing of the sort," Julia informed me. "Fausta thought

this dingy neighborhood was too cramped, so she had some of the tenements demolished. Milo already owned them, anyway. Isn't it beautiful?"

"It's pretty enough," I admitted. "But his whole point in putting the main door on this side was that the street was too narrow for his enemies to use a battering ram against it. They could build a siege tower in that park."

"It's worth putting up with a little danger to live with proper dignity. Come along, the guests are gathering."

We went inside, and a whole horde of pretty young slaves of both sexes swarmed around us, draping our necks with wreaths of flowers, placing chaplets around our brows, anointing our hands with perfume, and scattering rose petals before us. This was another change. I'd never seen anyone but strong-arm men in Milo's house before. His lictors had been dismissed for the evening, but the six *fasces* were ranged on stands by the door in token of his *imperium*.

The atrium was changed as well. Fausta had knocked three or four rooms into one huge one, and had raised the ceiling as well and added a window of many small panes above the door to admit the sunlight that was now available owing to the demolition of the buildings across the street. The walls were painted with wonderful frescoes depicting mythological subjects, and the floor was covered with picture mosaics of outdoor scenes. Picture mosaics were a new fashion, introduced by the Egyptian ambassador. Around the periphery of the room were statues of ancestors. Her ancestors, not his.

"Have you ever seen such an improvement?" Julia asked me.

"It's—different," I admitted.

"Fausta brought me here when she began the renovations." She shook her head. "As if Milo really expected her to live in that dark old fortress! I came to visit often while the work was going on. It gave me no end of ideas."

I felt the first, small ticklings of trepidation. Fausta was a Cornelian, and Julia was a Julian, and Julia would have to go Fausta one better. At the very thought I began to tremble.

"Ah, my dear, you realize that it may be quite some time before we can expect to live on such a scale—"

She giggled, covering her mouth with a palm fan to do so. "Oh, Decius, of course I know that! These things take time. But sooner or later you must inherit from your father, and of course Caesar will favor you after your service with him, and you'll have a praetorian province before long." She placed a hand on my shoulder and kissed my cheek. "I know that it will be four, maybe five years before we can have a place like this. Come on, let's see the rest!" Going shaky in the knees, I followed her.

We were headed for the *impluvium* when Fausta found us. She and Julia went through the customary embrace and exchange of compliments while I dawdled, wishing Milo would show up. Fausta was as golden blond as a German princess, one of the few Roman women who came by the look naturally. Her gown was likewise of Coan cloth, and it was of a single, transparent layer, but Fausta had the bearing to get away with it. She carried herself so regally that she could walk through a room naked and only after she was gone would anyone realize it.

"Come along," Fausta said. "I've finally got the *impluvium* stocked. You must see it." We followed her beneath an archway and into a vast area open to the sky. She had gutted the whole four-story structure and remodeled it. Where before there had been a vertical air shaft faced with windows of upper rooms, she had stepped each floor back from the one below so that now there were three balconies like theater seats built for gods. From each balcony were draped huge garlands, and upon them stood giant vases from which sprang colorful flowers and even small trees. Along the railings roosted pigeons and even peacocks, and incense burned in dozens of bronze braziers.

A change as great had been wrought on the floor. Before, there had been a modest catch-basin for rainwater. Now there was a veritable lake, and its pungent scent astonished me.

"Is this seawater?" I asked.

"Exactly," Fausta affirmed. "It's so tiresome having sea fish brought all the way up from Ostia on barges, and it's never really fresh when it arrives. I have the water brought up in casks. It has to be renewed frequently, but it's worth the effort. I get so tired of river fish."

I could see a variety of marine life disporting beneath the surface: mullets, tunny fish, eels, even squid. The water wasn't perfectly clear, but I could see that the bottom was another mosaic, this one a colossal figure of Neptune in his shell chariot drawn by *hippocampi*. His hair and beard were the traditional blue, the trappings of his chariot and the head of his trident gilded with pure gold leaf. I saw a wading slave armed with a similar, but more prosaic, trident. The weapon darted out, and he pulled it back with a wriggling tunny fish impaled on the tines. The onlookers applauded as if he'd speared a lion in the Circus. Around the periphery, other slaves plied the water with eel forks.

"Can't ask for anything fresher than that," I said, my stomach rumbling with anticipation. I knew that Julia would have to have a pond just like it, only bigger, but I was willing to worry about it later. I could see that Milo's previously Spartan concept of dining had gone the way of everything else.

"Decius," Julia said, "Fausta is going to show me her new wardrobe. Do try to stay out of trouble."

"Trouble? What sort of trouble could I get into in a place like this?" Julia rolled her eyes in exasperation and went off arm in arm with Fausta. Sometimes I had the feeling that my wife didn't trust me.

The place was thronged with guests and their attendants, and I was delighted to see that Fausta hadn't chosen the entire guest list. I saw Lisas, the seemingly perpetual ambassador from Egypt who had been in Rome as long as I could remember. He had a slave supporting him on either side, not because he was drunk but because he was so obese. His outrageous practices and unique perversions had been the subject of gossip for a couple of generations, but he was one of the most jovial and gregarious men I ever knew, which is just what you want in an ambassador.

Young Antonius arrived, already slightly tipsy, and began flirting with all women present, slave or free. I knew him slightly, and he waved to me with his wine cup. He was one of those ridiculously handsome, personable young men who never fear to do or say anything that comes into their heads, because they know they are universally adored and will always be forgiven.

I grabbed a cup from a passing server and began looking for Milo. I found his assembly room, which was filled with his thugs, all of them decently attired for a change, eating and playing games at long tables. Hermes was among them, playing knucklebones and probably losing. The walls were decorated with chariot races and animal hunts and gladiator fights, subjects dear to the hearts of Milo's men but undoubtedly not chosen by the lady of the house. The grand families happily sponsored the Games, but they considered them far too vulgar to be fit subjects for domestic ornament.

These men all knew me, and I was the recipient of much backslapping and congratulation and well-wishing. Should Milo and I ever fall out, they would cut my throat with equal enthusiasm, but until then they were my boon companions. Plus, they knew that someday I might be judging them in court, and it is always wise to be on good terms with a man who could send you to the mines or the lions or set you free at his whim.

"Decius! Welcome!" I turned and at last saw Milo coming through a side door. He clapped me on the shoulder, and, as always, I braced myself for a shock. He used no force, naturally, but the reaction was instinctive to one who knew how powerful he was. He had the strongest hands I ever encountered on a human being and could break a man's jaw with an open-hand slap. I had seen him, on a bet, tie a horseshoe into a knot with the fingers of one hand.

"The changes here have been—remarkable, Titus," I said.

"Has Fausta been showing you how she's ruining me?" His grin was rueful.

"Only a part, and it frightens me to see the look it puts in Julia's eye. How are you going to curb her extravagance when you go to govern your province?" We still had a rule that a promagistrate's wife had to stay in Rome while he was abroad.

He grimaced. "I don't plan to go. I'm like you, Decius: I don't want to leave Rome. I'll follow Pompey's example and send my legate to run the place and send me the money. It's the only way I'll ever keep up with her. Come along, let's eat. I'm famished!"

I went with him into the *triclinium*, which had been remodeled on a scale with the rest of the house. It was large enough for full-sized banquets, and for that evening it had been laid out with places for at least eighteen guests instead of the usual nine, apparently on the chance that each guest would bring along a friend, which was permitted under the newly loosened rules of etiquette.

Another departure from tradition was that the women reclined at the table along with the men, instead of sitting on chairs. I almost wished Cato could be there so that I could enjoy the shocked look on his face.

Julia came up to me, trailed by her maidservant. "Aren't these paintings wonderful?"

I studied them for a few moments. They depicted the banquets of the gods, with Jupiter taking his cup from Ganymede, Venus winking across the table at a sour-faced Mars, Vulcan enchanting his mechanical servitors, and all the rest of the company having a high old time while the Graces danced for them.

"Well," I said, "if Fausta gets tired of the guests, she can just look at the walls and feel she's among equals."

Julia swatted me with her fan, laughing. "You're incorrigible. She's put me next to that fat Egyptian. I hope he doesn't try anything disgusting."

"Just put up with him," I advised. "He can only dream. He's long past carrying out any of his intentions. Besides, he's one of my favorite people in Rome. And he's incredibly useful and a veritable mine of gossip. If Lisas hasn't heard about it, either it didn't happen, or it isn't going to."

"I'll see what I can get out of him."

She wandered off, and I was led to my place. I flopped down, and Hermes took my sandals and settled himself to wait on me, a duty he hated. I saw that there were seventeen places occupied, the place traditionally called the "consul's place" being left vacant, as it always was in a praetor's house, just in case a consul should decide to show up.

I was delighted to see that the man on my right was none other than Publilius Syrus, who was quickly winning a place for himself as Rome's most famous actor, playwright, and impresario. On my other side was Caius Messius, a plebeian aedile that year who had celebrated an uncommonly fine Floralia.

"This is extraordinarily lucky," I said to Syrus. "I've been meaning to look you up, since I'll be aedile next year."

"Spoken like a true Metellus," said Messius. "Already planning your *ludi,* and you haven't even been elected yet. Well, you can't pick a better man to arrange your theatricals than Syrus. The plays he put on for me went over wonderfully. My election to the praetorship is assured."

"I have two new dramas in the works," Syrus told me. "And six short comedies."

"Nothing about Troy, I hope. That war's been done to death."

Even worse, Caesar had been secretly hiring poets and playwrights to write about Aeneas, on the pretext that Caesar's family, the *gens* Julia, were descended from Julus, son of Aeneas. And the grandmother of Julus was none other than the goddess Venus herself. We had all been blissfully unaware of the divine ancestry of Caesar until he decided to tell us about it.

"One of the dramas concerns the death of Hannibal, the other the deeds of Mucius Scaevola."

"Those sound like safe, patriotic themes," I said. "Right now, anything about a foreign war looks like a reference to Caesar or Gabinius or Crassus. What about the comedies? I don't suppose you have anything that would poke fun at Clodius, do you?"

His smile was a bit strained. "I have to live in this city too, you know."

"Oh, well, forget it. I suppose the usual satyrs, nymphs, cowardly soldiers, conniving slaves, and cuckolded husbands will do well enough."

"I have a good one about King Ptolemy of Egypt," he said. "You know he came here last year, begging for money and support?"

"So I heard. I'll never understand how the king of the world's richest nation is always a pauper. But Gabinius put him back on his throne. It's not about him, is it?" The last thing I wanted to do was spend my money to help out someone else's reputation. Or even worse, risk making an enemy of a powerful man.

"No, this is about his coming here to beg before the Senate. Only I have him going about from door to door in the poorest parts of town, dressed in rags with a bowl in his hand, followed by a troop of slaves to carry his wine sacks. I've contrived a device that lets him drain the wine sacks one after another, right on stage."

I laughed heartily at the thought. I knew Ptolemy and his feats of wine-drinking were little short of what the actor described. "That sounds good. Go ahead with it. Egyptians are always good for laughs." Of course, we thought all foreigners were funny, but I didn't say that to Publilius, who, as his name attests, came from Syria.

"I recommend the new Aemilian Theater," Syrus said. "Have you seen it?"

"Not yet," I admitted. This was built the year before by the same Aemilius Scaurus whose baths I had enjoyed that afternoon. "Is it on the same scale as his new baths?"

"It's larger than Pompey's Theater," Syrus said. "Made of wood, but the decoration is unbelievably lavish, and it hasn't had time to deteriorate. Besides, Pompey's was damaged during his triumphal Games. The elephants stampeded and broke a lot of the stonework, and when he had a town burned on stage, the proscenium caught fire. The damage is still visible."

"Besides," Messius said, "Pompey's Theater will remind everyone of Pompey, and it's topped by a temple to Venus *Genetrix,* and that'll remind people of Caesar. Go with the Aemilian, and then all you'll have to worry about is a fire breaking out and cooking half the voters. It'll hold eighty thousand people."

"Plus," Syrus added, "most people won't have to walk as far. Pompey's is out on the Campus Martius, while the Aemilian's right on the river by the Sublician Bridge."

"I'm sold," I said. "The Aemilian it is." About that time the first course arrived, and we applied ourselves to it, and to those that followed. I was forced to admit that perfectly fresh sea fish was a rare treat in Rome, where the catch was usually at least a day old by the time it reached the City. These fish and eels were practically still gasping.

We were tearing into the dessert when there was a commotion in the atrium. A moment later a small knot of men came into the *triclinium.* One of them was none other than Marcus Licinius Crassus. Milo sprang to his feet.

"Consul, welcome! You do my house honor!" He rushed to

the old man's side and led him to the place of honor with his own hand.

"Nonsense, Praetor Urbanus," Crassus said, apparently in high good humor. "I'm just making a few calls after dinner with the Pontifical College. We've been meeting all day, and I'm bored out of my mind. I can only stay a short while."

"Stay until you depart for the East. My house is yours," Milo said, magnanimously. He clapped his hands, and the consul's place was immediately loaded with sweetmeats and iced wine. If Milo was being more than correct in receiving a consul, Fausta was not. She looked on with a coolness bordering contempt.

For my own part, I was shocked. This was the first close look I'd had of Crassus since returning to Rome, and the deterioration since I had last beheld him was marked. His color was high, but only in the cheeks and nose, and that only from the wine. Otherwise, his complexion was gray and deeply lined. His white hair was falling out in patches, and the cords of his neck stood out beneath his chin wattles like lyre strings. The neck itself was scrawny, and upon it his head wobbled like a ball floating upon agitated water.

"Won't be long now," Crassus said. "My legions will drive King Orodes of Parthea and his cowardly, savage horsemen to ground, and we'll bag the lot! Takes more than arrows to frighten Roman soldiers, eh?"

"Of course, you have our heartiest wishes for a swift victory, Consul," Milo said warmly, managing to keep his smile intact. Most of us shouted traditional congratulations. Even I managed a weak cheer.

Crassus contrived a lopsided, fatuous smile, as if he'd already won. "I'll bring Orodes home in golden chains and give Rome such a triumph as will make everyone forget Pompey and Lucullus and all the rest!" He raised his cup, slopping wine over his beringed hand. "Death to the Parthians!"

We returned the toast as if we meant it, covering our embarrassment with a lot of old battle slogans. Crassus seemed satisfied with this and nodded away as a slave dried off his hand.

"Jupiter protect us!" I whispered. "Is this really what we are going to send to command an army?"

"I'm afraid so," said Messius in a voice as low. "At least, he will if he ever leaves the City."

"What do you mean?"

"I've heard that a number of influential men have sworn to prevent him from going to join his army when he steps down from office. They say they'll restrain him by force if need be."

"I won't say it's a bad idea," I told him, "but I don't see how they can do that lawfully."

"People who fear a catastrophe don't worry much about fine points of law. They may whip up the Plebeian Assembly to stop him by mob action."

He was speaking of the tribunes, of course. They were the ones who had the greatest influence with that body, and of all the year's officials, Gallus and Ateius were the most venomously opposed to the Parthian war. This could mean blood on the streets again.

"What about that other one who got the law passed giving Crassus the command? Was it Trebonius?" I asked.

Messius nodded. "He was the only one among the tribunes who was really for the war, but with Crassus's money and Pompey's prestige behind him, one was enough. He managed to line up all the other tribunes except the two who're in the Forum every day. All the rest are a pack of timeservers who've spent the year dawdling over the minutiae of Caesar's agrarian laws and the doings of the land commissioners." He was referring to one of the burning issues of the day: a series of proposed reforms that were unendingly controversial at the time but are incredibly boring even to think about now.

Crassus chatted with Milo, and the rest of us returned to our small talk. When the dinner was concluded, we strolled about the renovated house, socializing and gossiping. I soon found fat old Lisas by the salt pool, talking with a sturdy-looking young man of soldierly bearing. The genial old pervert greeted me with a welcoming smile.

"Decius Caecilius, my old friend! I've just spent the most enjoyable evening speaking with your lovely and most noble wife. Have you met young Caius Cassius?"

"I don't believe so." I took the young man's hand. His direct blue eyes were set in a blocky face of hard planes, burned dark by exposure. He had the thick neck common to wrestlers and to those who train seriously for warfare, developed by wearing a helmet every day from boyhood on.

"The martial young gentleman accompanies Crassus to Parthia," Lisas said. "I have been telling him what I know of the place and the people."

"The honorable ambassador warns me not to underestimate the Parthians," Cassius said. "He says that they are more warlike than we imagine and treacherous in their dealings." He spoke with an earnestness rare in Romans of his generation. It went well with his soldierly bearing.

"For a people recently settled down from a nomadic existence, they are sophisticated," Lisas said. "They are cunning in the art of horseback archery, and one should always beware their invitations to parley."

"I don't expect that they'll have any cause to parley except when they surrender," Cassius said. "The bow hasn't been made that can send a shaft through a Roman shield, and they can ride around all they like. Sooner or later, they'll have to come to close quarters to decide the issue, and that's when we'll finish them."

"This is what we all hope," Lisas said, none too confidently.

"What will be your capacity?" I asked Cassius.

"Military tribune. I was sponsored by Lucullus and confirmed by the Senate."

Military tribune in those days was a most ambiguous position, a sort of trying-out stage for a young man embarking upon a public career. He might spend the campaign running errands at headquarters. But if he proved promising and capable, he could be granted an important command. All was at the discretion of the general.

"You have my heartiest wishes for a successful and glorious campaign," I said, with some sincerity. It wasn't his fault that he was to be commanded by one of the men I most despised.

"I thank you. And now, if you will give me leave, I must go pay my respects to the consul." He departed, and as he went, I felt cheered to know that we still produced dutiful young men. Because of his later notoriety Cassius's part in the Parthian war came into question, but as far as I was concerned, any officer who brought himself and his men out of that fiasco alive had my admiration, and I never really lost respect for him.

"An excellent young nobleman," Lisas said. "One could wish that he had a worthier commander."

"Don't tell me you're against the Parthian war, too," I said, snagging a full cup from a passing tray.

He shrugged his fat shoulders, and his slaves stood by, alert lest he should topple. "Elimination of Parthia would mean one less threat to Egypt. Were the Roman forces to be commanded by General Pompey, or Gabinius, or even Caesar, busy as that gentleman is, I would have no objection."

"Surely you don't object because Crassus is in his dotage?" I said. Ptolemy Auletes remained in power through Roman support, but I suspected that a slightly weaker Rome would be to his liking.

"You are unaware, perhaps, of the consul's activities when my sovereign master, the most glorious King Ptolemy, was here in

Rome almost from the time you departed until last year?"

I had some vague memory of letters mentioning something at the time, but I had been so diverted by terror for my own life that scandals in the capital interested me very little. "I'm afraid not. Will you tell me?"

"Gladly. When King Ptolemy came almost three years ago to petition the Senate for the restoration of his throne, that august body was at first more than sympathetic in hearing his suit."

"Support for the House of Ptolemy has been a cornerstone of Roman policy for generations," I said, pouring on the oil.

"And our esteem for Rome acknowledges few boundaries. Alas, Marcus Licinius Crassus proved to be less than wholehearted in his enthusiasm. Before the Senate, he questioned whether, with so many other military projects already undertaken, Rome should shoulder the burden of a campaign to replace Ptolemy upon the throne."

"The question was reasonable," I said. "We are stretched rather thin, militarily speaking."

"With this I am in full concurrence," he said smoothly. "However, I fear that Crassus resorted to unscrupulous means to reinforce his argument."

"Unscrupulous?" Roman politicians of the day were accustomed to employ means to gain their ends that would have shocked Greeks. And that was when they were dealing with their fellow Romans. When foreigners were concerned, few limits were observed.

"In his capacity as augur and *pontifex*, he demanded that the Sibylline Books be consulted."

This was a droll development even to my jaded sensibilities. "He consulted the old books? That's only done in national emergencies, or when the gods seem to be dangerously displeased with us—lightning striking a great temple or something like that. I never heard of them being consulted on a foreign-policy decision."

"Just so. Yet he did exactly that. He claimed to have discovered a passage warning against giving aid to the king of Egypt."

"A moment," I said, holding up a forestalling hand. "You say he claimed to have discovered it? I am not an expert on sacerdotal matters, but it is my impression that the keeping and interpretation of the books are entrusted to a college of fifteen priests, the *quinquidecemviri*."

"And so they are." He looked morosely down into the depths of his cup. "It seems that Crassus has means to get what he wants." A polite way of saying that he bribed the priests.

"Oh, well," I said, "Ptolemy is firmly back on the throne again, thanks to Gabinius."

"An excellent man. But now Rome is going to have an army in the East commanded by a man who is no friend of the royal house of Egypt." Meaning that, should Crassus have to call upon Ptolemy for aid, it would be very slow in coming. It was a diplomatic nugget of potential value, and it meant that Lisas was cultivating me in what I hoped was a friendly fashion. I thanked him and went to look for Milo.

I was not as shocked as I should have been. I never regarded the Sibylline Books with any great awe except for their antiquity. They were a foreign import dating from the days of the kings, in extremely antiquated language and couched in the customary obscure double-talk employed by sibyls and seers everywhere. On top of that, the original books had burned in a temple fire many years before, and they had been pieced together by consulting sibyls all over the world, and I had some doubts as to their similarity to the originals. The priesthood was not among the most prestigious.

I was skeptical of the value of sibyls and oracles generally, although most people believed in them implicitly. If you have something to say, why speak in riddles? Still, it was uncommonly brazen effrontery to falsify a sibylline consultation. But who was more brazen than Crassus? Even as I thought these things, the man himself appeared before me.

"Decius Caecilius! Allow me to be first to congratulate you on your election!" He grasped my hand and clapped me warmly on the shoulder, a sure sign that he wanted something from me. I was pretty sure I knew what it was.

"You are being a bit precipitate, but thank you anyway."

"Nonsense. We both know you're going to win, Metellus that you are, eh?" He grinned, a ghastly sight that exposed teeth as long as my fingers.

"Ah, so rumor has it." I had always disliked and feared Crassus, but this senile attempt at geniality was doubly unsettling. The Senate was full of dotty old men, but we didn't entrust the fate of legions to them.

"Exactly, exactly. Not a cheap office, aedile. Games, upkeep of the streets, walls, and gates—they're in shocking disrepair, you know. Next year is going to be a bad one on the aediles. Several of them have already come to me to help them with the burden."

"And I am sure that you received them with your famed generosity." He was as well-known for miserliness as for wealth, and he never turned a *sestertius* loose without expecting a fat return. Naturally, the irony sailed right past him.

"As always, as always, my boy. And I could do as much for you."

This was getting to be the theme of the day. The prospect was not made less tempting through repetition. I longed to grasp at it, but the repulsion Crassus always inspired in me made me draw back.

"But then you would expect my support in the Senate for your war, Marcus Licinius."

He nodded. "Naturally."

"But I oppose it. At least the Gauls and the Germans gave

Caesar some slight excuse to make war on them. The Parthians have done nothing."

He looked honestly puzzled. "What of that? They're rich." Always a good-enough reason for Crassus and his like.

"Call me old-fashioned, Consul, but I think Rome was a better state when we only made war to protect ourselves and our allies, and to honor treaty obligations. We've filled the City with other people's wealth and ruined our farmers with a flood of cheap, foreign slaves. I would like to see an end to this."

He leered hideously. "You are living in the past, Decius. I am far older than you, and I remember no such Rome. My own grandfather did not serve such a Rome. The wars with Carthage taught us that the biggest wolf with the sharpest teeth rules the pack. If we cease warring long enough for a single generation to grow up in peace, our teeth will grow dull and a younger, fiercer wolf will eat us." His voice steadied, and his eyes cleared, and, for a moment, I saw the young Marcus Licinius Crassus who had clawed his way to the top of the Roman heap during the City's bloodiest and most savage period, the civil wars of Marius and Sulla.

"The subjugation of Gaul will provide us with insurrections to put down for many years to come," I said. "Caesar is even talking about an expedition to Britannia."

"Caesar is still young enough to be thinking about such things. There is still one war to be fought in the East, and I intend to win it and come back to Rome and celebrate my triumph. Other members of your family have not been so delicate in their feelings for foreign kings. I strongly suggest that you consult with the greater men among them before making any unwise decisions. Good evening to you, Metellus!" He snapped out this last in a vicious whisper; then he whirled and stalked off.

I maintained my insouciant pose, but I was all but trembling in my toga. Yes, we still wore togas to dinner parties back then.

It was Caesar who introduced the far more comfortable *synthesis* as acceptable evening wear, and that was only after his stay at Cleopatra's court. Milo found me standing like that, and he wasn't fooled. He knew me far better than anyone else, except, perhaps, Julia.

"You look like a man with a viper crawling under his tunic. What did the old man say to you?"

I told him succinctly. I had few secrets from Milo, and we cooperated on most political matters.

"Personally," he said, "I don't know why you don't take him up on it. It really costs you nothing, and he's sure to die before he makes it back home, no matter how the war goes. His deterioration these last two years has been shocking."

"Clodius said almost the same thing to me earlier today."

"Even that little weasel is capable of wisdom from time to time."

"I'd rather not be known as another of Crassus's toadies, even if some of the other Caecilians have given in." My family, although still powerful in the Assemblies, had produced no men of great distinction recently. Metellus Pius was dead and his war against Sertorius all but forgotten. The conquest of Crete by Metellus Creticus really hadn't amounted to much. The Big Three understood that only *recent* glory counted for anything.

"It's a chancy time just now," he admitted. "It's hard to know exactly how to maneuver and how to vote. I find it all truly enjoyable, but a few years from now things are going to get vicious. Caesar, Pompey, and Crassus will all be heading for Rome and trying for the Dictatorship."

"They wouldn't dare!" I protested, with no great conviction.

He smiled indulgently. "Marius dared. Sulla dared. They'll dare. It's the main reason I support Cicero so strongly. He's a strict constitutionalist. If Caesar becomes Dictator, he'll get rid of me and make Clodius his Master of Horse." This ancient title meant the Dictator's number-two man and enforcer.

"And if it's Crassus or Pompey?"

"Then it's exile or execution for Clodius and me both. As long as they're engaged in foreign lands, they need men like us to control the City for them. With the Dictatorship they have it all, and they don't need us."

"You're talking about the death of the Republic," I said, shivering.

"It's been dying for a long time, Decius. Now come along. Cast off this gloom. Let's go talk to my men. Twenty of my best have agreed to fight in your funeral *munera* for Metellus Celer at a minimum charge, as a favor to me."

This cheered me, and I tried to shake off my mood of foreboding. Milo had some great retired champions working for him, men who were accustomed to getting huge fees to come out of retirement to fight in special Games. I grabbed another cup as we walked back toward his meeting hall.

"YOU DRANK TOO MUCH AGAIN," Julia informed me as we crawled into our detestably expensive litter.

"Do you think I don't know that, my dear? It's been an unsettling evening."

"You thought so? I had a wonderful time. Fausta has given me so many ideas."

"I feared that," I said, pinching the bridge of my long, Metellan nose.

"And Lisas is such an amusing dinner companion. You really must get us an invitation to the next reception at the Egyptian Embassy. I hear it is the most astonishing place."

"Such an invitation will be forthcoming. Lisas is now cultivating me, even though an aedile has nothing to do with foreign affairs."

"He knows you're on your way up," she said, patting my knee complacently. "So what soured your evening?"

"A little interview with our esteemed consul." I described our ominous conversation.

"That loathsome creature!"

"Oh, I don't know, someday I'll be old and decrepit, too, if the gods grant me a long life."

"That is not what I mean, and you know it!" she said, swatting me with her fan. "I knew him when I was a little girl, and he was still only middle-aged and relatively handsome. He was loathsome even then, the money-grubbing miser!"

"We can't all be patricians. As it occurs, I fully agree with your assessment of his character. Years ago, Clodia told me that Roman politics was a game in which all contended against all and there must eventually be one winner."

"She is an odious woman."

"But politically astute. It seems to be the general consensus that Crassus is soon to be removed from the playing board. All the rest have died or dropped out except for Caesar and Pompey. I fear civil war in the offing."

"Nonsense. Pompey is a political dolt, and he has separated himself from his veterans for too long. If Uncle Caius is forced to assume the Dictatorship—which is, I remind you, a constitutional office—I am sure that he will take only whatever measures are necessary to restore the Republic. He will then dismiss his lictors and hand his extraordinary powers back to the Senate, like all our great Dictators of the past."

So spoke the doting patrician niece. Her pessimistic, plebeian husband was far less confident. But he had many other things on his mind just then.

42

3

By THE NEXT MORNING I WAS A BIT fuzzy headed from the wine but otherwise ready to face another agreeable day of campaigning. Any day that began without the trumpets blowing to signal a dawn attack by the Gauls was a good day, as far as I was concerned. I left Julia snoring delicately and aristocratically behind me, splashed some water on my face, and went in search of breakfast. In my bachelor days I breakfasted in bed, but that luxury had gone the way of most of my bachelor habits.

Eating breakfast was one of those degenerate foreign practices to which I subscribed enthusiastically. Cassandra had laid a small table in the courtyard with melon slices, cold chicken, and warm, heavily watered wine. Nearby, Hermes, stripped to a loincloth, ran in place, warming up for a morning at the *ludus*. I noticed a slight hitch in his steps and looked for the cause.

"Come here, boy," I said. Apprehensively, he came to my

table, and I saw that he had a fresh, two-inch cut high on his left thigh, neatly stitched.

"That's Asklepiodes' needlework, isn't it?"

"Well, yes. He said it's nothing, just a skin cut. Didn't even nick the muscle. In fact—"

I brought my palm crashing down on the table, nearly up-setting my wine, which Hermes rescued. "I have ordered you *never* to train with sharp weapons! I'll not have my property risked need-lessly!"

"But all of the top men of the school—"

"You are none such! Practice with sharp weapons is strictly for veterans, the victors of many combats. They are men who earn fortunes by their skill and have no prospect of a future. As long as you belong to me, you are to stick to wooden swords. Sharp swords are for when we're in a war zone."

"It won't happen again, I promise," he said contritely. The evil little wretch was planning to disobey me at the first oppor-tunity. He always did.

"It was Leonidas, wasn't it?"

He looked surprised. "How did you know?"

"That backhand slice with the tip of the *sica* is his trade-mark. You were leading with your left leg and holding your shield too high. He always watches for that. If it had been a serious fight, he could have taken your leg off. The man's won thirty-two fights that I know of. You have no business sparring with him. Stick to the regular trainers and students of your own level. Do you un-derstand me?"

He hung his head with total insincerity. "Yes, sir."

"Then be off with you, and thank all the gods that you don't have to attend my morning calls." He was out the front door with-out bothering to put on his tunic. I returned to my breakfast, not totally displeased. If a champion like Leonidas thought Hermes was worth sparring with, he must be coming along nicely. Leonidas could behead flies buzzing around his helmet. The nick on the thigh had been a well-meant warning.

My clients met me in my atrium, and we went off to my father's house. As always it was mobbed with his clients. Since I was standing for office, I usually just paid my respects at the door, but this time his steward said that the old man wanted to speak with me. Knowing that this boded ill, I went in.

My father, the elder Decius, was one of the head men of *gens* Caecilia. He had held every public office including the Censorship and had commanded armies in the field, and his voice was one of the most respected in the *curia*. It was his continued longevity that kept me a legal minor. He could have manumitted me with a simple ceremony, but the old villain wasn't about to relinquish his hold. I found him alone in his study.

"Good morning, Father! How—"

He whirled around, his face red except for the great, horizontal scar that almost bisected his face and gave him his nickname: Cut-Nose.

"Did you really refuse Crassus's offer to cover your debts yesterday?"

"Well, yes."

"Twice, I understand?"

"How word does get around! Yes, I did. The second time to his face. You can't count the first time. That was to Clodius, and I'd never give him a positive answer."

"Idiot! You know how hard your family has worked to smooth relations with him, and with Caesar and Pompey!" These took the form of marriage ties: a son of Crassus married a Caecilia, I married Caesar's niece, and so forth. The fact that Julia and I actually wanted to marry had no bearing on the political matchmaking.

"I know you and the others have alienated Pompey."

He waved his big-knuckled hand. "No matter. He can manage the grain supply as long as he likes. He's done a wonderful job. We just have to keep him from command of the legions. Caesar has turned into a wild man, and he must be dealt with eventually, if he lives. But Crassus is vastly wealthy, and he could come back from Parthia a *triumphator!*"

"Everyone seems to think that he'll die before he gets home."

"How did I ever beget such a moron! No wonder you lose so much money at the races if that's how you place your bets!"

"Lose money? Me?" I cried, stung. "Just last month in Mutina I won—"

"Silence!" He leaned across his desk, supporting his weight on his knuckles, thrusting his head forward as he glared at me. "I know your memory is short, but I remember when Caius Marius returned from his last war. He was even older than Crassus and madder than Ajax! He seized power in the City and proceeded to kill more Romans than Hannibal! If Crassus comes back with a triumph and the wealth of King Orodes added to what he already has and a heart full of bile toward everyone he even imagines has offended him, a lot of us are going to die!"

"I hadn't thought of that," I admitted, chastened.

"And do you imagine the expenses of your office will be so slight that your family can afford to turn down a loan from Crassus? A loan that will be almost free from interest, I might add?" This was more like it: away from world events and back to the subject that touched us most intimately—the family purse.

"I'd rather go to the usurers than be owned by a monster like Crassus!"

"Nonsense! Crassus can't own you because I do! You will do as I say, vote as I say, and deal with Crassus as I say!"

At one time I would have erupted like a volcano at this, but the years had thickened my skin and leveled my temper. Besides, after you've been terrified by the likes of King Ariovistus the German, a father isn't all that frightening.

"I'll take your advice to heart, Father. But the damage is

already done. Maybe I can patch things up. The old fool may have forgotten the whole matter by now. But listen, Milo has made an excellent deal for me—" Father nodded, his color returning as I described the situation.

"Twenty of them? And some are Campanians, I believe. Yes, this will bring down the price of the funeral *munera* significantly. If we bring two or three pairs of the old champions on at the end of each day's fighting, that is what people will remember, not that you didn't have a hundred pairs earlier in the day. I've always held that it's the quality of fighting that counts, not how many half-trained amateurs and wretched prisoners you can crowd into the field. Why, in my younger days—" and so on and on.

Thus I left him in a somewhat better mood than I found him. This did little to improve my mood. He had upbraided me just as, earlier that morning, I had upbraided Hermes, and for the same reason. I was still his property. *Sometimes,* I thought, *the world is just not fair.*

Midday brought an unexpected invitation. A well-dressed man came up to me, and I greeted him as genially as I would have any other potential vote.

"Senator," he said, "I am Sextus Silvius, an equestrian. I come on behalf of the tribune Ateius Capito, who would greatly esteem your company at his house this afternoon. If you have no other plans, he customarily lays on an excellent midday meal. It will have to be quite informal. You know what a tribune's house is like."

I glanced at the *rostra.* "Your friend isn't in his usual place this morning."

"He knows that there is nothing more to be gained by talk. May I tell him that you will be coming? Or, better yet, will you come with me?"

I looked around the Forum, saw nobody I really wanted to associate with, heard my stomach growl, and decided. "It will be a pleasure." I took off my *candidus*, handed it to a client with instructions to take it home and inform Julia where I was going, and dismissed the rest.

"Why does this year's tribune want to cultivate next year's aedile?" I asked bluntly as we ambled toward the Via Nova, thence eastward into the warren of streets northeast of the Via Sacra.

"Both you and he are headed for higher office. The men who are to direct the great affairs of Rome in the future had better get to know each other if you are to work well together."

"That makes sense," I agreed, musing. "Silvius. Is that a Marsian name?"

He nodded. "Oh, yes. My family are Marsi from near the Fucine Lake. Roman citizens for generations, of course."

"Naturally." The Marsi were noted as splendid farmers and, less favorably, as practitioners of all sorts of magic. "Are you a relative of the tribune?"

"No, a friend. Along with others, I've been his assistant during his year in office. I will be more than relieved when that year is up."

"The tribuneship is a busy office," I said, putting it mildly.

The house of Ateius Capito took up the ground floor of a tenement block that faced an identical tenement block across a narrow street. The street itself was thronged with citizens: idlers, hangers-on, petitioners with rolled papyri to give to the tribune, and the generally disgruntled-looking, all come to press their suits upon the representative of the people. They made a path for me when they saw the senatorial stripe on my tunic. Some of the scroll holders tried to give their petitions to me in hope that I would bring them to the tribune's attention, but I begged off. The last thing I wanted to do was take on another politician's job.

The door was open, naturally. By ancient law the door of a tribune's house, even the door of his own bedroom, had to remain open during his year in office. He had to be accessible to the plebs every hour, day and night. Supposedly he incurred no danger through this practice because the sacrosanctity of his office rendered him immune from violence. Tribunes had been killed in past years of civil unrest, but that was considered very incorrect behavior.

It was just as crowded in the atrium, but there the great man's servants regulated the flow of callers so that they entered by ones and twos and small groups to present their petitions and questions and complaints. These servants stood aside as I passed through with Silvius.

"Tribune Ateius Capito," Silvius announced grandly, "I present the senator Decius Caecilius Metellus the Younger!"

"Welcome to my house, Senator," Ateius said, rising with hand extended. I took it and got my first close look at the man. He was lean as a dagger, with a dark, small-featured face dominated by unusually large, intense eyes. As a matter of fact, the whole man was intense. Even standing still, he seemed to vibrate like a plucked lyre string. "You do me great honor."

"The honor is mine. I can see how busy you must be."

"I am at the disposal of the citizens at all times," he said. "However, I think they will grant us a few minutes' leave." He went to the doorway and held up his hands. "My friends, fellow citizens, I must confer with the distinguished senator Metellus for a brief time. I promise that I will hear all your petitions." With sounds of disappointment, people backed away from the door, leaving us alone beside the pool of the *compluvium*.

Not that we were precisely alone. There remained behind a dozen or so friends of Ateius, most of them, like himself, of the equestrian order. They were all prosperous-looking men, as indeed was to be expected, a sizable fortune being the only real qualification for enrollment in that order. Ateius provided introductions.

"Private and formal meals are all but out of the question for a tribune," Ateius said, "but if you aren't finicky, I keep a simple buffet here." He led me to a long table heaped with food.

"This is more than adequate," I assured him, generously. Indeed, it was food of the plainest sort: bread and cheeses and fresh fruit, but that was to be expected. He couldn't rightly refuse food to his callers, and that mob would bankrupt him quickly if he laid on the delicacies. And for a man who had been living for months at a time on army rations when he could get them, there was nothing wrong with plain food. I heaped a plate and set it on a small table, and Ateius took a chair opposite me. The other men stood around attentively, far enough away to give us a sort of privacy, near enough so that Ateius could summon them without raising his voice. There is an art to this sort of attendance, although Romans have never mastered it the way they have in Eastern courts.

While we ate, we spoke of this and that, nothing serious. He bemoaned the travails of the tribuneship; I bewailed the forthcoming burdens of the aedileship; we both savored our own importance. Then, when we were finished eating, he got down to it.

"It's good to have you among us, Senator Metellus. The rest of your family have been maddeningly noncommittal."

It occurred to me that I had missed something important. "I beg your pardon? Whom have I joined?"

He smiled. "No need to be coy. By now everybody knows that you've turned down Crassus's offer to assume your debts, and did it at some personal danger, too. We admire that."

" 'We'?"

He waved a hand at the men around him. "The anti-Crassus faction. The men who know that the man is about to bring disaster upon us."

This was tricky. In the politics of the Republic, one never admitted to belonging to a *factio*. You, public-spirited statesman that you were, thought of nothing but the good of the State. On the contrary, it was your opponents, your enemies, whom you accused of belonging to *factiones*. Unlike you, they were self-seeking curs without honor or dignity.

It was all claptrap, of course. Everyone belonged to one *factio*, and many belonged to several. It was never formal or codified, like being a supporter of one of the racing companies in the Circus, where we Metelli had been Reds for centuries. In fact, it was from the Circus that we got the word *factio*.

At this time there were two major parties to which everyone subscribed to one extent or other. There were the Optimates: the "Good Men", i.e., the wellborn, and the Populares: the "Men of the People", i.e., all the rest. We Metelli were Optimates. So was Cicero. Clodius and Caesar were leaders of the Populares despite the fact that they were born patricians. Clodius was a Claudius and had changed his name when, with Caesar's collusion and over the objections of Cato and Cicero, he had been transferred to the plebs. He had taken this drastic step so that he could stand for the tribuneship, an office from which patricians were barred. Stripped of their powers by Sulla, the tribunes had gradually been regaining them in the twenty-four years since the Dictator's death, and now the tribuneship was in many ways the most powerful office in Rome.

Within these two major groupings were many smaller *factiones* representing more limited interests. I had the feeling that I was in the midst of one of these.

"Perhaps you had better elucidate, Tribune," I said. "It is true that I declined a loan from Crassus because I have no wish to become his lackey. I had no motive other than retaining my own political, not to mention economic, independence." This was not precisely true, but I did not feel that I owed this odd tribune any more.

"Oh, I quite understand that," he said. His tone said, on the contrary, that he knew a pack of lies when he heard one. "But you know that his proposed war is a disgrace."

51

"And yet," Silvius said in a well-rehearsed interruption, "the senator voted in favor of Crassus's command."

"As you all know perfectly well," I said, "the Senate voted no war. Crassus is to take over the Syrian promagistracy from Aulus Gabinius. What he does with his soldiers once he's there is up to him. It's a disgrace that the government has so little control over how our generals employ their troops, but that is the constitution as we have received it. As usual, I voted with my family on this. The Senate only ratified the law passed by your fellow tribune, Caius Trebonius. Blame him."

"Oh, I do, Senator, I do!" Ateius all but hissed, his fingers working reflexively as if on a dagger grip. Obviously, Ateius and Trebonius shared one of those Milo-Clodius relationships: each would happily drink the other's blood.

"Senator," Silvius said, "we must stop Crassus before he wrecks the Republic. Many, many Romans of all classes and all *factiones* agree with us in this. We have made it our business to appeal to all men of influence whom we know oppose Crassus to join us in this. We hope to number you as one among us."

"Gentlemen," I said, spreading my palms in an appeal to reason, "it is too late. There is nothing to be done. Whatever underhanded means were employed to secure him this command, the Senate and People have spoken. He has the backing of Caesar and Pompey. The Plebeian and Centuriate Assemblies have voted to pass the Trebonian Law, and the Senate has ratified it. The damage is done. There is no constitutional means to stop him."

"Then," Ateius said, his eyes glowing in a fashion not quite sane, "we may have to appeal to powers beyond the constitutional."

"I beg your pardon?" I said. "Admittedly, I am just back from Gaul after a long absence, but surely I would have been informed if our government had been set aside by, say, a Dictatorship or invading Libyans."

"I do not joke, Senator!" Ateius snapped. Clearly, here was a man of limited jocularity.

"Then what do you mean?"

"The Republic," he began, "has for many centuries rested upon a tripartite foundation. First," here he held up a knobby-knuckled finger, "there is the body politic—the Senate and People. Second," he raised a finger no comelier beside the first, "there is the constitution—our body of laws and practices, rigid in place but always changeable after due deliberation. Third," finger number three, somewhat shorter than the other two, and decorated by a ring in the form of a snake swallowing its tail, a tiny emerald for an eye, "the will of the gods."

I tried to think of other factors, but came up with none. "I suppose that about sums it up."

"As you just said, the possibilities of the first two have been exhausted short of violence. That leaves the third." He seemed quite pleased with himself for a man who was making no sense.

"The gods? I am sure that in this matter, as in all others, they were consulted, the proper sacrifices were made, prayers were offered, the auguries were taken, and so forth. But we all know that it is quite rare for the Olympians to take a direct hand in the affairs of Rome. At most they send us signs that we ignore at our peril."

"There are others," he said, portentously. "There are gods less remote than the official gods of the State—gods willing to aid those who know how to call upon them."

I felt a sudden chill. I had just come from a place where savage gods were called upon all the time and seemed more than eager to take part in the affairs of men—the bloodier the better.

"And you are one who knows how to bend these deities to your will?" I asked.

"I am," he said, smugly.

I stood. "Tribune, you tread close to the edge of sorcery.

There are laws against such practices—laws that carry with them terrible punishments. It is my firm belief that religion and trafficking with the supernatural should have no part in the conduct of State business, except for the sacrifices, festivals, and omen-taking sanctioned by the constitution, all of which are more than adequately defined by ancient law."

"Don't be a fool, Metellus!" he cried, dropping his geniality. "We are prepared to take the strongest measures to stop Crassus, and if you are not with us, we must regard you as an enemy."

The rest looked a little shamefaced, as if they were embarrassed by their colleague's excessive reaction. "There is no need for a breach between ourselves and the house of Metellus," Silvius said, trying to smooth things over. "The senator is clearly an anti-Crassan—"

"Join us, Metellus," Ateius said, "or suffer the consequences with the rest."

"Am I to regard this as a threat?" I said coldly.

"It is a warning I offer in good faith as tribune and priest," he said with the same lunatic certainty that characterized the rest of his drivel. Tribune and *priest?* The tribuneship carried no sacerdotal duties to my knowledge. Obviously, the man was mad. Of course, being crazy was no impediment to a successful political career. Look at Clodius.

"Then good day to you. I have kept you from the citizens too long." I swept out with what I hoped was imposing dignity. Behind me I heard an agitated muttering, as of an overturned beehive.

It had been one of the oddest interviews I had experienced in a career full of oddities. That night I described the bizarre business to Julia.

"Don't let it upset you," she said, sleepily. "The man is insane, and he'll be out of office in less than three months."

"Still, I dislike having a tribune announce himself to be my enemy, and lunatic enemies can be the worst kind. They are un-predictable."

"Out of office he'll be harmless," she insisted. "After that, your sane enemies will give you all the worries you need."

She made sense, but I had a definite feeling that sense would play little part in this matter, and I was right. I did not sleep soundly that night.

4

AND SO THE GREAT DAY DAWNED. Since it was one of the most famous days in the long course of those agonizing years, it behooves me to describe it in some detail. All the more so because it has been described wrongly by many who were not there or who were there but had reasons of their own to falsify the events, and by no few who weren't even born at the time.

Many, for instance, will tell you that it was a dark, gloomy day, with lowering clouds and ominous rumblings from the heavens, since this is supposed to be the sort of weather that accompanies dreadful events. Actually, it was a crisp, clear day in November. There was a bite to the breeze but the sun shone brightly. In truth, it was not the weather but the citizens who displayed every sign of depression. The streets were thronged as they were on all such occasions, and there was scarcely room in the Forum for a small dog to dart about between people's feet.

It was from this crowd, not from the clouds, whence came

the ominous rumblings. Ateius and Gallus and many others had whipped them into a near frenzy against the departure of Crassus. A riot was in the offing.

The Senate had assembled before dawn, and I was there, yawning and stamping my feet, trying to get warm. Things were better when the sun rose to display the senators in their full majesty, struggling hard not to look as cold as the citizenry. Working at this hardest of all was Marcus Porcius Cato, dressed as he was in his hideous, old-fashioned toga. This garment was of the antiquated, rectangular variety, which does not drape as gracefully as the conventional, semicircular type. It was so dingy that he looked like a man in mourning, and he did not wear a tunic beneath it, since the ancestors he worshiped had seen no need for more than a single garment. He was barefoot since those ancestors considered shoes or sandals likewise effete. Or so Cato thought and communicated at great length.

Every senator living in or near Rome and capable of rising from his bed was in Rome that morning. Marcus Licinius Crassus Dives was stepping down from his consulship, taking up his proconsular *imperium,* and departing for Syria. Everyone wanted to see whether he'd make it to the City gate alive. There was considerable doubt concerning the likelihood of this. His army was far away, and he had few friends in Rome. He had secured his elections through intimidation and bribery, and supporters secured by such means are not likely to come to one's aid when blood and teeth and random bits of flesh are being scattered in the streets.

As always happens on such occasions, the City buzzed with omens: a two-headed calf had been born in Campania, Aetna had erupted again, blood fell from the sky upon the patch of ground before the Temple of Bellona that is designated enemy territory, and so forth—all the usual bad omens. My favorite that morning was the reported sighting of an eagle that flew *backward* through the Temple of Janus, in the back door and out the front. It is so rarely that one hears of a truly original omen. It occurred to me to wonder how anyone knew which door was which, since the god faces both ways.

More disturbing were the accurate reports from the temples, where the sacrifices had been almost uniformly disastrous. Sacrificial animals had struggled; the priest's assistant had needed more than a single blow of the hammer to stun them; unclean animals had intruded; or priests had stumbled over the ancient formulae. In front of the Temple of Jupiter *Stator,* an Etruscan *haruspex,* upon examining the liver of the sacrificed bull, had fled in horror. It is my own tendency to flee in horror from any liver, but *haruspices* are expected to be made of sterner stuff. Even as we waited at the base of the Capitol, Crassus was atop it sacrificing to Capitoline Jupiter.

My fellow senators were crowded onto the steps of the Temple of Saturn, and all around us were the members of the various priestly colleges wearing their insignia. The Vestals stood on the steps of their temple, surrounded by a well-behaved crowd made up mostly of women.

There were senators present who rarely came into the City twice in a year. I saw Quintus Hortensius Hortalus, my father's old patron and colleague, who had retired to his country estate when his career in the courts was eclipsed by Cicero's. He was deep in conversation with Marcus Philippus, one of the previous year's consuls. I knew exactly what they were talking about: fishponds. Since the death of Lucullus the year before, Hortensius and Philippus had been unrivalled for the extravagance and magnificence of their fishponds, which contained both salt and fresh water, were the size of small lakes, and were surrounded by colonnades and porticoes, and whose every last mullet and lamprey they seemed to know by name. I suppose every man needs a hobby.

Cicero himself was there, back from exile but not really safe in the City. That morning, however, all the malice in Rome was directed elsewhere.

I thrust my way through the press to Cato's side. "The betting is five to three that he doesn't make it alive past the Golden Milestone," I said. "It's ten to one and climbing that he doesn't get to the City gate on his feet."

"I loathe the man," Cato said with some degree of understatement, "but a Roman magistrate should be allowed to depart for his province without interference."

"They just shouldn't be allowed to take office, eh?" I said, studying the fine new scar on his forehead. In the elections of the year before, he had tried to stop Pompey and Crassus from standing for consul. In the subsequent riot he had been badly injured.

"It was Crassus's hired thugs who started the brawl," Cato said, stiffly.

"I'm sorry I missed it." I sighed.

"You'd have been in your element." He looked uphill. "Here they come."

A hush fell over the great mob as the procession made its way down the steeply sloping Capitoline Street. First came two files of lictors, twelve in each file. One file, Pompey's, wore togas. The lictors of Crassus wore red tunics cinched with broad, black leather belts studded with bronze—field dress for lictors accompanying a promagistrate in his province. Behind them strode the consuls.

"Pompey is with him," Cato said, relieved. "He may make it to the gate yet."

It was a splendid gesture on Pompey's part. He had set aside his personal animosity to see his colleague safely out of Rome. Pompey was still an immensely popular man, and his presence just might avert violence. Close behind Pompey, I saw an enormous man who had a mustache in the Gallic fashion. He wore a toga the size of a ship's sail, so I knew he was a citizen. I had never before seen a Roman citizen wearing a mustache.

"Who's the hairy-lipped giant?" I asked.

"Lucius Cornelius Balbus," Cato said. "He's a close friend of Pompey and Caesar. He soldiered under Pompey against Sertorius. Pompey gave him citizenship as a reward for heroism." Of course, I had heard the name, and Caesar had spoken to me of him often, but this was the first look I'd had of him. He was from Gades, in Spain. The people around there are a mixture of Carthaginian and Greek and Gallic, with the latter predominating and probably accounting for his lip adornment.

The year's praetors walked behind the consuls, and I saw Milo and Metellus Scipio and a few others I knew. One of the Censors, Messala Niger, was with them, but his colleague, Servilius Vatia Isauricus, was not. Vatia was very elderly and probably had stayed home. I saw a man come from the crowd and fall in beside Milo. It was his brother-in-law, the almost equally handsome Faustus Sulla.

"Senators!" Cato called. "Let us fall in behind the serving officials. We must not allow the dignity of public office to be molested by an unruly mob." *Nicely put,* I thought. Nothing to indicate support for Pompey or Crassus, whom everyone knew to be among his personal enemies. Cato stepped forth fearlessly, muttering out of the side of his mouth: "Decius, stay close to me. Allienus, Fonteius, Aurelius Strabo, and Aurelius Flaccus, come to the front." He called for others, assembling all the Senate's most notorious veteran street brawlers; there was no lack of such men in that august body. When a man like Milo could make it all the way to praetor, you can imagine what the back benches were like.

Slowly, we walked behind the men with the purple borders on their togas. There was still grumbling from the crowd, and Crassus made a show of ignoring it, but the presence of Pompey kept things from getting violent. I almost thought they were going to pull it off.

61

The first disturbance came before we were out of the Forum. As if by magic the crowd parted before the lictors, and there stood the tribunes Ateius and Gallus with their staffs ranged behind them. Ateius raised a palm and cried out: "Marcus Licinius Crassus! As Tribune of the People, I forbid you to leave the City of Rome!"

"Stand aside, Tribune!" Pompey shouted in a parade-ground voice that cracked through the Forum like a stone from a catapult.

Ateius pointed at Crassus. "Arrest that man!" The tribunal assistants surged forward, but the lictors closed ranks. With a few brisk strokes of the *fasces*, Silvius and his companions were laid out on the pavement. People cheered this rare entertainment.

Abruptly, another man rushed at Ateius. "Let our consul proceed, idiot!" he cried, even as he punched Ateius in the mouth.

"This man has laid violent hands upon a tribune!" Ateius screamed. "This is sacrilege!"

"Trebonius is a tribune, too," Milo shouted. "Can't do a thing about it. He's sacrosanct."

Purple in the face, growling like a dog, and bleeding slightly from the lip, Ateius whirled around and pushed his way into the mob. Shakily, his men got to their feet and hustled off after him.

The procession continued on its way. The little farce seemed to have put everyone in a better mood. There were no cheers, but the threatening noises had subsided to a few rude shouts and derisive laughter aimed at Crassus.

"I think he's going to make it to the gate," someone said from behind me.

"I hope so," I said fervently. "I've bet a hundred and fifty sesterces he'd get all the way out of the City." The senators who had bet he wouldn't even make it out of the Forum alive were already paying the winners, sour faced and with one more grudge against Crassus to add to the rest.

We marched all the long way to the ancient Capena Gate,

which gave onto the Via Appia. Crassus was going to travel the Appia all the way to its end, in Brundisium. Thence he was going to sail to Syria, so eager was he to get there fast. A man who would set sail in November was capable of any folly.

Ateius was waiting for him upon the city wall atop the gate. "What's that fool up to?" Cato said, as mystified as the rest of us. The procession and the whole following crowd, as well as the multitude that had been waiting by the gate all morning, stood goggling at this unwonted spectacle.

Ateius was transformed. Not only did he stand in this rather unorthodox spot, but he had discarded his toga for a bizarre robe striped red, black, and purple, bordered with Greek fretwork in gold thread, and spangled with embroidered stars, scorpions, serpents, and other symbols, many of them unfamiliar to me. The left side of his face was painted red like that of a *triumphator,* the right side painted white. On his head was a close-fitting cap covered with what looked like a multitude of tiny bones. Before him a fire burned in a bronze bowl mounted on a tripod. The flames were an ugly green.

"Hear me, Janus!" Ateius cried. *Conventional enough so far,* I thought, *despite the strange getup.* When we invoke the gods, we always invoke Janus, god of beginnings, first. "Hear me, Jupiter Best and Greatest! Hear me, Juno, Minerva, Mercury, Venus, Saturn, Mars, Neptune, and all the Olympians! Hear me, Bellona, Ops, Flora, Vulcan, Faunus, Consus, Pales, Vertumnus, Vesta, Tiberinus, the Dioscuri, and all the gods of the City, the river, the fields, and the woodlands of Rome! Hear me, the Unknown God!" *A comprehensive but not unusual invocation,* I thought.

It was an unprecedented display. Ateius belonged to no priestly college I was aware of. He was not performing his ceremony, whatever it was, at a temple, shrine, or other sacred site. Still, despite its boldness and effrontery, nobody sought to stop him. It was not that any authority restrained us. It was just that, as Romans, we were terribly reluctant to interrupt a ritual in progress. From earliest youth we were drilled in the rule that a rite must be performed from beginning to end without interruption and without mistake. Ateius was taking advantage of our unthinking adherence to ritual law.

Now he pointed at Crassus, using a wand wreathed with myrtle and tipped with what appeared to be an infant's skull.

"Immortals! Marcus Licinius Crassus has ignored the many and profuse omens you have sent to make plain your displeasure with his impious expedition to make war against the will of the Senate and People!" All this he spoke in a hieratical chant, the sort of voice one is accustomed to hear priests using, for they must often recite formulae in language so antiquated that even the best scholars disagree on their exact meaning, and the only way to speak them intelligibly is to chant them rhythmically. Priests are so accustomed to this mode of speech that they use it even when reciting prayers in Latin or Greek. Now he raised hands and wand high, and he shouted in a voice louder than ever.

"I curse this man! I curse his expedition, and all who take part in it! I curse all who support it in Rome! In the name of all the gods I have invoked thus far, I invoke the most terrible execrations upon the head of Marcus Licinius Crassus!"

Every jaw of the multitude sagged with disbelief. Unconsciously, we covered our heads as if attending a sacrifice. Everywhere, people were pulling out protective amulets and making the ancient hand gestures to ward off evil. A geniune, priestly curse was a great rarity, usually invoked only against a foreign enemy or, very rarely, a Roman traitor. Curses were only performed by qualified priests and then only under rigidly prescribed safeguards to prevent the curse from rebounding upon the priest and anyone else standing nearby.

Thus far? I thought. Who was left to invoke? I soon learned. Ateius reached into a fold of his weird robe and took out something that looked like a dried snake. This he cast into the flames, releasing a foul-smelling smoke. He drew forth a similarly dried human hand and cast it in. Herbs, roots, preserved animal and human parts went into the green flames. He snapped the wand in two and placed it on the flames. Then he drew a small, hook-bladed knife. With this he opened a vein on his forearm, and, as his blood dripped sizzling into the fire, he resumed his chant.

"Father Dis, Plutus of the Underworld, Eita, Charun of the Hammer, Tuchulcha, Orcus, and all the Manes and Lemures, summon to the enforcement of my curse all the unspeakable minions of your realm!" And now he got down to the real business of the day.

"Immortals! I invoke—" and here he spoke a name that was forbidden for any man below the priestly rank of *flamen* to pronounce, and even then only in the company of enrolled priests of the State. And then he spoke another. And another. These were unthinkably ancient, half-forgotten gods, most of them worshiped in Italy before the foundation of the City. Some were Etruscan gods, and Etruscans were the most powerful magicians outside of Egypt. Even now, all these many years later, the pen trembles in my hand as I think of that day. Well, my hand trembles these days anyway, but this is worse.

I heard him speak the name of a god I had thought was only known within my own family, one we called upon to communicate with our dead ancestors at special Caecilian rites, after the *paterfamilias* had performed all the protective and purificatory rites. I looked around me and saw every major priest of the State gone dead white. The *virgo maxima* had her hands clamped tightly over her ears, and all the Vestals behind her did the same. The other citizens stood with looks of stupefied terror. One rarely sees people who are both panic-stricken and absolutely still.

Ateius's voice rose to an eerie, wailing shriek. At first the words were in one of the ancient, ritual languages that even Etruscans no longer understand, but that are terrifying just to hear. Then, in Latin:

"I curse him forever, in life and in death! I curse his friends and followers! In the name of all the gods and demons I have invoked, I curse them all forever! Immortals, hear me!" With the last word, he kicked the brazier over, and it toppled from the top of the gate to the pavement, scattering flame and hot coals and foul-smelling substances indiscriminately. People drew back shrieking as clothes were set smoldering, and when we had wit to look up again, Ateius was gone. For a long time, nobody spoke.

At last Cato uncovered his head. "What a time for the *pontifex maximus* to be out of the City! He's the only one with authority over this sort of thing."

Cicero came up to us. "At least Caesar would be able to control this crowd," he said. "They're like stunned cattle now, but in a few moments they'll come halfway to their senses, and there will be a riot such as we've never seen before! They are terrified!"

"There's one they'll listen to," I said. "Wait here."

I went over to the huddle of Vestals. The *virgo maxima* was an aged aunt of mine, and the most revered person in Rome. The priests and augurs were mostly politicians, and viewed as such except when conducting rituals, but the Vestals were the embodiment of Rome itself.

"Auntie, dear," I said, "you had better speak to this crowd, or they will tear the City apart. Assure them that this curse will not fall upon them."

"I can assure them of no such thing," she said. "But I will do what I can."

She strode to the center of the plaza, awesome, but serene, in her dazzling white robe. A jerky, spastic muttering had broken out among the crowd, but it stilled when she went to stand by the consuls.

"Romans!" she called out. "Our ancient and sacred City is

unclean. I forbid all work, all celebration, all activities save those for the maintenance of life. There will be no sacrifices, no funerals, no manumission of slaves, no courts, no official business of any sort." She turned to Crassus. "Marcus Licinius Crassus, leave the City of Rome instantly, and bear your curse with you. Go forth to take up *imperium* over your province and accomplish whatever mischief is in your heart, but leave."

Crassus wore the most frightful expression, compounded of rage and terror, his teeth grinding audibly. "That tribune has robbed me!" he finally choked out. "Today was to be glorious!"

"Go!" she said coldly.

"I do not care!" he screamed at the multitude. "He has taken my setting forth, but I will return in glory, and then I will kill him and all his friends!" He whirled and stalked out beneath the gate, where a small party of horsemen awaited. A great, collective sigh escaped the crowd.

"Consul," the *virgo maxima* said to Pompey, loud enough for all to hear, "I instruct you to convene a full meeting of the Senate, to include all the priestly colleges. We must devise a way to avert the wrath of the gods. This is a religious matter, so the convocation escapes my ban on secular business."

"You have heard the august lady," Pompey called. "All senators and priests: to the *curia now!* All other citizens, foreigners, and slaves, go to your homes and allow the duly constituted authorities to deal with this matter. I dismiss you!"

Slowly, frightened still but no longer panicky, the crowd began to break up. The situation was in competent hands. People believed in Pompey, and everyone revered the Vestals.

We all began to trail back the way we had come, but I looked back over my shoulder and saw the dwindling figure of Crassus riding amid his escort, framed by the Capena Gate. It was the last I ever saw of Marcus Licinius Crassus. Within eighteen months he would be dead along with most of his army in one of the greatest military disasters of Roman history. That was one powerful curse.

THE *CURIA* WAS PACKED, WHAT with so many more senators than usual being in town. It was also noisy. We usually adhered to a grave, dignified demeanor when the commons were watching, but we carried on like supporters of rival factions in the Circus when we assembled in one of the meetinghouses. The Curia Hostilia was the most venerable of these, and it was right in the Forum. The new meetinghouse attached to Pompey's Theater was far more spacious, but it was a long walk out over the Campus Martius, and it was usually used only in summer, when the heat made the old *curia* stifling.

When Pompey made a point of summoning the priests, that had been mostly a gesture to reassure the people, since most of the priests were senators anyway. At least it was more colorful than usual, since most of the members of the various priestly colleges wore their robes and insignia of office. The Arvals wore wreaths of wheat ears, the augurs wore striped robes and carried their crook-headed staffs, the *flamines* wore their conical, white caps, and so forth. There was no *Flamen Dialis* that year. In fact, there had been none for more than twenty years. The duty was so laden with taboos as to make it too onerous for anyone in his right mind to want. The *virgo maxima*, rarely seen in the *curia*, sat next to Pompey, attended by her single lictor.

Pompey stood from his curule chair, and the room fell silent. Well, almost silent. It was, after all, the Senate.

"Conscript Fathers," he began, "today Rome has suffered an unprecedented misfortune. A man who may not be touched by any legal authority has taken it upon himself to perform a terrible ceremony within the *pomerium* and before the assembled people. The implications of this ritual must be interpreted for us by the highest religious authorities, and a suitable remedy and course of action must then be found. None here may speak of our deliberations outside this chamber. A single report will be written, and this will be delivered under seal to the *Pontifex Maximus,* Caius Julius Caesar, in Gaul. In his absence the next-highest authority will address us first. *Rex sacrorum,* speak to the Senate."

Pompey resumed his seat, and the King of Sacrifices rose from his front-row bench and turned to face the assembly. He was an aged priest named Lucius Claudius. He had held the office since he was a young man, and because it barred him from political life, he had devoted himself to the study of our religious institutions. Although he had never held public office, like all the highest priests he had a seat in the Senate with all its insignia and privileges, except that he had no vote.

"Conscript Fathers," he said, "I was not present at this desecration of the City, but the curse has been related to me in its entirety by qualified colleagues, and rest assured that this was a ritual of the utmost power, and one nearly certain to fall back upon the one who pronounced it. Furthermore, it was of a deadliness sufficient to destroy the City of Rome itself. Our City and our people have become ritually unclean and abhorrent to the immortal gods!"

This pronouncement was so terrible that the whole Senate was actually silent for a while.

"Tell us what we must do," Pompey said, more frightened than he had ever been in battle.

"First, and immediately, there must be a *lustrum.* Censors!" Servilius Vatia and Messala Niger stood. Vatia was a *pontifex* as well as a Censor. "Have you chosen the sacrificial victims for the *lustrum* required by your office?"

Messala, the younger of the two, answered: "The ritual is always performed in May. We have been too occupied with the Census to look at sacrificial beasts."

"Then send out your assistants immediately. The rite must begin before sunrise tomorrow, and it must be completed, without failure or interruption, before sunset!"

Vatia said: "That should be plenty of time—"

"You misunderstand," said the *rex sacrorum*. "This is not to be the conventional *lustrum*. The entire City must be purified before we can resume relations with our gods. That means that the sacrificial animals will not merely be carried around the citizens assembled by centuries on the Field of Mars. They must be carried around the entire circuit of the Servian Walls! Three times!"

At this a great collective gasp went up. It would be an absolutely Herculean task, but nobody thought to protest. If we lay under so great a curse, no mere formality would impress the gods. I felt sorry for the men who would have to accomplish the feat. Pompey must have been reading my thoughts.

"The people must see how seriously we regard this matter," said the consul. "I want those animals carried by senators! Every man of this body who is under his fortieth year, and especially those who have recently returned from military service, are to report to the *rex sacrorum* at the end of these deliberations!"

I closed my eyes and buried my face in my palms. I should have stayed in Gaul.

Pompey recognized Cato. "I think," Cato said, "that we should look into reviving the old custom of human sacrifice. That would be pleasing to both the gods and our ancestors."

"Isn't that just like Cato?" I muttered, this novelty taking my mind temporarily from my upcoming torment.

Cicero rose, and I knew from his malicious smile that he had been waiting for just this proposal from Cato.

"My learned colleague, Marcus Porcius Cato, raises an interesting point. While, as all men know, human sacrifice was forbidden by senatorial decree many years ago, it has been revived under circumstances of very special danger to the State from time to time. This particular instance presents us with certain problems in choosing a suitable victim. The usual sacrifices have been foreign captives or condemned criminals. However, this offense has insulted all the greatest gods of the State. Such a sacrifice would be contemptible to these deities. On the contrary, when sacrificial animals are chosen for sacrifice, they must be perfect in all respects.

"If we transfer this consideration to a human victim and choose him with the same rigor, ruthlessly rejecting those who display any defect of body or character, we should be hard put to find one pleasing to all the gods. He would have to be highborn, of the highest moral character, of unimpeachable honesty, and of perfect piety. In fact, since Marcus Porcius Cato is, by his own admission, the only Roman of this generation who possesses all these virtues, he must be the only suitable sacrifice! Cato, do you volunteer?"

Face flaming, Cato resumed his seat. There was much choking, coughing, and clearing of throats. If it hadn't been such a solemn occasion, the *curia* would have experienced its greatest outburst of hilarity since the day Caesar had said his wife must be above suspicion, seven years earlier.

One after another, the heads of the priestly colleges spoke, as did others who were experts on ritual law. Pompey appointed a special commission, headed by Cicero, to examine all the religious implications of what had happened and come up with remedies. The *lustrum* was only the beginning, allowing us to address the gods in greater detail.

"Now," Hortensius Hortalus said, "what are we to do about this renegade tribune, Caius Ateius Capito?"

"Nothing can be done to him now," Pompey said, "but in less than two months' time, both he and I will step down from office, and at that time I intend personally to prosecute him for sacrilege, for *perduellio*, and for *maiestas!* For offense against the gods, for offense against the State, and for offense against the Roman people! I want you, Hortensius, and you, Cicero, to assist me in this."

"Gladly!" said both men at once.

Pompey turned to face the door outside of which was the bench of the tribunes. "Publius Aquillius Gallus!"

The man came to stand in the door, white faced. "Yes, Consul?"

"Of all the Tribunes of the People, you have been closest to Ateius in opposition to Crassus. What was your part in this matter?"

"Consul, I had no idea that he would do this! Like most of Rome, I oppose the aims of Crassus and will do so until I die or he does, and all men know this. But I never knew Ateius intended this impious act and would have done all in my power to stop him. This I swear—that is, after the *lustrum* tomorrow I will swear it before all the gods!"

"I am prepared to believe you," Pompey said, grimly. "But in this matter mere words are not enough. Tomorrow evening you will go with me to the Temple of Vesta and swear exactly that before her altar and fire, and so will every other tribune, even Trebonius, whom I know to be the enemy of Ateius. As far as I am concerned, the whole institution of the tribuneship has been disgraced."

After that, there were more speeches and more debate, for men never talk so much as when they are most afraid. This time it was as if a million Gauls were camped outside the gates, or Spartacus were risen from the dead and sitting out there with all our slaves behind him.

I returned to my house after sundown, famished and ill-tempered. I had not eaten since early morning, and nobody in Rome could bathe or shave until the *lustrum* was finished, which didn't improve things. Julia was wide-eyed with apprehension when I came in. The figures of the household gods were covered with cloths. The slaves went around on tiptoes.

"The whole City knows what that awful man did," Julia said. "The most terrible rumors are flying about. What did the Senate decide?"

"I'm forbidden to speak of it," I told her, "but I can tell you what we are going to do in the morning. The people are being told by the heralds now." In the distance, I could hear the loud shouts as the heralds went through the streets, telling everyone of the ceremony to be begun before dawn. I described the trial that awaited me.

"Will it be possible?" she said, putting a hand on my shoulder.

"Just barely, I think. The worst of it is, I can't even go sacrifice at the Temple of Hercules for strength."

"At least you're in the best condition of your life," she said encouragingly. "I know that better than anybody!"

5

For once, I wasn't grousing and complaining at having to rise before dawn. I was too apprehensive for that. I breakfasted lightly, but drank plenty of water, for I was all too aware of how hard I would soon be sweating. I dressed in a red military tunic and *caligae,* since that was the ancient custom when performing the *lustrum.*

"All the patrician women are gathering at the Temple of Vesta," Julia told me. "That is where I will be." She had put on her aristocratic Roman lady persona, as she had been drilled by her grandmother to do in times of crisis. I shuddered to think that one day she might turn into Aurelia.

"I will meet you back here, then, my love, although I may have to be carried. Hermes, do you have all my things?"

"Got them right here." He patted the bulging hide bag that contained most of my military gear, which might be needed at some stage of the ceremony. Surely, I thought, they would not demand that we wear armor the whole time. But anything was possible.

I kissed Julia and made my way into the street with Hermes close behind me. All the way to the front door, aged Cassandra sprinkled me with dried herbs and called upon obscure rural deities to lend me strength. On that particular morning they probably weren't listening, but I was not about to turn down any aid, however slight, and it could do no harm.

The streets were crowded as people left their homes to find viewing places atop the wall. Despite the solemnity of the occasion, there was a certain subdued holiday feeling in the air, as there always is when routine is broken for an extraordinary event.

The Senate assembled by torchlight outside the gate nearest the base of the Capitol. Had this been the conventional, five-yearly *lustrum,* the citizens would have been drawn up by centuries, for this ceremony in former times was the purification of the army, and, by extension, of the populace as a whole. Of course, the armies were now far away, and the centuries had become mere voting categories, but we adhered to the ancient forms. The Censors were required to perform the *lustrum* before they left office.

But this was an extraordinary ceremony, and nothing was as usual. We had to hope that the *rex sacrorum* knew what he was doing.

"Senators!" Pompey shouted. "The sun will be up soon, so there's little time to get organized. The lictors will direct each of you to his place along the support poles. Since there will be a bit of sag to the poles, the shortest men will be nearest the center, the tallest at the ends. Many of the older senators have volunteered to go a part of the way. I'll take a hand myself for part of the course. But the senators under forty will make the whole three circuits—is that understood? Any of them who fall out had better recall that the Censors will be watching and they haven't purged the senatorial roles yet. Personally, I want to hear death rattles from anyone who drops. Lictors! Get them lined up."

With brisk efficiency, the lictors lined us up by height, with the shortest on the left end of the line, the tallest on the right. I found myself standing next to Cato, and he was dressed in full legionary gear, including a shield slung across his back.

"How far are you planning to carry it, Cato?" I asked.

"What do you mean? The full three circuits, of course."

"You don't have to, you know," I said. "Only those under forty have to go the whole course."

"I was born when Valerius and Herennius were consuls," he said stiffly.

"The same year I was born?" I said, aghast. "Unbelievable!" Cato was one of those men who give the impression of being elderly from childhood. I had always taken him to be at least ten years my senior, and probably more.

"Ah!" Cato said, ignoring me. "This is splendid! The gods will have to be pleased with this!"

Dawn was creeping over the field, and at last I saw clearly what we had to carry. "Oh, no!"

The priests and the temple slaves had indeed outdone themselves to honor the gods. The litter was the sort that is carried in triumphs, but this one was huge even by triumphal standards, with two support poles the size of ship's masts. It was beautifully made of the finest woods and decorated with gold, draped heavily with such flowers as were available in November. And atop it, on a high platform, rested the sacrifices.

The *lustrum* always takes the form known as *suovetaurilia*, in which three animals are sacrificed: a boar, a ram, and a bull. In the countryside near Rome there are sizable farms that do nothing except breed the exceptional animals required for the major ceremonies. The ram atop the float was not the wooly little creature you picture in hearing those awful pastoral poems, where lovesick shepherds tootle their pipes while mooning over some nymph named Phyllis or Phoebe. This one was the size of a small horse, with huge, curling horns and a haughty look on his face. The boar was the size of a common ox—a fierce-looking creature I wouldn't want to meet if he were fully conscious. The bull was, I believe, the largest such creature I had ever seen, larger than the fighting animals bred in Spain. He was pure white and was, as required, an absolutely perfect specimen of the breed.

All three creatures has been drugged so that there would be no unseemly bleating, squealing, or bellowing to disrupt the proceedings. Their legs had been doubled beneath them and bound with ropes entwined with fine, golden chains. Horns and tusks were gilded, and the beasts themselves had been heavily sprinkled with gold dust.

"Gold," I said, disgusted. "Just what we needed. More weight."

Pompey strode down the line, inspecting. Like most of us, he wore a plain military tunic and boots. He stopped before Cato.

"Senator, all that ironmongery will not be necessary."

"Consul, I am quite prepared to carry out this ceremony in the ancient fashion, fully armed."

"Senator—"

"I think it would be most pleasing to the gods if we all did so, in fact," Cato maintained stoutly.

"Senator!" Pompey snapped, out of patience. "We are losing time! If Cnaeus Pompeius Magnus," here he poked a finger into his own chest, just in case Cato was in some doubt as to whom he meant, "twice consul, winner of more victories than any other general in Roman history, finds a military tunic the proper uniform for this ceremony, then a senator who has held no offices higher then quaestor and tribune should not find this beneath him!"

"Yes, Consul!" Cato said, with a fine, military salute. While his slaves helped him out of his gear, Pompey addressed the rest of us.

"The pacesetters will take the front position on each pole. These will be the *praetor urbanus* Titus Annius Milo and Lucius Cornelius Balbus, whom the Censors have just enrolled as a senator in recognition of his heroic military service. They are undoubtedly the two strongest men in this august, but usually out-of-shape, assembly."

This was the first I'd heard that Balbus was a senator. There was an ancient tradition that heroism could win a man a seat in the *curia* and a stripe on his tunic, but Sulla had instituted the law that a man had to be elected to at least the quaestorship to be enrolled. But Pompey usually got what he wanted. It was one more piece of evidence that Sulla's constitution was crumbling and that we were heading back into the anarchic old days.

The lictors positioned me on the left-hand pole, the one Milo captained. I noticed that Clodius was a few men behind me. I wished that he had been placed ahead of me, so that I could watch him suffer. It would have made up a bit for my own agony to come. Two other stalwarts took the rear positions, and we were all arranged.

"Now, Senators," Pompey said, "I want no one to try to run, no matter how late it gets. We'll never make it that way. We can get this done on time if we keep to a legionary quick pace. You've all been drilled in that since you were boys. Rome will rest on your shoulders today. So, lift!" Again came the word, hurled like a deadly missile, and we all stooped, laid hold of the poles, and lifted the tremendous parade float onto our shoulders. Upon the walls the people sighed with satisfaction. The animals seemed not to notice, merely blinking with lordly equanimity.

The *flamines* and other priests set out before us, some of them swinging censers in which incense burned. Atop the walls more incense smoked in braziers. We were burning enough that day to cause a serious shortage of incense throughout Roman territory.

"By the left," Milo said quietly, "quick step, *march.*" As one man, we all stepped off, left foot first.

In the beginning, the weight seemed quite tolerable, but I knew that would change. Soon the older senators would start dropping out. Then fatigue would take its inexorable toll. And even among the younger senators, for years many had performed no exertion more strenuous than crawling from the cold bath to the hot. They would not last either. I wanted no part of Cato's foolish nostalgia, but it seemed even to me that we were growing too soft. Unlike Cato and his ilk I did not blame this on foreign influence, but upon our increasing reliance on slaves to do everything for us.

The wall built centuries before by Servius Tullius had once marked out the boundaries of Rome. The City had long since spilled out of its confines, onto the Campus Martius and even across the river into the new Trans-Tiber district, and Sulla had even extended the span of the sacred *pomerium*, but these changes were too recent to make much of an impression. To all Romans of that day, the Servian Wall, following the line of the old *pomerium*, still defined the City.

Much building now lay outside the old wall, but it was surrounded by a span of sacred open ground on which nothing could be built and in which the dead could not be buried. This open ground formed our processional way. It was relatively level, going around the bases of the hills, and it was grassy, for no trees or shrubs were allowed to grow upon it. The old wall was still one of the military defenses of Rome, and you don't just give your enemy effective cover.

We started out northeast along the base of the Capitol, circling the city to the right. All around us the temple musicians played their double flutes, striving mightily to drown any sound that might disturb the ceremony or be interpreted as an evil omen. Before we had made a half-circuit, I was sweating despite the crisp breeze. Others were in far worse condition. I heard gasping from the older men and from those less well-conditioned.

Between the Colline Gate and the Esquiline Gate, all the elderly senators stepped away from the litter. The weight on our shoulders grew fractionally heavier. When we reached the embankment where the river runs along the base of the wall, the middle-aged men were dropping out fast.

About an hour before noon we reached our starting point. Four hours for the first circuit. Here Pompey left us, red faced and puffing.

"Keep it up, men," he gasped. "At this pace, we'll finish before sundown handily."

But there was more to it than time and pace. For the second circuit, we had perhaps half as many men to shoulder the burden. Granted it had been the weaker half that had left, but the willing backs of even old men had been a great help. By noon my shoulder was aching, and the sweat streamed off me by the bucketful. At least, to cheer myself up, I could always look back at Clodius, who was wheezing like a punctured bellows.

From atop the walls whole troops of little girls showered us with flower petals. They must have raided every garden and flower box in the City, and most of the petals were rather withered at that time of year, but we appreciated the gesture. All along our route, lesser priests and temple slaves dipped olive branches into jars of sacred, perfumed water and splashed it over us liberally, like the Circus attendants who dash water on the smoking chariot axles during the races. This we truly needed and appreciated, although ritual law demanded that we drink nothing during the ceremony.

We completed the second circuit of the wall by mid-afternoon, and some of us were in serious condition. My shoulder, neck, and back felt like molten bronze, and spots swam through my field of vision. My right arm was all but numb, my knees were shaky, and my feet were bleeding despite the hard marching I had been doing in Gaul. I was in better shape than 90 percent of those who were left. Clodius was in a near-coma, but still gamely on his feet. I no longer took delight in his discomfiture. Cato was hanging on stoutly to his Stoic demeanor, but I could see the signs of deathly fatigue in him. Milo and Balbus seemed not to be distressed, but neither was an ordinary mortal. Many of my colleagues would clearly not make it for another quarter-circuit, and I was having waking nightmares about the drugs wearing off and those huge animals setting up a struggle, rocking the litter.

"Good, men, good!" Pompey said as we set out on the third and final circuit of the walls. "Just one more little march, and it's done! We will be here, ready for the sacrifice, when you return."

"He's assuming a lot," wheezed somebody as we set off again.

"That's Pompey," said someone else in a phlegm-clogged voice, "always the optimist."

"Save your breath," Milo cautioned.

"Right," Balbus said in his faintly accented Latin. "Now comes the hard part."

And hard it was. Almost immediately, men dropped in their tracks, causing those behind to stumble and the float to lurch. Now I had another terror to add to the others. If the litter toppled, which way would it fall? The men on the wrong side would have a ton of wood and livestock fall upon them. But then, I thought, maybe that was what the gods wanted. A few squashed senators would make an impressive and, certainly, a unique sacrifice.

Somewhere near the Appian Aqueduct I decided that my right shoulder was now permanently six inches lower than my left. I was half-blind, but I looked around me anyway, and I saw the final, hard core of the Senate soldiering grimly on. Not many were friends of mine, but all were men whose reputations for toughness would not let them give up short of their final breath. I saw tunics stained with vomit and others stained with blood from lacerated shoulders. Blood poured in a steady stream from Clodius's nostrils, drenching his tunic and running down his thighs. I didn't dare look down at myself for fear of what I might see.

I heard a gentle grunt that didn't sound much like anything a human might perform. Then a lowing sound, followed by a quizzical baa. I looked up in pure horror.

"Hercules help us!" I said, forgetting that because of the curse he didn't hear. "They're waking up!"

"Steady, back there," Balbus said. "Not much farther to go now. They'll stay quiet." I saw that the back of his tunic, and Milo's, were soaked with sweat. They were human after all.

But the beasts began to shift, and the litter rocked, and when that happened, we lost step. Each time, it took us longer to get back in step again. This was looking bad.

"How far is it to the river?" I gasped, sweat obscuring what little vision I had left.

"We passed the embankment awhile ago," Cato growled out. "Are you blind, Metellus?"

"Just about." Past the river? I tried to remember how far it was from the river to the gate, but I couldn't, despite having walked the route a thousand times. Rome seemed like a totally strange place—a place I had never visited before. I had no more idea of its geography than that of Babylon. I wasn't even sure that we were going in the right direction.

I had a sensation of floating. Gradually, a sense of pressure told me that I was lying on my back. My vision cleared enough to see that I was looking up at the clouds of late evening, tinged red on their westerly edges. I knew then that we had failed. And ritual law prescribed the procedure when a ceremony was not performed properly: you do it all over again, right from the first.

"Pity Pompey didn't let us do this in full gear," I remarked. "I'd like to fall on my sword."

"Are you still alive, Metellus?" I'd have known that voice on the bank of the Styx.

"So I seem to be, Clodius. But I'm just not myself without lunch and my afternoon bath. How far did we get?"

"I don't know," he groaned. "I fell down awhile ago, and I haven't been able to turn over."

"On your feet," said Milo. Something grabbed the front of my tunic, and I was hauled to my feet as easily as a doll of straw. I saw that Milo and Balbus and a few others were reviving the fallen and that the priests were leading the sacrificial beasts from the platform.

"We made it?" I asked.

"Of course we made it," Milo said. "We're Romans, aren't we? But nobody attends a sacrifice on his back, so everyone stand up until it's over. As long as you keep on your feet, we can continue, although a sorrier-looking lot I never saw."

At last I looked down at myself, fighting off a wave of dizziness and nausea as I did so. I was covered with blood and less-reputable fluids, to which handfuls of flower petals adhered. My companions were in equally disheveled shape, and some of them far worse. But we had done something never attempted in living memory, and if the animals would just die without fuss, we could all go home and then brag about it for the rest of our lives.

A number of men staggered in while the final preparations were made. I later learned that only twenty of us made the entire three circuits, somehow carrying that tremendous weight for the last quarter-mile on our shoulders. Later, the Centuriate Assembly voted us special oak wreaths in honor of our feat. Those of Milo and Clodius were later burned on their funeral pyres, and I believe Cato had his with him when he died at Utica, many years later. My own still hangs among my achievements in the family atrium. I don't know what happened to the other sixteen.

Just before the upper rim of the sun disappeared below the horizon, the priests finished their droning chant, and the flutes were stilled. The *rex sacrorum* nodded, the hammers swung, the knives flashed, and the beautiful but weighty beasts fell with their blood gushing out onto the sacred soil.

The *rex sacrorum* raised his hands and intoned: "The gods are pleased. Rome is purified. All may return home now and sacrifice to their household gods. Worship of the immortals may resume."

And that was that.

With an arm over Hermes' shoulders, I lurched slowly toward home through a City that seemed much relieved. We weren't out from under the curse yet, but progress had been made.

"Maybe we should stop off at the baths first," I said, my chest sending pains through my body with every word.

"You need it," Hermes said, "but they've been closed down since yesterday morning. I don't expect to see them back in operation before tomorrow."

"Right. I forgot."

I vaguely remember people shouting congratulations at me and people offering me wine that I tried and immediately threw up. I had been in pitched battles far less strenuous than that day's exertion.

To my great amazement, my father reached my door at the same time we did. I was amazed because for my father to call on me rather than the other way around was all but unheard-of.

"Well-done, my boy," he said as he went in through the front gate. Coming from him, that was the equivalent of triumphing and winning at the Olympics on the same day.

Julia gasped at the sight of me and immediately had the slaves hustle me off to the tiny bathing room just off the kitchen. There I stripped off my unspeakable tunic, and Hermes sluiced me down with lukewarm water while I stood in the little stone tub.

Damp-haired and still unshaven, but washed, dressed in a clean tunic, and feeling far better, I went to join my family. I found Julia making a fuss over my father in the *triclinium*. I took a chair, and Hermes began to knead my shoulder, which was already turning a lurid purple. Cassandra gave me a large cup of warm, honeyed water, and I found that, if I sipped at it slowly, I could keep it down.

Julia beamed at me proudly. "The whole City is buzzing with your praises," she said. "Word reached the Temple of Vesta just moments after the sacrifice."

"I have a summons to deliver," Father interrupted, apparently thinking that I had already received more praise than a mere mortal could ever deserve. "While you were carrying out your duties, I was meeting with some of the sacerdotal authorities, and they wish to meet with you under conditions of utmost privacy. What they have to say to you must be heard by no others."

"I'm not sure I understand," I said.

"Of course you don't understand!" he snapped. "Why should you? It is sufficient that they want to talk to you."

"Do they wish to honor him in some way?" Julia asked innocently. She was anything but innocent.

"No, nothing like that. Your husband's reputation as a snoop precedes him. They have an investigation for him to undertake."

I thought I saw where this was leading. "Has anything been heard from Ateius?"

Father shook his head. "No, the villain's vanished. It's at times like this that we need a Dictator. The evil demagogue should be impaled on a hook and dragged down the Tiber steps. As it is, we'll have to wait until he's out of office, and then the best we can do is exile him."

"I suppose they'll want me to find him. As far as I know, he can be interrogated before a pontifical court, tribune or not. They have no *imperium*, but they can make it impossible for him ever to show his ugly face in Rome again. That's not too far from being a death sentence."

Again Father shook his head. "I don't think it's that. They

wouldn't tell me, of course, but I think it is something far more serious than that."

I began to get an uncomfortable sensation, the sort I had often felt just before the Gauls attacked. "More serious? What could be more serious than—"

"I don't know, and I won't speculate," Father said. "Just meet with them. They'll tell you."

I sank back in my chair, groaning. "I hope they don't want to meet too soon."

"No, you'll have plenty of time to recuperate," he assured me. "Be at the Temple of Vesta at dawn."

"Dawn!" I shouted, appalled. "By morning I'll be unable to move! I'll be lucky if I can get out of bed three days from now!"

"Nonsense," he said, standing. "A few hours of sleep will set you up; no man needs more than that. Be there. Good evening to you." With that he swept out in a cloud of *gravitas*.

"What am I going to do?" I moaned, covering my face with my hands.

"If I may make a suggestion," Julia said, "you'd better get to bed right now."

THE FIRST, GRAY LIGHT OF DAWN found me on the steps of the beautiful little temple. True to their duty, Julia and my household staff had accomplished the formidable task of getting me out of bed and out the front gate while it was still dark. In the neighborhood Julia had found a masseur to loosen my limbs and a barber to make me presentable, and between poundings and scrapings Cassandra had forced me to down honeyed milk, fruit, and bread. With Hermes dogging my steps lest I collapse, the long walk to the Forum completed my awakening process so that, by the time I reached the temple, I was actually feeling rather human.

Metellus Scipio was there, along with the Censors, both of whom were *pontifices*. Soon we were joined by the *Flamen Quirinalis*, a kinsman of my wife's named Sextus Julius Caesar, and the *rex sacrorum*. Cornelius Lentulus Niger, the *Flamen Martialis*, arrived, and we stood there uneasily for a while, no one wanting to breach the subject of the day. The *flamines* wore their robes of office and their peculiar headgear: the close-fitting white cap topped with a short spike of olive wood. Passersby on early errands blinked to see such an assemblage at that hour.

A young Vestal came to the doorway of the temple. "The *virgo maxima* requests that you come inside," she said. With that we passed within. The most powerful, arrogant men in Rome would never enter this particular temple without invitation.

The small, circular temple was one of the least pretentious in the central part of the City, but it was the most revered by the citizenry, who held it in greater affection than the Temple of Capitoline Jupiter. Its proportions were perfect, and it was built of white marble, inside and out, every inch of it scrubbed to an immaculate gleam. Citizens rarely saw the interior, except during the Vestalia in June, when mothers of families brought food offerings. For the rest of us, it was enough just to know it was there.

We found the *virgo maxima* seated by the fire, which was tended day and night by the Vestals. It was the hearth and center and in many ways the most sacred spot in Rome. There were a number of chairs placed in the sanctuary, and at her gesture we sat.

"After the hideous events of two days ago," she began, "the *rex sacrorum* and I conferred, and we determined that this would be the best place to hold our meeting. It is as holy a place as Rome affords. *Rex sacrorum*, please begin."

"Some of you," said Claudius, "already know what I am about to impart. Others are not yet aware of how serious a sacrilege was committed."

This sounded bad.

"When the unspeakable tribune Ateius Capito pronounced his execration," Claudius went on, "he departed from the forms generally used in such cases. All were struck by the extreme obscurity of some of the deities upon whom he called. Most of them have not been recognized in Rome since the days of the kings, when the Etruscan influence was very strong in our territory. Others are wholly foreign. But in the midst of them he spoke a name that it is forbidden to pronounce, that is supposed to be known only to a handful of the most deeply consecrated *sacerdotes* of Rome. He spoke—" at this the *rex sacrorum* trembled, and his throat closed up.

My aunt leaned forward, and in a voice that was firm yet tense with emotion, she said: "That monster spoke, aloud and for all to hear, the Secret Name of Rome!"

Metellus Scipio gasped loudly and gripped the front of his robe in palsied fists. I thought that Servilius Vatia, the ancient Censor, would drop dead on the spot. His colleague, Messala Niger, was not taken by surprise, and neither was Sextus Caesar.

As for me, I was as shocked as anyone, although I was too sore for any extravagant demonstrations. The Secret, or Hidden, Name of Rome was an ancient and incredibly potent talisman. Legend had it that Romulus himself, when he marked out the *pomerium* with his plow drawn by a white cow and bull, gave his City this name, which was to be used only during specific rituals. Publicly, it was to be known by a variant of his own name—Rome. Names, as all men know, have power. To know the true name of a thing gives one power over that thing. At least, the superstitious believe this. I am not personally superstitious. Nonetheless, I was trembling like a dog caught in a Gallic rainstorm.

"The incident may not be as catastrophic as it seemed at first," the *rex sacrorum* assured us, having regained his composure. "He spoke in a number of old, ritual languages. To almost all who heard, that name was just one more word in a great flood of gibberish, and all but impossible to remember. At least, so we must hope. With the Secret Name of Rome at his disposal, a foreign enemy would have Rome at his mercy."

"In accordance with practice laid down at the very founding of the Republic," said the *virgo maxima,* "only six persons are to know that Name, and each is to pass it on only to his successor. These are the three major *flamines*—" she nodded toward Messala and Vatia, "of whom the *martialis* and the *quirinalis* are here with us. Rome has lacked a *dialis* for far too long. The other three are the *rex sacrorum,* the *virgo maxima,* and the *Pontifex Maximus.*"

"How," said Scipio, "did a wretch like Ateius Capito learn this name?"

"We would very much like to find that out," said Claudius. "In fact, it is for this reason that we summoned your kinsman, Decius Caecilius."

I was afraid of that. "Ah, I expect you want me to locate Ateius. That should not be difficult, but he may have fled—"

"While it may be desirable to find Ateius," said Claudius, "we are far more interested in learning who imparted to him the Secret Name."

"I see," I said, trying to think of a way out of this. "It is likely that the only way I can find that out is by interrogating Ateius himself, a man who may not be arrested for nearly two months. And I hope you will forgive me for suggesting it, but the list of likely suspects is rather limited."

"You mean it was probably someone in this room," said Claudius. "If so, we must know. Caesar is of course in Gaul. But," he spread his hands, "I think there may be other possibilities. The lands of Latium, Etruria, Samnium, and Magna Graecia and all the rest of Italy and Sicily are full of ancient cults and priesthoods of an antiquity comparable to our own. It is not impossible that some cult, or some family of sorcerers, at some time in the past learned the Secret Name and have kept it as a weapon against need."

"That is, indeed, a possibility," I admitted. "However, such cults are, by their very nature, rather secretive, and it might be quite difficult to—"

"Nephew," my aunt interrupted briskly, "we are not asking if you can find time in your busy schedule to assist us in this matter. We are telling you to drop all lesser things and find this offender. It must be done at once!"

"Exactly," said Claudius.

"Lesser things to include the upcoming election?" I said.

"Don't worry, Decius," said Scipio. "You are one of what the citizens are already referring to as the Twenty. You'll be a hero for weeks to come, until they find someone else to idolize. You couldn't lose if you set fire to the Temple of Castor and Pollux."

No way out. Oh, well. "How much of this may I divulge in the course of my investigation?" I asked. "That is to say: who knows about Ateius using the Secret Name, and whom may I inform of this?"

"The members of the Pontifical College who were not summoned to this meeting may be told," Claudius said. "Beyond those, we do not wish anyone to know that this catastrophe has befallen us."

"That could hamper my investigation," I protested. "Should I need the aid of a praetor, for instance—"

"You are not to spread this about," said Messala. "As Censor I forbid it. The mere rumor of this would be sufficient to panic the citizens, to encourage Rome's enemies, to bring about chaos. We are engaged in wars at the fringes of the world, but our hold on the peninsula of Italy is not so secure that we can afford to ignore unrest in nearby territories. Most of us remember the Samnite army camped outside the Colline Gate just twenty-seven years ago. The Umbrians, the Lucanians, even the contemptible Bruttians bide their time, watching for some great disaster to befall Rome and planning to seize upon this to rise in arms once more. None of these peoples are extinct. No, Decius, you must not give these people encouragement."

I didn't think much of this line of reasoning, but I was far too lowly to rebuke a Censor, especially in company as exalted as I found myself in that morning.

"You must not waste any time," Claudius said. "I shudder at the thought of what our foreign enemies might do with the Secret Name."

"And when I find this excessively knowledgeable person?" I asked.

"He must not be allowed to live, of course," said Vatia.

"I can't just kill him!" I protested. "I'm an investigator, not an executioner. The man may be a citizen, and the laws are quite specific concerning who gets to kill citizens. He will have to be tried in a praetor's court."

"A trial would be bad," Claudius said. "Not only would Rome's honor be besmirched, but the Secret Name might be uttered. No, this will have to be settled in some other fashion."

They were talking as if sacerdotal courts still had power of life and death, as they had many centuries ago. Yet, with the exception of the *virgo maxima* and the *rex sacrorum,* all of them were Roman politicians of many years' experience in the Senate, the Assemblies, the courts, and the army. They were certainly not naive. They were playing some deeper game of their own, either collectively or individually. Just my luck.

"To whom do I report?" I asked, knowing I would not be able to weasel out here. I would just have to weasel out somewhere else.

"It would be best if you were to report to the Censors," Claudius said. "The *virgo maxima* and I are not always approachable. The Censors are men of the highest honor, and one of them is the

Flamen Martialis. They will in turn report to the rest of us."

Now for the big question. "Has Pompey been told? And if not, is he to be told?"

"The consul," my aunt said, "although we esteem and honor him most highly, is an initiate of no priestly order save that of the augurs. He is neither *pontifex* nor *flamen*. He is aware that this extraordinary meeting has been called, but he very wisely did not seek to learn the reason for it."

There was no love lost between my aunt and Pompey. She was a younger sister of Metellus Pius, who spent years putting down the rebellion of Sertorius in Spain. Pompey, in his usual fashion, mopped up the shattered remnants of the rebel army and then claimed sole credit for winning the war, robbing her brother of his rightful glory.

Claudius stood and bowed toward the *virgo maxima.* "Honored Lady, most of us have duties to perform. The morning sacrifices will begin soon." Then he turned to me. "You have been charged with your sacred duty. When you have information, report at once to the Censors. If it should be necessary that we all meet again, you shall be informed. I dismiss this meeting."

Hermes read my expression as I walked down the temple steps.

"Bad?" he asked.

"Hermes, kiss the easy times good-bye. We have work to do."

6

Of course, I told Julia all about it immediately. We hadn't been married long, but I had already learned the futility of keeping anything secret from her. We sat in the small garden, and I sent the slaves away, out of earshot, for whatever good that might do. Julia looked somewhat aghast when I told her about the compromising of the Secret Name, but she quickly recovered her patrician aplomb.

"I think it's very wise of you to tell me this, Decius, even though you were expressly forbidden to do so by such high authority."

"Of course it's wise to tell you, my dearest, but I don't think the matter will remain secret for long, in any case."

"Why not?"

"Except for my aunt and Claudius, every man there this morning was a senator. There is no way such men will keep a juicy bit of political gossip like that quiet, not if they see the slightest chance of using it to their own political advantage."

"You have a low opinion of the Senate."

"I am a senator. I rest my case, my little white Falernian heifer."

"The mantle of Cynicism sits ill on your shoulders," she said. "Cynicism is Greek, and you are always saying that you detest Greek philosophy."

"Even a Greek may be correct once in a while, my little jug of vintage *garum*."

"And stop devising ridiculous endearments!" she snapped.

"It's just a sign that I'm deep in thought. This is by far the strangest investigation I have ever been handed. I'm not sure even where to begin. I would like to go and lean on Ateius Capito. His invulnerability is a legal fiction, but the supporters of tribunes can be extremely violent these days."

"Will the people support him after what he did?"

"Yes, they will. The shock is over, and he will be out of office soon, anyway. The Assemblies have spent the last twenty years fighting tooth and nail to restore the tribunician powers stripped away by Sulla. They'll rally even to this fool if they see a threat to the institution."

"Do you think he is in hiding?"

"I don't know. Supposedly, if he does not keep himself accessible to the plebs, he forfeits his office. But who pays all that much attention to the laws anymore? My guess is, he's hiding right at home, behind a heavy bodyguard."

"Leave him alone, then. Milo's thugs might force you a way in, but a street riot is no way to conduct an investigation."

"I did not contemplate such a thing. No, I'll have to be more decorous. I need to find someone not connected with the Senate, who is knowledgeable concerning the old religions, the mystery cults, that sort of thing."

"A rather large subject," she said, "but you probably needn't concern yourself with the Eastern sort, the slave cults, and other such nonsense. I'll make inquiries among my friends. Some of them are dreadfully superstitious. They trade the names of their magicians the way they do those of their jewelers or their perfumers. What will you do?"

"I'll look into the records of the aedile's office, to begin with. They have the task of expelling magicians from the City. I won't waste much time with it. I suspect that the bulk of them are nothing but mountebanks, and that goes for the ones your lady friends frequent as well."

"Do you think I don't know that? But please recall that some of them are priestesses of very respectable cults and can be expected to know things to which very few men are privy, especially senators, who care far more about war and politics than about religion."

"I knew being married to you was going to come in handy."

"Something else strikes me," she mused. "Crassus himself is a *pontifex*. Do you think he had any idea of what was being used to curse him?"

I thought back over the scene at the gate. "I don't think so. If he had, he probably would have turned right around and gone home. Surely even his lust for loot has limits."

"So one would think."

Soon I was back in the Forum, but this time I wasn't wearing my *candidus*. Instead, dressed as an ordinary citizen, I went to the end of the Forum where the men standing for the office of quaestor were lounging about, cadging votes. Among them was Faustus Sulla, looking uncomfortable the way an aristocrat always does when he has to go about the low-bred process of vote-grubbing. Near him was the younger Marcus Crassus, who looked much more at home. He grinned engagingly when I walked up. We went through the usual, overdone public greeting.

"Taking the day off, Metellus?"

"Yes, but not willingly. Not much longer until the elections,

97

anyway. Will you be joining your father in Syria to be his quaestor?" Like me, he was almost certain of election. Nobody could outbribe a Crassus.

"No, I'll be with Caesar in Gaul. My brother Publius will be leaving Caesar's army early next year to take some Gallic cavalry to Father's war with Parthia."

"Lucky you. I spent my year in the Treasury."

"Safe but unprofitable," he said. "I hear Caesar's doing rather well." In peacetime a general's quaestor was little more than a paymaster, but in a great war he could get rich. Besides disbursing pay for the troops, he let contracts to businessmen supplying and serving the army, divided and accounted for the loot, and sold prisoners to the slave traders who followed the army like a bad smell. A bit of every transaction could stick to his fingers, and I had no doubt that the younger Marcus Crassus had been an apt student of the elder.

"Your father's campaign certainly had an ill-starred beginning."

He shrugged. "It takes more than maledictions mumbled by a swine of a tribune to frighten the old man. Spells and curses are how our nurses make us behave when we're children. They have no place in the real life of men of affairs. If magic were any real use, how did we ever whip the Etruscans? And why does everyone push the Egyptians around with impunity? Everyone says they're great magicians."

"An astute observation. So your father didn't act as if this curse was anything especially menacing?"

"No. Why do you ask?" His eyes sharpened on me, bright with suspicion.

"I've been charged to investigate the incident." This much at least I could admit to. "You're probably right, and it's nothing but a lot of mumbo-jumbo to impress the masses."

"The curse is nothing. The insult—well, that's another matter. The second that viper steps down from office, I'm going to be waiting there with my *flagrum*. My slaves will tell you that I don't wield it with a light hand when I'm annoyed. I'll flog him from here the whole length of the Via Sacra and out of the City."

"That'll serve him right," I commended. "Well, I have to go and catch up on some paperwork. Good luck, Marcus."

He shrugged again. "All this is a waste of time if you ask me. I've bought the office already."

Spoken like a true Crassus, I thought.

My steps next took me south through the Forum Boarium and past the Circus Maximus to the Temple of Ceres. There, amid the archives of the aediles, I found one of the year's plebeian aediles, a man named Quintus Aelius Paetus, who never achieved any greater distinction that I ever heard about. He lifted an eyebrow when he saw me come in.

"Starting work a little early, aren't you, Metellus?"

"I have no intention of assuming office one minute too early," I assured him. "I'm here to look something up."

"Ah! Here I can be of aid." He turned his head and bellowed over his shoulder: "Demetrius! Come in here!"

A middle-aged slave came from the back. "Sir?"

"The honored senator Metellus, soon to be your supervisor, has something he wants to look up. Assist him."

"Certainly. How may I help you, Senator?"

"I haven't been here in a few years. I don't recall seeing you before."

"I have been here most of my life, but usually in the back rooms. I became head archivist last year. What might you be looking for?"

"I need to examine records concerning aedilician investigations or expulsions of sorcerers and priests of non-State cults."

"Let me see," Demetrius mused. "We have several centuries'

worth of such documents. I take it you do not wish to view them all?"

"Just the most recent will do," I informed him. "When was the last such suppression?"

"Three years ago, when Calpurnius Piso and Gabinius were consuls," said the slave. "You may recall that Piso was very keen to expel the Egyptian cults from Rome."

"Actually, that was my first year with Caesar in Gaul. We were more concerned with the Gauls and Germans than with the Egyptians."

"As generally happens in such operations, the expulsion took in foreign cults as a whole, including those of Italy outside Rome."

"Then that is what I'm looking for. I'm not interested in the market women who tell fortunes or the poisoners or abortionists we're always expelling from the City—just the major practitioners of magic and advocates of non-Roman gods. I'm especially interested in the Italian cultists, although I suppose the Egyptians will bear looking at."

"I take it this has something to do with that business at the gate two days ago?" Paetus asked.

"Yes, the pontiffs want to know where Ateius got that elaborate curse. They've charged me to investigate."

"What's the authority?" he asked. "A pontifical investigation is rare. I'm not even sure of its legality."

"This is informal, of course. I'm standing for aedile and will have access to the records after the elections, anyway."

"With your family, I suppose you can take the election for granted," he said enviously. "Well, I don't see why not. Demetrius, the archives are at the noble senator's disposal."

"Who was charged with the task of routing the Egyptians?" I asked the slave.

"The curule aedile Marcus Aemilius Scaurus."

"He must have been a busy man," I said. "I've been to the

baths he built that year, and they're magnificent. I hear the same of his theater."

"It was a remarkable tenure of office," Demetrius said.

"His Games were of unmatched splendor," Paetus said, "even by the standards Caesar set. Pity the poor Sardinians. They're having to pay for it all, now."

"Squeezing them pretty hard, is he?" I asked.

"Sardinian property owners he's extorted are already in town, lining up prosecutors. He'll be up before the courts the minute he sets foot inside the gates."

"I'm always out of town when the best shows are on," I groused.

"Of course, he had the leisure to plan his Games and build his baths and round up all the mountebanks," Paetus said. "He was curule. He could sit around in the markets half the day and assess fines. Plebeian aediles have to spend all day inspecting every street, warehouse, and foul tenement in the City." He seemed to be a man with a lot of grievances.

"If you will come with me, Senator," Demetrius said. I followed him into the musty warren of rooms beneath the temple proper. Aemilius had been a curule aedile, while the temple was the headquarters of the plebeian aediles, but the records of both were kept there.

"Since it was a recent year," Demetrius said, "the records will be easy to find."

I wasn't looking forward to going over the documents in a tiny room by the smoky light of an oil lamp and was much relieved when the slave showed me to a room with a large, latticed window through which I could see the imposing superstructure of the Circus Maximus.

"I shall be back in a few minutes, Senator," Demetrius said. He disappeared into an adjoining room, and I heard him giving instructions to some other slaves.

I sat at a long desk, groaning as my knees bent, all too aware that, if I sat too long, I would probably be unable to get up. Still, it was pleasant to sit there, listening to the clamor of the market below and the screeching axles of the chariots in the Circus, where the horses were being exercised. A few minutes of this, and Demetrius returned with a slave boy, each of them bearing a basket laden with papyrus scrolls and wooden tablets.

"Here they are, sir," he announced. "All still in one place, luckily."

"Would you happen to have a list of that year's magistrates handy?" I asked him.

He turned to the slave boy. "Bring my writing kit and some scrap papyrus." The boy went away, and I began arranging the documents on the table. When he returned, Demetrius took his reed pen and began writing down the names of the serving magistrates of the third previous year, neatly and from memory: consuls, praetors, aediles, tribunes, and quaestors. "Do you need the promagistrates serving outside of Rome?" he asked. "I'll have to look some of them up."

"No need," I assured him. "I can see you're going to be invaluable to me next year."

"I look forward to it," he said, apparently without irony. "Will there be anything else?"

"I don't think so."

"I will leave Hylas here with you. If you should need anything, he will see to it."

I thanked him and set to work. The boy named Hylas sat on a bench. After a while I became aware that he was staring at me.

"What is it?" I asked.

The boy blushed. He appeared to be about twelve years old. "Excuse me, sir. Are you a charioteer?"

This was a new one. "Nothing so exalted, I am sorry to report.

I am a mere senator. What causes me to resemble the racing gentry?"

"It's just that, well, the only men I've ever seen bruised up like that are charioteers who've been in wrecks."

"Am I that colorful?"

"The whole side of your neck and half your face are purple," he reported.

"Sometimes," I told him, "the gods are demanding. Now, I have work to do."

Scanning the list of magistrates, I saw immediately the one name I knew I would find: Clodius. He was one of the tribunes, and the main reason I was out of Rome that year. He had been another busy man. Besides his scandalous legislation to distribute grain to the people free of charge (his promise to do so had secured him the election), he had worked furiously to get Cicero exiled, to get the proconsular provinces of Macedonia and Syria for the year's consuls, and to do more besides. It seemed unlikely, however, that he would be concerned with the aediles' persecutions of foreign cults.

The earliest dated document of the year was an instruction from the consul Piso to investigate and scourge from the City the Egyptian cults, which were distracting citizens from observance of the State religion and, more seriously, sucking money from Rome to Egypt.

Next, Aemilius Scaurus reported on the proliferation of Egyptian temples in Rome, in the surrounding *municipia,* and in Italian towns as far afield as Capua and Pompeii. Most of them were dedicated to the Isis cult. This caused me some amusement. Having spent some time in Egypt, I happened to know that the cult of Isis and Osiris was just about the dullest, most respectable religion imaginable. The whole College of Vestals could attend the Isis ceremonies for years without being exposed to the mildest impurity.

Now, the Egyptians had some truly scabrous cults, but they kept the good stuff at home, to themselves. What these guardians of public morals really needed was to attend one of the festivals of Min or Bes, gods who delivered their worshipers a good time.

Once the unfortunate followers of Isis had been dealt with, the aediles turned their attention to other cults and to magicians practicing solo. The tally of names looked like one of Sulla's proscription lists, although they probably weren't as profitable to those denouncing them. I thought it might be amusing to find out how many of these men were still practicing in the City. That would tell me how many had been able to bribe their way out of the ban.

I noted that most of the names were foreign. Some were Etruscan, many were Marsian, and the rest were Greek, Syrian, and so forth. I was willing to bet that many were ex-slaves with fake names and accents. For some reason, those who believe in magic are always ready to credit exotic foreigners with greater power in these matters than their own countrymen.

"Listen to these," I said to young Hylas. "Hezzebaal the Paphlagonian, Chrysanthus of Thebes, Cinnamus of Lydia, Euscios the Arab, Ugbo the Wonder-Worker—Ugbo! What sort of name is that? It sounds like a dog gagging."

"I'm afraid I don't know, Senator. Sorry."

"Don't be. It's what we educated people call a rhetorical question. It doesn't call for an answer. Can you write?"

"Certainly, sir."

"Excellent. I want you to copy this list of names for me while I study these other documents."

The boy took the reed pen, and I gave him the scrap of papyrus with the list of magistrates. Carefully and with great concentration he began copying the names in a blocky, workmanlike hand. Like so many young slaves he had the name of one of the famous pretty boys of antiquity, but he wasn't an especially attractive youth—not that my tastes run that way. He was snub-nosed with protruding upper teeth, but he seemed to be intelligent. I have always been willing to overlook ugliness in a slave if he has some redeeming quality.

"Be sure to copy the descriptions as well," I admonished.

"I am doing that, sir," he said dutifully. Next to each name were a few words describing the putative magician's speciality: "necromancer," "spirit medium," "astrologer," "summoner of Eastern gods," and so forth. One was described, alarmingly, as "raiser of corpses."

Besides these practitioners there were organized cults whose supposed indecent practices were catalogued in some detail. There were the usual ecstatic dancing, public fornication, self-mutilation, drug-induced intoxication, unnatural acts with animals, mass flagellation, and loud music. I have always objected to loud music myself.

I found a certain unworthy pleasure in reading about these supposedly disgraceful practices adjacent to that list of prominent public men. I was familiar with many of those men, and knew some of them to be addicted to things far worse than any attributed to the religious libertines. The difference was, they were senators while these cults attracted slaves, freedmen, the lowest of the *proletarii*, and the resident foreigners.

This is nothing new, of course. We are always anxious to protect the lower orders from vices that we ourselves practice with great enthusiasm. We know that we have the inner, philosophical strength to resist carrying our pleasures to excess, while the childlike masses are apt to be corrupted by them.

Follow-up reports gave details of suppression and expulsion. Most of the leaders were foreigners and were simply banished from Rome. Some of these were branded so that they would be unwelcome anywhere in Roman territory. The way our Empire was growing, these unfortunates might soon have to take up residence somewhere around the headwaters of the Nile or in the land of the Seres, where silk comes from.

The ones who could claim Roman citizenship were mostly let off with an admonition, any repetition of their scandalous behavior to be dealt with sternly. I had every expectation that these people had also proven able to come across with a few thousand sesterces to make the aedile's life more comfortable and help defray the onerous burdens of his office. It was an unspoken but well-recognized fact of political life that cult leaders could deliver substantial bloc votes come election time.

When the reading and copying were done, I tipped young Hylas with a sesterce and turned away discreetly while he disposed of it somewhere about his person. Slaves, especially small ones, must resort to certain subterfuges in order to prevent larger slaves from acquiring their wealth, and it is often inadvisable to wonder too much about where our money has been.

With my papyrus tucked into my tunic, I left the temple, thinking about the man now looting Sardinia, and others of his sort. From what I had learned of him so far, Marcus Aemilius Scaurus was nothing unusual, just a typical Roman politician of the times. At some time he had been a quaestor, doing scut work for the government, perhaps accompanying some general and profiting from it, making valuable political and commercial contacts in the process. He had then been elected to the aedileship and had not stinted himself on largesse to the populace with his Games and his theater and his baths. Undoubtedly he had gone deeply into debt to do this, besides squandering whatever wealth he had inherited.

Riding on the great popularity of his aedileship, he stood for praetor the very next year and won the office handily. Then he had been given a propraetorian province, Sardinia, which he was now looting so merrily. It had become common practice, and it did much to ruin the Republic. Provinces that had been Roman territory for centuries were treated like newly conquered nations, with extortions and oppressions that would shame an Oriental potentate.

The provincials had recourse in our courts. Cicero had made his legal reputation prosecuting a man named Verres who had given Sicily a sacking that was breathtaking even in that jaded age. The Sicilians had come to Cicero because they had been very pleased with the honesty of his own administration of the western part of the province when he was quaestor there under Peducaeus.

Not that even Cicero hadn't come back from provincial administration well-off. There were plenty of ways to accumulate money that were considered legitimate, if not exactly high-minded: there was nothing wrong with accepting handsome "gifts" from contractors; people currying favor were always happy to sell land, property, and artworks at extremely favorable rates; and any over-age in the revenues might be divided among the promagistrate and his assistants. Plus, never forget, today's quaestor might be to-morrow's praetor, consul, even Dictator, administering provinces, commanding armies, and making policy for the Empire. It was always advisable to be fondly remembered by such people.

One thing was certain: an aedile always needed money, and a suppression list like the one tucked into my tunic was a match-lessly handy way to raise cash.

I returned home to find Julia glowing.

"Decius!" she bubbled, first rushing to embrace me, then drawing back at my involuntary groan of pain. "Oh! I'm sorry, I forgot. But guess who was here a few minutes ago!"

"Uncle Julius, back from Gaul?"

"No! A man from the Egyptian Embassy! He arrived in a litter carried by Ethiopians with feathers in their hair and big scars carved in patterns all over their bodies. He wore a huge black wig and a white kilt made of linen so stiff that it crackled when he walked, and he had on all sorts of gold and jewelry."

"I am familiar with Egyptian fashions," I told her. "What was the brunt of this dignitary's mission?"

Cassandra appeared with a tray bearing cups and two pitchers, one of wine and one of water. I reached for a cup, but Julia got it first, added extra water, then handed it to me.

"He brought this," she said, beaming. She held up a papyrus, beautifully decorated with Egyptian drawings in colored ink and gilding. It was an invitation, praying that the "distinguished senator Metellus" and his "goddess-descended lady Julia" attend a reception being given in honor of King Ptolemy's birthday.

"I'm just distinguished while you're goddess-descended?" I said.

"I am a Julian, while you're a mere Caecilian," she told me, as if I didn't know. "I've been so hoping for this! It's the day after tomorrow. What shall I wear? How shall I do my hair?"

"My dear, I trust your patrician instincts in this. I just ask that you do not—do *not*, I say, consult with Fausta."

We meandered into the *triclinium*, where the slaves laid out our dinner. It was a rare dinner at home for us, and while we ate, Julia went on happily about the upcoming party at the embassy. While I tried to look bored, I was cheered by the prospect. Lisas gave wonderful entertainments, and I was in need of such. After the dishes were cleared away, I steered the conversation toward more serious things.

"Did you get to circulate among your lady friends today?" I asked Julia.

"I started out at the new baths this morning," she reported. At the time it was the custom for women to use the facilities in the morning, men in the afternoon. "And after that I went to the perfume market and the jewelers' market, and then to the Temple of Juno Moneta on the Capitol."

"The Temple of Juno?"

"Every month at this time the patrician ladies gather there to practice the songs for the Matronalia."

"I see." Another of those women's things I was going to have to get accustomed to. "And did this activity reap a rich reward?"

"Well, first off, everybody has an astrologer. But you aren't interested in astrologers, are you?"

"As it happened, references to astrology were about the only occult things left out of Ateius's curse."

"I thought so. Once I'd cleared away the clutter of abortionists and fortune-tellers and so forth, I kept turning up three names: Eschmoun of Thapsus, Elagabal the Syrian, and Ariston of Cumae."

"Ariston of Cumae? That doesn't sound like a magician's name. It sounds more like a professor of rhetoric."

"Nonetheless, a good many well-born women regard him as an infallible seer and spirit-guide. He is supposed to be on familiar terms with the powers of the underworld."

"It might have been worse. At least he's not Ugbo the Wonder-Worker. And what business have these ladies with such powers?"

"A number of things. Communicating with dead relatives, who give them guidance during difficult times, and underworld spirits are supposed to be good at spying. The women ask what their husbands are up to."

"Hmm. No wonder the Senate is always trying to drive them out of the City. Speaking of which—" I took the papyrus from inside my tunic and spread it on the table. "Just as I thought. All three of them are on the list of foreign magicians supposedly driven out of Rome three years ago."

"What is that?"

So I explained to her about Aemilius Scaurus's somewhat conditional zeal in suppressing the foreign cults.

"Then why are they still here?"

"Presumably, they were able to come up with Aemilius's price."

"That is a disgraceful way for a Roman official to carry on," Julia said.

"Oh, I don't know. I'll be an aedile myself next year. I may have to accept the occasional handout from a questionable source, too."

"But surely you would never deal with people as loathsome as these?" she said.

"Oh, I would never do that," I murmured.

"Look. By all three names it says, 'trafficker with the chthonians.' None of the others has that particular description."

I took the list and examined it. "You're right. What a pity Aemilius Scaurus is in Sardinia and I can't touch him. I'd love to question him as to why he let these three slide. Oh, well, I can do the next best thing, which is question the men themselves."

"They're an oddly assorted lot," she noted. "A man from an old Carthaginian city with a Carthaginian name—Eschmoun was a god of Carthage, I believe—a Syrian, and an Italian Greek."

"It does sound odd," I agreed. "But then, they could be three slaves born within brick-throwing distance of this house, tricked out in foreign clothes, beards, and fake accents. That's a pretty common dodge with frauds. Did you happen to find out where these three exotic specimens live?"

"Of course. Which will you begin with?"

"Whichever of them lives nearest. I have a suspicion that I won't be up to much walking tomorrow."

7

ELAGABAL THE SYRIAN, IT TURNED
out, had his dwelling in the northern part of the Subura, near the
Quirinal. This was a relief because, as I had predicted, I awakened
in even worse shape than the day before. Amid much loud groaning I was once again massaged and shaved and shoved out the
front door. I dismissed my solicitous clients and trudged through
the cheerfully raucous morning bustle of my district. Here and
there people recognized me and called out congratulations or
wished me good fortune. Yes, it was good to be back in Rome,
even in the poorest district.

There was no mistaking the house of Elagabal when I came
to it. The facade was painted red, and flanking the doorway were
a pair of man-headed, winged lions. Over the door was painted a
serpent swallowing its tail. Not your typical, cozy little *domus*. It
was two stories, and a trellis ran around its upper periphery,
draped with climbing plants spangled with multicolored flowers.

When I tried to enter, a hulking brute stood in the doorway, arms folded across his chest. He had a black, square-cut beard and suspicious little eyes flanking a nose like a ship's ram.

"Do you have business with my master?"

"Is your master Elagabal the Syrian?"

"He is."

"Then I do."

The man stood, unmoved. Perhaps the little exchange had been too complicated for him. While he sought to sort out its nuances, someone spoke up from behind him.

"This man is a senator. Let him in."

The hulk stood aside, and I passed within. I found myself in an atrium that had been converted into something resembling a ceremonial temple entrance. Several statues stood there, in human form but in very stiff poses.

"I apologize for Bessas. He defends my privacy with great skill but little wisdom." The man was thin with a vaguely Eastern cast of countenance, wearing a long robe and a pointed cap. His beard was likewise pointed.

"I take it that I address Elagabal?"

"At your service," he said, bowing with the fingers of one hand spread over his breast.

"Decius Caecilius Metellus the Younger, senator and current candidate for next year's aedileship."

"Ah, a most important office," he said.

"One with which you've had some official dealings, I understand."

"Is this an official visit, Senator?" he asked.

"Of a sort."

He appeared unapprehensive. "Official or social, there is no need to be uncomfortable. Please accept the hospitality of my house. If you will follow me, we may be comfortable above."

We went up a flight of stairs and came out onto a splendid little roof garden, some of the plantings of which I had seen from the street below. At the corners, orange trees stood in great earthenware pots, and the trellises arched overhead so that, in summer, they would provide shade. Now, in November, the growth had been trimmed back but was still luxuriant. In its center a tiny stream of water bubbled in a delightful little fountain. There were few parts of Rome with sufficient water pressure to get even that much water up to what was, in effect, the third floor of a building.

At Elagabal's gesture I took a seat at a little table, and he sat opposite me. Moments later a young slave woman appeared with a tray set with the expected refreshments, along with some strips of flat bread strewn with granules of coarse salt.

"If you will indulge me in a custom of my country, bread and salt form the traditional offering to a newly arrived guest. It is the ancient token of hospitality."

"I am familiar with the custom." I took one of the strips of bread and ate it. It was still hot from the oven and astonishingly good. The serving girl stood by silently. She was barefoot, wearing a simple wrap of scarlet cloth fringed with yellow yarn that covered her from armpits to knees. Bangles at wrists and ankles were her only adornments. Her heavy, black hair was waist length, and she kept her gaze demurely down, with none of the offhand insolence you so often see in Roman slaves. Maybe these Syrians were onto something, I thought.

Unlike many Romans I have a certain crude regard for other people's customs, and I knew that, in the East, one did not bring up the subject of business immediately. To do so was a sign of rudeness and ill breeding.

"The gods in your atrium," I said, choosing a mundane subject, "which of them is Baal?"

He smiled. "They all are."

"All?"

"*Baal* in my language just means 'Lord.' In my part of the world, we seldom or never use the actual names of our gods. This practice is so ancient that those names have sometimes been forgotten. So we address each deity by his best-known aspect or his location. Thus Baal Tsaphon is Lord of the North, Baal Shamim is Lord of the Skies, Baal Shadai is Lord of the Mountain, and so forth. A goddess is *Baalat,* which means, of course, 'Lady.' "

"I see. Is this true of all the lands east of Egypt?"

"To an extent. In the various dialects Baal is honored. To the Babylonians he is Bel, to the Judeans El, to the Phoenicians and their colonies, Bal. The word forms a part of many names. My own name translates, from very archaic language, as 'My Lord Has Been Gracious.' *Baal* is also a part of the Carthaginian name best known to you Romans: Hannibal."

"Fascinating," I said. He seemed to be a learned man, not the wide-eyed fanatic I had half expected. "I have never been to that part of the world—no farther east than Alexandria."

"Perhaps your duties will take you to my homeland someday. Even now your proconsul Crassus wends his way thither."

"It is concerning something touching that expedition that my errand brings me here this morning."

"I am far from the high ranks of power, merely a humble priest. But whatever poor knowledge I have is at your disposal; this goes without saying."

"Undoubtedly you know of the scandalous act of the tribune Ateius Capito upon the departure of Crassus?"

He raised his hands in an Eastern gesture imploring protection from baleful powers. "All Rome has heard of this! I rejoice that I was not there when it happened. Such a curse contaminates all who witness it. He is lucky to be a serving official of Rome. In my own land he would be subjected to the most terrible punishments for such an offence to the gods."

"I am pleased that you appreciate the gravity of the act. I have been commissioned to investigate this sacrilege."

"I am flattered to be called upon. But the curse, as it was

repeated to me, involved none of the Baalim. This is the plural form," he added, although I had guessed the meaning already.

"Even so, it is thought that foreign influence may be present."

"Ah," he said, ruefully. "And your Roman officials are always wary of the corrupting influence of foreigners, despite your habit of packing the City with them in the form of slaves."

"Precisely. Three years ago, during the aedileship of Marcus Aemilius Scaurus, there was a purge of Rome's foreign cults. Your name was on the list of those to be driven from the City, yet I find you still here. How comes this about?"

He made a truly comprehensive gesture involving hands, shoulders, neck, and head, indicative of all things unknowable and unavoidable, combined with all things eminently mutable and subject to arbitrary change, ever altering, yet ever remaining the same. I have never known a people as eloquent in their gestures as the Syrians.

"The honorable aedile and I came to an agreement whereby I was to remain in the City, so long as I refrain from any unnatural practices and do not disturb the neighbors." He smiled broadly. "You have said that you stand for that same office, and surely so eminent a gentleman as yourself will have no difficulty in securing it. I do trust that we shall be able to come to a similar understanding?"

So he thought I was here soliciting a bribe. He knew his Roman officials, all right.

"That's as may be," I said vaguely, knowing how strapped for money I would soon be, "but just now I am more concerned with that curse. The list of foreign priests to be sent away listed you and two others as 'traffickers with the chthonians.' How does this refer to you?"

He quirked an eyebrow upward. "*Chthonian?* That is not a

115

word I encounter every day. Greek, is it not? Indicating things of the underworld?"

"Yes. In Rome, our chthonians mostly came to us by way of the Greeks and Etruscans. We Romans were a rustic lot. Our gods were those of the fields and rivers and the weather."

"I see. This must account for your fondness for pastoral poetry."

"Please," I said. "I regard pastoral poetry as one of the blights of this age. Epic is the only worthwhile verse form as far as I am concerned."

"Spoken like the scion of an heroic people. Now, as to the chthonians, some of the Baalim are lords of the underworld and have as their servants whole legions of imps ever eager to torment the living. These can deliver to my—my associates," he chose a legally innocuous term, "certain valuable services, always protective and always secured by means of perfectly respectable ceremonies, I assure you."

"But none of these deities were named in the tribune's curse?"

"None."

"Two other such traffickers were named along with you on Aemilius's list: Eschmoun of Thapsus and Ariston of Cumae. What can you tell me about them?"

Another gesture, this time contemptuous. "As for Eschmoun, you will waste your time talking with him. He is a fraud from Africa, of mixed Libyan descent. He claims to commune with the underworld through a serpent that resides in a golden egg. What he actually does is bilk wealthy ladies of large sums of money by bringing them messages from their dead husbands, children, and other relatives. He is exceptionally good at discerning what it is that his clients long to hear. He has purloined the name of a Carthaginian god and taken upon his shoulders the mantle of power still clinging to that thankfully destroyed city."

" 'Thankfully'?" I said. "You have no esteem for Carthage? And yet were the Punic people not relatives of yours?"

He grimaced. "Distant kin at the very most. The Phoenicians founded Carthage many centuries ago, and the Punic race worshiped the Baalim, but their practice grew very degraded even as the city grew rich and powerful. As you are aware, they performed the most frightful acts of human sacrifice."

"They were barbarians, however well they dressed," I said.

"Even so, their practices must have given some satisfaction to their gods, for those deities blessed them with many victories. In the end, of course," he added hastily, "the gods and arms of Rome prevailed, praise be to all the Baalim."

"It was a rough fight," I admitted, "but it made soldiers of us."

I was putting it mildly. The First Punic War alone had been twenty-four uninterrupted years of solid campaigning—land battles, sea battles, and sieges. The Carthaginians had thrashed us far more times than we beat them, but in the end we were a matchlessly warlike, military nation for good or ill. Before, we had just fought our Italian neighbors and expanded our territory incrementally in the peninsula. But we won Sicily from Carthage, and with it our first taste of empire. By the end of the Third Punic War, we had holdings in Spain, Gaul, and Africa, and Carthage was a pile of rubble.

"Ariston is another matter. He is a very deep scholar of the ways of gods and spirits. Many aspiring scholars and historians consult him on these matters."

"And what sort of cult does he lead?"

A shrug. "I was unaware that he had any such. Of course, men involved in arcane studies often excite malicious and fearful rumors. Perhaps some superstitious or malevolent person gave false information against him."

"That may have been it." I stood. "Well, I thank you for your help and hospitality. I am sure that I shall be able to report that you had nothing to do with the tribune's scandalous behavior." I was sure of nothing of the sort, but neither was I under oath.

"I rejoice in meeting you, Senator," he said as he led me back to his door. "Soon you will be an official of great authority, and I have learned that previous acquaintance makes one such far more approachable." He was still expecting to bribe me. I said nothing to discourage his assumption.

It was a fairly lengthy walk to the house of Eschmoun, which was just off the old Forum Boarium, in a block of tenements that were foul even by Roman standards. Beside his doorway were painted all sorts of trashy mystical signs, and I was sure I would find a filthy, wild-eyed loon within. What I found instead was the well-appointed town house of a man of considerable means.

Eschmoun himself was a plausible, smooth mountebank, as described by Elagabal. The rogue proudly displayed his mystical egg, a handsome object of smooth gold the size of a child's head. I had to take for granted the residence within of the holy serpent. Eschmoun, too, tried to bribe me, and again I ignored the attempt, while leaving the impression that I might be back sometime. His occult knowledge clearly extended only to his confidence spiel, and fleecing wealthy, gullible ladies is far down on my list of intolerable offenses.

It was another long walk to the dwelling of Ariston, and I stopped on the way for lunch and a brief rest. I was loosening up, and walking had become moderately tolerable. Passing through the Forum, I saw Milo returning from his morning court. I asked him if anything had been heard from our eccentric tribune.

"Not a word or a sighting since the curse," he informed me. "He has a gang surrounding his house, but no petitioners have been able to get through to see him."

"Then he can be impeached," I said.

"If someone is willing to bring charges. And if he can be

located. The house may be empty. The *populares* are concerned for the institution of the tribuneship. If he's disappeared, they may be pretending to protect him from assault to prevent a wider scandal."

"I suppose it's too much to hope that the bugger's hanged himself."

"He didn't strike me as so obliging a man."

So I continued on my walk, all the way to the Esquiline Gate and out of the City. This was one of the most undesirable districts of Roman territory, where the poor were buried. Besides the depressing clay tombs of the poor, a part of the district included the notorious "putrid pits," where the poorest of the poor, the unclaimed slaves, and foreigners and dead animals unfit for salvage were thrown into lime pits. In the hot days of summer, the wind blowing from that quarter carried an utterly appalling stench. It was none too fragrant in winter, for that matter.

In more recent years, Macaenas has covered over these pits and replaced them with his beautiful gardens. For this civic improvement I can almost forgive his being the First Citizen's crony.

The learned Ariston actually lived in a house not far from these notorious pits. It was a two-story affair standing by itself, like a country villa, only much smaller. Its only plantings consisted of a small herb garden, and its only neighbors were some very modest tombs and a few small shrines.

At least his doorway and walls were devoid of magical images, I noted with some relief. My tolerance for supernatural paraphernalia has never been high. The slave who answered my knock at this unadorned portal was a middle-aged man. When I announced my name and mission, he ushered me inside, where an undistinguished woman his own age was sweeping. Ariston didn't seem to share Elagabal's taste for attractive, docile young serving women. Stoic, probably. Minutes later a man entered the atrium.

"Yes, what may I do for you?" No extravagant signs of welcome or offers of hospitality, just this rather abrupt greeting. The man had a tangled, gray beard with matching hair, and he wore Greek clothing. I took this for an affectation. Cumae was once a Greek colony, but it had been a Roman possession for two hundred years.

"You are Ariston of Cumae?" I asked.

"As it happens, yes. Aside from being a senator, what distinguishes you from the rest of the citizenry?" Obviously, this fellow was going to be difficult. Maybe he was a Cynic rather than a Stoic.

"My commission, which is to investigate the curse delivered by the Tribune of the People Marcus Aemilius Capito. Living where you do, you might not have heard of the affair."

"I've heard. I live here by choice; I'm not an exile on some island. Come along, then. I have to look at my garden."

I followed the peculiar specimen back outside. "I rather thought you lived here because you were driven from the City three years ago by the aediles."

"Nonsense. I'm a Roman citizen; I can live anywhere I like." He stooped to examine a sickly looking plant.

"Then why here? Most don't consider it a desirable district."

He gestured toward the surrounding tombs and the pillars of smoke ascending from the lime pits. "The neighbors here are quiet and don't bother me much. That way they don't disturb my studies."

"You're sure it's not because proximity gives you the opportunity to commune with the dead?"

He straightened and glared from beneath tangled brows. "Most of those interred here were ignorant fools whom death has improved in no way whatever. Why should I want to talk with them?"

"Report has it that necromancy and trafficking with the

chthonians are your specialties," I said, undeterred.

"There is a difference between being a scholar of these things and being a fraudulent sorcerer," he informed me with great dignity.

"And yet you enjoy a great reputation among my wife's more superstitious lady friends, who can scarcely be accused of scholarship."

His face clouded. "And what if I sometimes sell them the occasional charm or counsel them concerning the fate of the dead? Even a scholar has to eat."

"I quite understand," I said with patent insincerity.

"Listen, Senator," he said, nettled, "Marcus Tullius Cicero himself does not scorn to come to me with questions about obscure gods and ancient religious practice. He has come here many times in the course of his researches and has asked me to read the drafts of his writings on the ways of the gods, solar and lunar, earthly and chthonian."

This actually was most impressive. A man as deeply learned as Cicero would not allow anyone to edit his work except a scholar of equal credentials. I made a mental note to question Cicero about the man.

"Then you must indeed be what you say. That being the case, you are probably an authority on the extraordinary and alarming deities invoked by Ateius Capito some few days past."

"I am. And if there is one thing I hate, it is the performance of dangerous, exacting rituals by an amateur!"

"You mean the curse was not well-done?"

"Oh, he carried it off well enough. Magical practice, on the level of ritual, is simply a matter of memorization; and if there is one thing every politician can do, it is memorize. The schools of rhetoric teach little else."

"I knew that conventional temple ritual works that way. The *flamines* and *pontifices* have to memorize interminable formulae in languages nobody understands anymore. Is it the same with sorcery?"

"Oh, yes." He lost some of his irascibility as he launched into his favorite subject. "The greatest difficulty may be encountered in assembling the very specialized apparatus and materials required to carry out a particular ritual. If, for instance, your ceremony requires the mummified hand of an Egyptian pharaoh, it isn't something you can just pick up in the stalls around the Forum. You might have to travel all the way to Egypt to secure such a thing, and even then it can be difficult to distinguish such a hand from the appendage of a lesser person."

"I can well imagine. The Egyptians are sharp traders." I said this with considerable conviction, having been there.

"Even with something as simple as herbs and other plants," he gestured to his well-kept garden, "it is best to grow your own. That way you are sure of purity and authenticity."

I found myself fascinated despite my skepticism. It is always interesting to hear a real expert expound upon the arcana of his realm.

"How do men of learning such as yourself acquire these—these objects and assure yourselves of their quality?" I was remembering the nameless things Ateius had tossed into his brazier.

He glanced at me shrewdly. "If you need leopards for the shows you will be giving, how do you expect to get them? They aren't sold in the Forum Boarium."

"I'll contact one of the hunting guilds in Africa Province."

"And you will probably do this through the propraetor governing Africa, will you not? And is he not a man who was once an aedile himself, required to do exactly the same thing?"

"I see where this is leading. There is a sort of brotherhood of magicians who know how to contact one another and trust each other's honesty and expertise?"

He actually smiled. "Exactly! Throughout the lands around

the sea, there are scholars like myself, practicing sorcerers, priests of many deities, all able to call upon one another at need. It takes a lifetime to build up such an acquaintanceship, but it is an invaluable resource."

He walked to a small marble bench beneath a stately cypress and sat. While we had been talking, the slave woman had brought out a pitcher and cups. I sat by him and accepted one.

"So, what did you mean when you said that Ateius is an amateur, even though he performed his curse competently?"

He brooded for a moment. "Sorcery, the deepest practice of magic, is a terribly serious business. I do not speak here of the petty magics practiced by witches. I mean the summoning of the often malevolent spirits of wasteland and underworld. It is not sufficient that this work be done by knowledgeable persons. It should be approached only by those who possess great strength of character, inner fortitude, and true nobility of soul."

"And why might this be?"

"Because one who is easily corrupted by the temptations of power will be instantly and utterly corrupted by the beings whom the greater gods have driven into the wasteland or beneath the earth. The practice is intensely dangerous to the practitioner. Cicero is a splendid man, and deeply learned, but he knows better than to practice any of the arcane arts we have discussed. Not only does he consider them ignoble, but he is very aware of his own weaknesses in this area."

This was a shrewd comment. I admired Cicero above all other Romans of the day, but I, too, had seen how his thirst for power and distinction had lessened him. Once a young orator with all of Cato's rectitude and none of Cato's repulsive bigotry, he had over the years acquired an unseemly self-importance and a querulous indignation at being thwarted and denied the highest levels of influence and prestige. How interesting to learn that he recognized this himself.

"I take it that Ateius Capito is not such a man?"

"He is not."

"Then you know him?"

"I do. Like many another, he has come to me over the years for instruction, which I imparted to him freely, as I do to all serious students. I daresay that some of the obscure deities he invoked are ones he learned from me."

"And you taught him these things knowing him to be a man of poor character?"

He snorted. "Those names possess little power in themselves. They have been largely forgotten, not suppressed. The Romans came to a respect for the chthonians late in their history, but it was not so for the other Italian peoples—the Samnites and Campanians, the Falisci, the Sabines, the Marsi, the Paeligni, the Umbrians, above all the Etruscans. And I need hardly point out that southern Italy was largely Greek until a short time ago. My own home city of Cumae was founded as a Greek colony more than a thousand years ago, and my ancestors knew all those people well. In fact, the people of this peninsula have been more intimate with the underworld than all the rest of the world together."

"I've had some experience with the local witch cults," I admitted. It was an episode I preferred not to think about.

"Then you have some understanding of this. Well, Ateius Capito was a rising young politician and a minor scholar. He was agreeable, as politicians usually are when they want to be; he was quick and intelligent. But I soon discerned that he wanted the knowledge I had to impart in order to gain political advantage over his opponents, as such men often do."

This caught me by surprise. "He was not the only man in Roman politics who has come to you?"

"Far from it. Power is power to them. When I was still living in Cumae, I was even consulted by the Dictator Sulla, who was famously attached to magical things, attributing all his successes to a unique relationship with the goddess Fortuna. He was also, I might add, easily duped by frauds. A man who is incredibly astute in his chosen field is often an utter fool in another.

"But whether intelligent and statesmanlike or merely grasping, such men care only for power, not for knowledge. A genuine scholar, like a philosopher, cares only for knowledge."

I had my reservations about that. "When did Ateius last come to you?"

"Let me see, it could not have been in this year; his office has kept him far too busy for that. He came rather frequently beginning about four years ago, but his visits became fewer as he realized that I was not going to impart to him any genuinely fearsome secrets. I suppose he was last here about eighteen months ago, and then he was so preoccupied with his campaign for the tribuneship that his visit was at best perfunctory."

"And what was he after that last visit?"

"Words and names of power, what else? He wanted me to help him influence the election! Absurd!" He snorted, above all such petty considerations as he was.

I had been wondering how to lead into the crux of my investigation without giving too much away, and this provided me with an opportunity.

"There are some in our higher pontifical offices," I said delicately, "who suspect that he may have employed just such words or names." I could not be more specific than that. "Would you know if he did?"

His look was frosty. "If he did, he learned none such from me!"

With this rather conditional denial he rose, and taking his cup, he walked into the nearby field, studded with its humble graves. He stopped at one of them, a mere stone marker crudely carved with a name. Beside the stone was a clay pipe that led into the ground below. Into this pipe Ariston emptied his cup.

"This one was a terrible drunkard," he said. "He murdered his wife and children, then hanged himself. If he doesn't get a drink from time to time, he disturbs the neighborhood." He favored me with a less frosty glance. "It doesn't pay to underestimate even dead men."

We walked back to his house, and there I took my leave of him. "I thank you for your cooperation. This has been most informative. I may need to call upon you again."

"Feel free to do so. Please give my regards to Cicero. Tell him it has been too long since I have seen him." With that, he went back inside.

I began to walk back toward the City. As I made my way homeward, I reflected that this extraordinary investigation was bringing me into contact with some decidedly odd people. In the course of a single day, I had interviewed a priest of Syrian gods, a mountebank with a magical egg, and now a proud scholar-philosopher and friend of Cicero who was not above selling the occasional spell, charm, or cantrip to gullible customers. Rome is a city of such incredible variety. No wonder I have always hated to be away from her.

That evening, I discussed my findings with Julia, while she displayed, for my horrified edification, the clothing and adornments she had purchased for the reception at the Egyptian Embassy.

"I think Eschmoun sounds the most promising," she said. "What do you think of these earrings?" She held them up to her delicate lobes.

"Lovely," I said, a sudden pain shooting through my head. "Emeralds go so well with your eyes. Why Eschmoun? The man is nothing but a mountebank."

"That is why I suspect him. He convinced you so easily that he is just a cheap trickster. That means he is hiding deep secrets. What about these green-tinted pearls?"

"They go well with the emeralds. No, I am not entirely satisfied with Ariston of Cumae."

"Cicero's friend? He seems to have been open and cooperative."

"That means little. Every villain who knows his business knows how to seem open and cooperative."

"But you pride yourself on spotting these subterfuges," she pointed out. "This gown is half silk. Shall I wear it?"

I didn't even want to think of what it cost. Half silk! "Please do. What he said didn't rouse my suspicion. What he didn't say did."

"How subtle. Do go on." She admired herself in a polished silver mirror.

"He was on Scaurus's exile list, but he is still in Rome. Well, just outside the City, but you know what I mean. Elagabal as much as admitted that he secured his own situation with a substantial bribe and would be all too happy to perform the same tribute to me. So did Eschmoun."

"And did you ask Ariston?"

"You don't ask a citizen a question like that except in court or at least with a praetor's authority, as an appointed *iudex*. No, a certain indirection was called for."

"Are you sure he's a citizen?" She tried pushing her hair into a pile atop her head.

"The Cumaeans have had full citizenship at least since Marius's day, maybe before. If he's really a Greek, he must be one of the last Cumaean Greeks alive. The place was taken over by the Campanians centuries ago."

"You rarely hear about Cumae, except for the sibyl. Everybody knows about the Cumaean sibyl. Well, we already know Scaurus went easy on the accused citizens."

"I'm sure he required hefty payments from them, though," I said. "And that's what bothers me. Here is a prestigious, but penurious, scholar, reduced to selling spells, living frugally in a humble house on what has to be absolutely the cheapest real estate in all of Roman territory. What did he bribe Scaurus *with?*"

This, finally, took her mind off her preparations. "That is a good question. Might it have been the bribe itself that impoverished him?"

"That's a thought, but he spoke as if he's lived there for longer than just the last three years. I'll have to ask Cicero."

"Do that," she advised. "Do you think Cicero will be at the embassy tomorrow?"

8

Do you think she got my hair right?" Julia asked.

"You look superb, my dear," I assured her. In fact, she was better than superb as we rocked along in our hired litter to the admiration of all eyes. The sides were rolled up to give those eyes the best possible view. Julia, dressed in her half-silk gown and decked in her emeralds and pearls, her face made up by an expert and her hair dressed in a high-piled lattice of curls, could have modeled for one of the goddesses. I didn't look so bad myself, with my bruises fading and wearing my best toga. The winter sun of late afternoon, low in the south but shedding a clear light, flattered us both. Behind us, as usual, walked Hermes and Cypria.

"I am so excited," she said, fanning herself unnecessarily.

"I don't see why. You've attended the festivities at Ptolemy's own court. This won't be nearly so lavish."

"You know it's not the same. In Alexandria, I could only stay for the first part of the evening. For the sake of my reputation, I had to leave before things got really scandalous. Besides, those were the revels of a barbarian court, full of half-mad Egyptian nobles and Persian degenerates and Macedonian brutes. Lisas's entertainments are attended by the cream of Roman society."

"I've seen the cream of Roman society behave like a shipload of drunken pirates plundering a coastal villa," I told her. "Part of a diplomat's art is getting people to loosen up, and Lisas really knows how to do it."

"Then you will have to protect me," she said.

The Egyptian Embassy was situated on the lower slope of the Janiculum, in the relatively new Trans-Tiber district. Free of the cramping walls of the City proper, the estates on the Janiculum sprawled amid generous grounds, and much of the property was the domain of wealthy foreigners. At the top of the hill was the pole, from which fluttered a long, red banner, which was taken down only if an enemy approached.

We were carried across the Sublician Bridge, pushing past the throngs of beggars who always haunt bridges, thence up along the line of the old wall built by Ancus Martius to connect the bridge and the Servian Wall to the little fort surrounding the flag-pole. Both the wall and the fort were in ruins, despite occasional calls for their restoration.

At length we arrived at the embassy, where flocks of slaves doused us with flower petals, sprinkled us with perfume, and generally behaved as if we had just stepped down from Olympus to let mere mortals bask in our radiance. They even draped our slaves with wreaths.

The place was a marvelous jumble of architectural styles, decorated with the most extravagant paintings, frescoes, and picture mosaics, the buildings and grounds populated with Greek and Egyptian statuary and planted with ornamental shrubs and trees from all over the world.

Lisas himself came to greet us, swathed in a tremendous,

gauzy robe dyed with genuine Tyrian purple, his face plastered with heavy cosmetics to disguise the ravages of his legendary degeneracies.

"Welcome, Senator Metellus! And this must be the niece of the great conqueror, the beauteous Julia of whose innumerable graces and accomplishments His Majesty and all the royal princesses have sung praises. King Ptolemy was devastated that you had to depart his court. Princess Berenice has been sunk in melancholy since your departure; young Princess Cleopatra asks daily for your return. Welcome, welcome, goddess-descended Julia!" He took her hands but, to my relief, did not kiss them.

"I am so charmed and flattered. I count your king and his princesses among my dearest friends, and I cannot express how highly my uncle, Caius Julius Caesar, esteems them."

"I am enraptured by your words," he said, seemingly about to faint from sheer ecstasy. Then he snapped out of it. "But the consul Pompey arrives! I must fly to him! Be free of my house and all it offers, however humble. Enjoy my esteem and affection forever, my friends!" And off he went, gauze flapping.

"You see now what makes a truly great diplomat?" I said.

"It's breathtaking! I've never felt so much like royalty. I never saw Ptolemy sober enough to remember me the next day, and Berenice is a bubblehead, but Cleopatra was a sweet child, with more brains than the rest of the royal family combined. Give me the tour."

So I conducted her through the labyrinth of rooms, all of them full of guests, entertainers, servants, and tables laden with delicacies. Lisas did not believe in formal dinners except when entertaining small, restricted groups like serving Roman magistrates and ambassadors from other countries. Instead, he let people wander as they pleased and made sure there was plenty to divert them wherever they happened to be. Naked nymphs disported themselves in the many pools. At least they looked like nymphs. Close enough for my eyes, anyway.

I showed Julia the infamous crocodile pool, full of the ugly, torpid reptiles and presided over by a marble statue of the crocodile-headed god, Sobek. No nymphs in that pool, naked or otherwise. Romans were always telling their slaves that, should they run away, they would be sold to Lisas to feed his crocodiles. I doubt that it ever happened, but I could not discount it entirely. He was a man of decidedly unusual tastes.

"What a monster!" Julia cried, pointing at a twelve-foot specimen that lounged sleepily on the bank of the pool. His back was laced with scars of many battles with the other crocs. "Does he have gold in his mouth?"

I leaned forward and saw that the brute had gold wire wrapped around the top of one of the fangs of his upper jaw. "Amazing. The Egyptians have marvelous dentists. I've known men who had false teeth laced to their own adjoining ones by Egyptians, using fine gold wire. I knew they mummified crocodiles after they died. I didn't know they took such care of their dentition." One more Ptolemaic extravagance.

We encountered a number of friends and started the inevitable round of socializing. Besides prominent Roman statesmen and their wives, Lisas had invited exotics like the ambassador of Arabia Felix and a wealthy merchant from India. Lisas had brought in some poets and playwrights, chosen for their wit and conversational skills, and some courtesans chosen for exceptional breeding and beauty. He knew how to create a well-balanced crowd, and throughout the evening he circulated, making sure that everyone met everyone else and that nobody got bored.

Pompey was there (Lisas had to invite the consul, naturally), and so were Milo and several of the other praetors, but not Clodius or Antistius or anyone else likely to start a flaming argument to mar the festivities. He neatly avoided inviting deadly enemies on the same evening. The man was the soul of diplomacy.

I endured many congratulations and backslaps for my feat in carrying the sacrificial litter. The congratulations were all right, but the backslaps were quite painful. We were in the main room of the villa (I am not sure what you would call such a room; it rather resembled Ptolemy's throne room, but was smaller) when there was a disturbance. From the direction of the entrance came a pair of lictors, flanking a public slave wearing the brief tunic, high-strapped sandals, and cap of a messenger. He carried the white wand that opened all gates and doors and gave him the right to commandeer any horse or vehicle.

"Is he a Senate messenger?" Julia asked me in the sudden hush.

"Of praetorian rank," I told her. "The highest."

The man went straight to Pompey and spoke to him in a low voice. The consul's face was a study in consternation.

"Do you think it's a battle report?" Julia said breathlessly. "A disaster?"

"He's not carrying a dispatch case," I pointed out. "Whatever his message is, it's a short one."

Pompey raised a hand and snapped his fingers, a military signal you could hear through the whole villa. "All senators to me!"

"Wait here," I told Julia. I hustled over to him along with about two dozen others. Milo already stood next to Pompey, and we gathered close to him, knowing that it boded no good. Like an ebbing tide, those of no official standing drew back toward the walls, leaving the men in the variously striped tunics and togas standing as it were on an island in the center. Lisas looked on with anxiety, but also with a sort of gloating anticipation. A real catastrophe would be the perfect capstone to his party.

"Senators," Pompey said, "I have just received news of the

gravest importance. The Tribune of the People Caius Ateius Capito has been discovered, murdered."

"Hah!" said a vinegary old senator named Aurunculeius Cotta. "Serves the bugger right!" He was a well-known adherent of the aristocratic party. There were many murmurs of agreement.

"My sentiments to perfection," Pompey said, drily. "But the man was a tribune, and at this moment the commons are in a frenzy, assembling in the Forum and ready to burn the City down. We have to go there at once and calm them, or there will be a riot such as Rome hasn't seen in a generation."

I went to Julia. "We're in for a riot. Don't try to go back home tonight. Stay here or with friends in the Trans-Tiber. Hermes!"

"Here, Dominus!" He was this formal only when he knew the situation was serious.

"You have your stick?"

"Right here." He patted the rather indecent bulge in the front of his tunic. "I'll guard your back."

"No, stay with Julia. I want her—"

"Take him," Julia urged. "I'll go to Grandmother's summer house; it's just a short walk from here."

"I'd forgotten about that place. Yes, go there. I'll arrange with Lisas for an escort." Even if the rioting spilled out of the City and across the river, no mob would ever have the courage to assault Aurelia's property.

"You're exaggerating the danger," she said.

"Not in the least. A tribune has been murdered. That hasn't happened in nearly thirty years, and the last time the mob rioted for three days without letup."

"And I thought your life would be a little quieter away from Gaul." Like the other wives present, she made no motion to embrace or kiss me. Such a public display would have been unthink-

134

able for a woman of her breeding. Sometimes I think we carry this business of *gravitas* too far.

"Of a certainty," Lisas said when I spoke to him. "I am already assembling my soldiers. They cannot pass through the gates, but I shall provide my guests an escort to any place they choose on this bank of the river. Of course, the lady is welcome to stay here if she so chooses."

"I am most grateful," I assured him. "I shall not forget." He appeared about to faint at the prospect of receiving my gratitude, and I left him there, my mind set much at ease. The embassy guards were all hard-bitten Macedonians—not an Egyptian in the lot.

"Lictors to the fore!" Pompey shouted as we assembled in the courtyard. With the consular and praetorian lictors in a double file, we made a formidable procession.

"March!" Pompey called, and we set off with Pompey in front, Milo behind him, the other praetors there behind Milo. We lesser senators followed in a gaggle. Behind us strolled a fairly substantial force of bodyguards, mostly *ludus*-trained slaves like Hermes, forbidden to bear arms but handy with fists and clubs. I was all too aware that they would be little protection against attack by a real mob.

However, I also knew that Milo's crowd would be there in the Forum, and Pompey's many clients, and the personal followings of the other important men, and these might be able to hold the mob at bay long enough for us to escape, should worse come to worst.

We passed across the bridge and through the gate, where the guard saluted us. Pompey paused there for a moment.

"Can you see anything?" he called up to the men atop one of the gate towers.

"No fires, Consul," the man answered.

"Good. Things haven't properly started yet." He led us off

across the Forum Boarium, past the ghostly bulk of the Circus Maximus, and then around the base of the Capitoline Hill. The Tuscan Street would have been more direct, but this brought us out at the Basilica Julia, which had a more commanding view over the Forum and offered a better escape route up to the Temple of Capitoline Jove, should the worst happen. Either way, the walk was all too short.

"When we get to the basilica," Pompey said, "I want the lictors in a line halfway up the steps. Senators at the top of the steps, serving magistrates nearest me. Milo, I trust your boys will be there?"

"They have their orders for situations like this, Consul," he said. "Every man will be there, in place, to give us the best protection. The question is: which way will Clodius jump?"

The same question had been running through my own head. "Clodius won't want a riot unless he controls it, and *nobody* will control this mob once it loses its head," I said.

"Metellus is right," Pompey said. "Milo, I don't want anything to break out between you."

"I won't start anything," Milo said.

We had been hearing the roar of the crowd ahead from the time we entered the Forum Boarium. The noise abated as we went into the Basilica Julia through a rear door and crossed its cavernous interior, inhabited only by the night cleaning crew of public slaves who huddled in the corners, wide-eyed with fear. Then we walked out onto the colonnaded portico, and the full roar of the mob struck us.

Beside me I heard a senator mutter, "A white boar to Hercules if I get through this night alive."

For my part, I was ready to pledge a whole herd of bulls to Jupiter. The Forum was a seething, storm-tossed sea of people, alight with waving torches, further illuminated by the bonfires that, for some unknown reason, mobs always feel compelled to ignite.

The fires were fed with furniture and building materials plundered from all the nearby buildings. At least they were burning on the pavement and hadn't yet spread to the houses and public buildings, but that was just a matter of time. A mindless mob is always happy to burn its own homes and shops, only to wake up when the hysteria has passed and look for someone to blame for its own beastly behavior. That part is usually good for another riot, one with more bloodshed than arson.

The lictors took up their station on the steps, standing shoulder to shoulder, their *fasces* held at a slant across their chests. Some of the mob caught sight of them, and then of the knot of dignitaries on the terrace at the top of the steps. As word spread, an extraordinary motion, something like the way water moves when it is disturbed, swept through the crowd. A bit at a time, starting at the forward fringes and amid little concentrations here and there, the inchoate, antlike swarming began to assume a common direction, and then the whole mass was surging toward the basilica, except for those who had already secured points of vantage on the bases of monuments or who hung, apelike, from the great statues and monumental columns.

In the fore of the crowd, I saw Clodius, dressed in his workingman's tunic. He was a few steps ahead of the mob and running for all he was worth, not escaping them, but leading.

"Let that man through!" Pompey ordered the lictors, "but no other who is not of senatorial rank."

From behind us, more senators quietly came from the depths of the basilica. They were the braver members of the order, who had been watching from hiding places around the Forum, waiting for a signal to assemble. To my relief I saw Cicero, along with Cato, Balbus, and some others. With so much courage and prestige present, we might just pull it off. I scanned the crowd, and saw that Milo's thugs had taken up a position well to the fore, ready to turn and hold off the mob on their master's order. In fact, the whole section of the mob nearest the steps were his adherents and Clodius's. I felt a sort of perverse pride in the sight. Romans can even organize a bloodthirsty mob. Let the barbarians match that, if they can.

Clodius rushed up the steps, his face in a wild grimace, gesturing madly with his arms, waving them and shaking his fists as if he were berating Pompey just short of physical attack. But these were broad actor's gestures for the delectation of the mob behind him. His words were those of a sane, calculating man.

"Pompey! You're the only man in Rome this night who can quiet this crowd. I've done my best, but even I have never seen them like this! Do something quickly!"

Pompey came down the steps with an arm extended, which he draped over Clodius's shoulders in a gesture of concern and conciliation. The two turned and went back up the steps. Behind them, the noise of the crowd muted a bit, not calm yet, but indecisive.

"A screen, here," Pompey said. The other senators closed around them, and Pompey, Milo, Clodius, Cicero, and Cato got their heads together for some hasty planning. It was amazing to see how this group of men, among whom there were far more poisonous hatreds than fast friendships, could drop their animosities in an instant and cooperate for the common good. Another aspect of the Roman genius, I suppose: political compromise.

After a few minutes' conferral, they broke apart. Behind the screen of senators Clodius and Milo worked their way to the edge of the steps while Pompey and Cicero went through the center. Cato came to stand beside me.

"What did they work out?" I asked him.

"A makeshift," he said, his mouth a grim, tight line. "It might work. Be ready to jump forward when your name is called."

Oh, no, I thought, my heart sinking. They had involved me!

Pompey strode superbly to the front of the terrace and held

up his hands for silence. Gradually, the shouting died down, then the muttering and murmuring, and after a few minutes there was silence. Even the waving of the torches grew less wild until they were held steady, and then the only noise was the not-unpleasant crackle of the bonfires. Clodius had been right: on that night, only Cnaeus Pompeius Magnus could have quieted such a mob. The only other man who could have done it was Caesar, and he was far, far away.

"Citizens!" Pompey shouted in his parade-ground voice, echoing off the buildings on the far side of the Forum, "a great evil has befallen us! The gods have not yet forgiven us for the sacrilege committed five days ago, when my coconsul, Marcus Licinius Crassus, departed for his proconsular province." Good phrasing, I thought. Whatever had happened, this would remind people that Ateius had brought his fate upon himself.

"Now another sacrilege has been committed!" he went on. "A Tribune of the People, holder of a sacrosanct office, has been foully murdered! Like all Romans, I fear the anger of the gods! All our animosities must be put aside until justice has been done, and we can once again discern clearly what our gods want of us!"

He went on for a while in that vein, speaking of the gods and conciliation, staying rigidly away from partisanship and faction. It was an excellent performance. Pompey wasn't much of a politician, but he knew how to harangue the troops. While he was speaking, I saw Clodius and Milo down at the corner of the steps, in a dim spot behind an old monument to Scipio Africanus where they couldn't be seen, briefing their men. One would get his orders and rush off into the crowd. I saw one man there who belonged to neither of their gangs: a well-known Forum loudmouth and malcontent named Folius. He formed a sort of party of one, with no clear political agenda, but always ready to mouth off to the mighty.

After a few minutes, Milo and Clodius rejoined us. "They're primed now," Milo said to Pompey. The three conferred in low voices for a moment, and the crowd murmur began to rise again. Then Pompey stepped forward.

"Bring forth the body of Ateius Capito!"

Another surge swept through the mob. From somewhere near the center of the Forum, there was a stirring, then a massive shape rose and began to come toward the basilica. It was an eerie sight, as the thing parted the crowd and its torches, like a ship passing through an unearthly sea, and for a moment I shuddered at its fancied resemblance to Charon's ferryboat conveying the souls of the dead across the Styx.

Then it was near, and I saw that a group of men bore a corpse laid out on a makeshift catafalque: a platform of scavenged timber atop which they had set a couch, doubtless looted from some house or store. On the couch lay something vaguely man shaped and blood-soaked, wrapped in a weirdly striped robe with which I was all too familiar.

"Pompey!" I saw the man Folius push through the crowd and stop short only at the line of lictors. He pointed at the consul. "The people of this City will have justice for the sacrosanct blood of Ateius! Will you satisfy us, or will we hang every aristocrat in Rome by his own white toga?" At this a great shout went up from the mob.

Pompey pressed a hand against his breast and looked mortally hurt. "My friend! Has Cnaeus Pompeius Magnus, victor on land and sea in all parts of the world, *triumphator,* and twice consul, ever failed his masters, the Roman people?" Approval and applause from the crowd this time. This was great theater.

"It is not enough to rest on past victories, Pompey!" shouted Folius. "This time the enemy is neither barbarian nor pirate! It must be one of your own little well-born crowd, the Senate!" Roars of agreement. Foreigners are always astonished at the way Roman commoners speak right up to the highest officials. They used to, anyway. Much as I detested him, a man like Folius was worth more than all the lickspittles who fawn on the First Citizen these days.

"Was Quintus Sertorius not a noble Roman and a senator?" Pompey demanded. "And when he offended Rome, did I not hunt him down and slay him?" Leaving aside for the moment the fact that Sertorius bested him in every fight until he was assassinated by his own second-in-command, Perperna. It was Perperna whom Pompey defeated. He got Sertorius's head secondhand. No matter. The crowd was accustomed to attributing all glory to Pompey, and they cheered mightily.

"Who is to prosecute, Pompey?" Folius shouted. "Who is to investigate?"

"This case," Pompey cried, "will be handled by the highest judicial authority in Rome, the *praetor urbanus,* Titus Annius Milo!" He clapped Milo on the shoulder. There was a great roar from the crowd. "I hereby clear from his docket all other business. This murder shall take precedence over all other legal matters before the Roman bar!"

Milo stepped forward. "With the approval of the Senate and People, I will appoint Decius Caecilius Metellus the Younger as *iudex* to investigate this murder. He is to have full praetorian authority, equal to my own, save that I will retain my praetorian *imperium.*"

"Does this satisfy you, Romans?" Pompey cried.

Now another man pushed forward. I knew him as a supporter of Clodius: a man named Vetilius. He shoved Folius aside, and there was a moment of lively, but fake, scuffling; then Vetilius stretched a pointing hand toward me.

"Everyone knows Milo and Metellus are close as teeth in a comb! Name someone else!"

Yes, please do! I thought.

"And yet," Pompey said, "is Decius Metellus, one of the Twenty, not known to you all as a great man-hunter, who has brought many a malefactor to justice and revealed more than one plot against the State? He is the son of a Censor, a veteran of many wars, scion of an ancient and distinguished house, and nephew by marriage of our great, conquering general, Caius Julius Caesar!" I could almost hear Pompey's teeth gritting through his praise of another man's military glory.

"That is not good enough!" Vetilius shouted. "The People must have a representative here!"

"Then," Pompey said, "overseeing this investigation on behalf of the People, I name the former tribunes Publius Clodius and Marcus Porcius Cato. Clodius voluntarily gave up his patrician rank to serve as your tribune, and Cato is famed for his honesty and integrity above all other Romans of his generation. Will *that* satisfy you, Citizens?" Everyone knew how Clodius and Cato detested one another.

Now Cicero stepped forward. There was a little muttering from old Catilinarians in the crowd, but mostly they were respectful.

"Romans! Citizens and Conscript Fathers assembled here on this dire night, listen to me! It is time to put aside politics and faction! In some terrible way we have offended the immortal gods, and we must not fight with one another while our sacred City lies beneath this cloud. I call upon the Pontifical College to review all this year's ceremonies and festivals, to see if anything was ill done or omitted through oversight or malice.

"In the meantime, I call upon you all to reconcile yourselves while we determine where lies the guilt in this foul murder. I call upon those who stand here upon these steps to demonstrate their reconciliation, putting aside their disputes to serve the gods and the State as Romans used to, in the days of Scaevola and Fabius Maximus." *Good show, Cicero,* I thought. Appeals to religion, history, and patriotism all at once.

Well-distributed voices in the crowd began to cry out, "Yes!" and "Show us!"

First, Milo put out his hand. Slowly, reluctantly, Clodius took it. Then both of them grinned, their eyes shooting flames all the while. Pompey put an arm around the shoulders of both. Then Cato and Cicero and I joined the loving little ménage, and there was a veritable orgy of hand-shaking, back-patting, and embracing. The crowd loved it. They had never seen so many deadly enemies standing so close together without their swords drawn.

We drew apart and resumed our *dignitas*. I heard Cicero say, out of the corner of his mouth: "And I thought Plautus wrote implausible comedies!"

"Citizens!" Pompey shouted. "Disperse now to your homes, committing no unlawful acts to further anger the gods toward us. I bid the body of Ateius Capito be taken to the Temple of Venus Victrix, above my own theater. There, on the third morning after this, we shall celebrate for him as splendid a funeral as Rome has ever seen, at my own expense!" At this, a cheer went up.

Slowly, from its corners and fringes, the great mob began to break up. Like streams of light, torches meandered up the side streets, clumps of people broke away and dispersed, until finally only the hard core of the mobs of Milo and Clodius remained, along with the strong-arm supporters of some of the senators.

Pompey let out a gusty sigh. "Well-done, everyone."

"How much of this was constitutional?" I asked.

"We'll sort out the legal niceties later," he said. "The important thing is, we've saved the City from destruction."

"For tonight, anyway," said Cicero. "By the way, that was an excellent idea, using your theater for the funeral. A funeral mob can turn ugly as any. This way, if they riot, we can close the gates and confine the destruction to the Campus Martius."

"Of course," I pointed out, "your theater and temple will almost certainly be destroyed."

Pompey shrugged. "It needs repair, anyway. Those damned elephants." He looked at me. "And, Decius, do try to find the guilty man or men before the funeral. It will do wonders to quiet the mob."

"I hardly know where to start," I said. "It's not as if there were a shortage of suspects."

"Just find us *somebody*," Pompey insisted. "Rome is full of people who aren't really necessary." He had a true military man's disregard for the innocent victims of war, be it military or civil. "Well, let's have a look at the wretched bugger."

We walked down the steps. At the bottom, a few thugs lounged around the catafalque. Some of them, already bored, were rolling dice and knucklebones.

A senator let out a low whistle. "Someone did a thorough job. Looks like the lions have been at him."

The body was indeed an alarming sight. The bizarre robe was in rags, and the remainder of his clothing was little more than bloody ribbons. A huge variety of wounds covered it—everything from round punctures to long, parallel gashes like those made by an animal's claws. Clodius pointed to one such set of marks.

"I've seen gouges like that made by spiked *caesti*." He looked up at me and smiled. "That's your favored weapon, isn't it, Metellus?"

"You should know," I said. "You've kissed it often enough." Amid laughs at his expense I took out my own *caestus* with its bronze knuckle-bar set with stubby spikes and held it against the indicated wounds. "If it was a *caestus*, it had longer spikes than mine, and they were wider set. Besides, even I could never hit that hard."

"Milo could," Clodius said. "Or even Senator Balbus here. We all know how strong they are."

"Let's have none of that," Pompey warned. "We told the people that we'd set aside our differences and cooperate, and we will.

Any of you who violates that agreement I'll hound into exile and then to his death. There isn't a man here who didn't want to see this rogue dead, so there's no sense pointing fingers just yet. I want full reports of this investigation every evening starting tomorrow."

I could not tell whether Ateius met his fate with fear or anger or resignation, since his face was too lacerated to read any expression. Even the eyes were gone, and you could see every tooth in his mouth. Most of his scalp hung away from the skull in hairy, bloody flaps. It was ghastly, but I'd seen bodies mauled worse after gang fights, and all the damage done by bricks and nail-studded planks.

"Don't get blood on your best toga!" Hermes hissed in my ear. "Julia will skin both of us!"

"Gentlemen," Pompey said, "good evening to you. Once again, well-done. This was a good night's work. We might not have been able to pull it off except that four of the men I named to the commission were seen by everyone carrying the sacrifices for the full three circuits a few days ago. The people still feel good about that. But this is not over yet—far from it."

Clodius pointed to several of his men in turn. "You men haul this carrion over to the temple. Mind you be respectful."

I addressed the remaining idlers. "Do any of you know where he was found?"

Vetilius came up to me. "I heard that some night-fishermen found him on the riverbank this evening, just before nightfall. Bodies aren't all that rare in the river, but after the curse, everybody in Rome knew about that robe. They alerted the gate watch, and pretty soon the word was all over the City."

"Do you know which bank they found him on?"

He shrugged. "I didn't hear that, but it was those boatmen you see fishing with nets and torches at night between the Sublician and Aemilian Bridges."

"Then I know who to ask. Thanks." I turned to Hermes. "Come along."

"Where are we going?"

"I'm going home, to bed. You go to Aurelia's summerhouse and tell Julia that I'm all right."

"I can't pass through the gate by myself," he pointed out. "Don't worry. She'll have Cypria sitting on the roof, watching for fires in the City. As long as there are no buildings burning, she'll know there's no riot." The boy had a positive genius for avoiding exertion.

"Oh, I suppose you're right. Tomorrow morning, when you go to the *ludus,* tell Asklepiodes to meet me at the Temple of Venus Victrix at his earliest convenience."

"Right." He yawned as we trudged toward home. "This is more exciting than Gaul."

"No rest for a servant of the Senate and People," I said. Now I had two thorny investigations to conduct. But I knew that, when I found the answer to one, I'd have solved the other.

9

THE STRETCH OF THE TIBER BE-
tween the Aemilian and Sublician Bridges was rich with history,
for these were our oldest bridges and the scene of legendary battles. It was also rich with smell, for the great sewer, the Cloaca
Maxima, discharged its effluent into the river at this spot, along
with some of the lesser sewers. The adjacent Forum Boarium, together with the Circus Maximus and all its attendant stables, had
to be cleaned daily, and the resulting product, if not sold to farmers
for fertilizer, was dumped by the wagonload into the murky water
between the bridges.

All this enrichment of the otherwise nutrition-poor water resulted in abundant schools of fish, making this intrapontal stretch
of river the most desirable fishing ground anywhere near the City.
The fishing was dominated by a few families who had for generations defended their territory against all interlopers. They had
their own customs, sacrificed to their own gods and to Tiberinus,
the personified river. They even spoke in a dialect of their own.

There were, roughly speaking, three groupings of these families: those who fished from the banks and bridges with poles, those who fished with nets from boats during the day, and those who fished at night, with nets and torches.

At dawn on the morning after the near-riot, I waited on the riverbank, grateful that the coolness of winter kept the stench within tolerable boundaries. We Romans are inordinately proud of our sewers, but they came about more or less by accident. The Forum was on swampy ground, so the early settlers dug a ditch to the river to drain it. From the Etruscans they learned how to encase the trench in vaulted stone and cover it. It turned out to be a convenient place to throw all the city's waste, and now we have a whole system of sewers, although the City always seems to grow a little faster than the capacity of the sewers to keep it clean.

The day-fishermen were readying their boats to go out as the night-fishermen came in, and as the latter began to unload their fish, I accosted an older man who seemed to be in charge of several of the fishing craft.

"I am Decius Metellus, *iudex* appointed to investigate the murder of the tribune Ateius. I need to speak with whoever found the body."

The gray-haired fisherman spoke slowly, and I will not try to reproduce here his river-fisherman's dialect. "Was young Sextus, the one we call Cricket, that spotted the corpse; then we all rowed over for a look. Would've left it till morning and reported it then, but the other Sextus, the one we call Mender because he's so handy mending the nets, he leaned close with a torch and sang out. The dead man was wearing a strange robe and looked like lions had been at him. We'd all heard talk about the crazy tribune who'd cursed Crassus, so I went over to the gate and reported it right away."

"Admirable. Which bank was he on?"

The man turned and pointed to the far bank, opposite the City. "The Tuscan."

"Did you carry him in?"

He shook his head vehemently. "No, we don't touch no corpses. You do that, you'll never catch no fish till you're purified by a priest. The gate captain rounded up some night-cleaning slaves from the Forum Boarium, and they carried him through the gate. By that time, word was spreading fast. There was already a crowd waiting at the gate."

"An excellent report," I told him. "I am obliged to you." I turned to go, but he spoke up.

"Senator?"

I turned back. "Yes?"

"You're up for aedile next year, aren't you?"

"I am."

"You get elected, the big sewer's clogged real bad, been needing cleaning for years."

"I'll remember," I said, sighing with resignation. I would be paying for my predecessors' neglect. Scouring the sewers was one of the very worst jobs on the aedile's docket. We usually employed condemned criminals to do it.

"Do it as soon as you're in office," he admonished me. "Or it'll be too late."

"What do you mean?"

"Flood coming next year, a big one. We've seen all the signs," he nodded dolefully.

"I'll see to it. Thanks for the warning."

I made my way toward the Campus Martius, brooding over the prospect of the year ahead. I didn't doubt the man for an instant. This wasn't an old woman seeing warnings from the gods in every bird that flew past her window. These were people who lived their lives on the river and knew all its moods. If they said a flood was coming, then, barring freakish circumstances, it would come.

I skirted the edge of the Forum Boarium and went out through the Carmentalis Gate and took the long street that led to Pompey's Theater. The street was lined with some of our smaller but nonetheless most beautiful temples. Pompey had had the street widened and improved to facilitate access to his theater, which was the first permanent theater built in Rome. For centuries, the Censors tried to keep degenerate Greek influences out of the City, regarding them as a danger to public morals.

The great complex of interconnected buildings bulked up from the flat plain of the Campus Martius like a beached whale. At one end was the vast theater with the temple atop it, and from it stretched the extravagant portico and the Senate meetinghouse, all surrounded by splendid gardens. Pompey could do some things right, if he hired someone competent to think it up for him.

I passed into the theater and stood within the great half circle of seats, said to have a seating capacity of forty thousand. On the stage, an acting troupe was rehearsing what appeared to be a tragedy, the actors looking strange without their masks. At the top of the seats, before the temple, I could see a small crowd gathered. I began to climb, feeling like a slave at the Games, relegated to the highest seats with the most distant view of the action.

A pack of thugs stood as a sort of honor guard around the mangled remains of the late, unlamented Ateius Capito. I didn't bother to look him over, since I had come here to get a professional opinion. Instead, I admired the temple, which I had not seen since it had been completed.

The Temple of Venus Victrix was, of necessity, rather small. You do not build a truly huge temple atop a theater, even if you are inclined by nature to such odd architectural juxtapositions. Its proportions, however, were exquisite. The slender, delicately fluted

Corinthian columns, topped with their sprays of acanthus leaves, were especially pleasing.

"No signs of action from the City?" I asked the man in charge of the thugs, one I vaguely remembered seeing with Clodius's escort.

"No. My guess is, everyone will hold off till the funeral. The other tribunes will give a rousing funeral oration and carry on just like they didn't hate his guts. Then, if you haven't found the killer or killers, they'll start taking the place apart."

"There'll be no end of fun if that happens," agreed another. These men were connoisseurs of mobs and riots.

I wandered over to the edge of the top terrace next to the temple and looked over the waist-high railing. The building with its tiered rows of arches below me looked like a huge marble drum. Statues stood inside every arch, all of them specially commissioned for the theater. We had looted all the Greek cities so thoroughly that there was little original artwork left worth taking, so now we brought in expert sculptors to make copies for us of famous sculptures.

I leaned out for a better look, bracing a hand against one of the masts set in massive, bronze sconces at intervals along the top of the outer wall. On days of theatricals, these masts supported the *velarium*, a huge awning. Pompey's *velarium* was striped with purple, because he was never shy about reminding people of his military glory. Of course, the stripes were not made with the true, Tyrian purple used for the *triumphator*'s robe. That much Tyrian dye would have cost more than the whole theater complex. Rather, it was made with dye extracted from the common trumpet-shell and mixed with various native dyes. I learned this from an old dye merchant of Ostia. The effect was almost the same as that of the true purple, but unlike Tyrian dye this imitation faded with age and exposure to the sun.

Beyond the theater stretched the sprawling buildings of the

Campus Martius. They were not stacked as high as those crowded within the walls and so gave a finer sense of space. Largest of them was the Circus Flaminius. It was smaller than the Circus Maximus, but constructed largely of stone, while the Maximus was mostly of wood. Between the clusters of buildings were broad stretches of greenery. This part of Rome was actually far more pleasant to live in than Rome within the *pomerium,* but a native just didn't feel that he was in Rome unless he was within the walls.

"An imposing view, is it not?"

I turned to see Asklepiodes behind me. He was a small man, wearing a traditional physician's robe, his gray hair and beard dressed in the Greek fashion, with a fillet of plaited silver encircling his brow. He was physician to the gladiatorial school of Statilius Taurus and an old friend. He was also, by his own modest claim, the world's leading authority on wounds inflicted by weapons. In this professional capacity he had aided me in many investigations. In his other capacity he had bandaged, stitched, and anointed me more times than I could readily count. I took his hand, which was astonishingly strong for a man his size.

"It is good to see you again," I said, studying him. "You're a little grayer, but otherwise unchanged."

"You are likewise the same except for a few new scars. Young Hermes tells me the two of you have been conquering Gaul virtually without help."

"He's young and inclined to boast. Right now it seems as if someone is trying to start a good-sized war right here in Rome."

"Truly? How might that be?"

"You haven't heard of what's been happening? The departure of Crassus and the curse and last night's murder?"

"I heard some rumors at the school, but I am very busy and pay little attention to the political life of Rome. I am a foreigner and cannot vote, so what would be the point?" We strolled toward the catafalque, and he looked over the temple with a critical eye. "This is a very strange place to build a temple, is it not?"

"You don't know that story, either?"

"There is much about Rome that I do not understand, long though I have lived here."

"Well, for centuries the Censors have fought any attempt to build a theater in Rome. They say that plays are a passing frivolity, and besides, they're foreign and degenerate and, if you will forgive me, Greek. So Pompey, when he wanted to polish up his reputation by giving us a permanent theater, put this temple at the top of the seats so he could say that the seats are actually a stairway leading to the temple."

He smiled. "That is a tortuous subterfuge, considering the reputation you Romans have as a straightforward people."

"We have our moments."

"And your concept of corrupting influence mystifies me. I spend my days patching up the men who fight in your funeral Games, who die by the score in those spectacles and whose practice bouts are as bloody as some conventional battles. You enjoy chariot races that are scarcely less dangerous than wars and are conducive to mob violence. Yet you fear contamination from Sophocles and Aeschylus?"

"But the *munera* are religious services in placation of our dead," I told him.

"Drama and comedy are likewise celebrations to honor the gods."

"But," I pointed out, "they encourage the softer emotions, like fear and pity, whereas our Games encourage the virtues of sternness and manliness. Believe me, with the way we've treated the rest of the world, if we show a moment's softness, we'll have Persians and Syrians and Libyans and Iberians at our throats in seconds, and that's not mentioning the Gauls and Germans, who are halfway to our jugulars already."

"If you insist," he muttered, grumpily. "But how you can reconcile your abhorrence of human sacrifice with dosing the shades of the dead with human blood challenges my powers of rationalization."

"But the gladiator has a better-than-even chance of coming out of the fight alive," I told him. "You see? It's different." Sometimes I just don't understand Greeks.

"I shall defer to your command of the subject. Now, let's have a look at this unfortunate politician." He clapped his hands, and two men came running up the steps. They were his slaves—Egyptians who spoke only the native tongue of that land and who were expert surgeons in their own right. They had a skill of bandaging possible only to the people who invented mummies. At Asklepiodes' wordless gesture they peeled the ragged cloak and clothing from the corpse, leaving it all but naked. Unlike Romans, they had no superstitious dread of touching corpses. The thugs looked on curiously.

"You may have consulted the wrong man, Decius," said Asklepiodes. "I treat the gladiators, not the *bestiarii*." He referred to the men whose specialty it was to fight wild animals in the Games. It was a much lower calling than that of swordsman.

"Do you think it was an animal? *Caesti* and spiked clubs can leave wounds similar to these."

"Who is the expert here?" he said, testily. "Actually, I think it might be several animals. There are claw marks and teeth marks, and there is a wound here," he indicated a huge slash that slanted across the unfortunate man's ribs, "that looks like it was made by a great whip." He bent closer and had his slaves turn the body over on its belly. "There are other marks here, cuts and—" he mumbled some foreign words, and one of the slaves probed delicately at a bloody depression on the back of the skull "—a depressed fracture that might have been made by a club. It is as if he was attacked with weapons from behind and by beasts from in front."

"Like a condemned man pushed to the lions by men with spears?"

"Possibly, although these attacks from behind were more than mere proddings. How did this man come to rate so colorful and thorough a demise?"

I gave him an abbreviated version of the story, leaving out, of course, the part about the Secret Name of Rome.

"Ahh," he said, clapping his palms together with delight at so utterly bizarre a story. "This is far better than the usual sordid murder for gain or for revenge. It is like something from one of the dramas," he waved a hand toward the stage, where the actors still pranced through their paces. "In fact, thinking of them," his face grew more solemn, "if I were a more religious man, or one more superstitiously inclined—" he let it taper off portentously.

"Then what?" I urged.

"The man committed a great offense against the gods. In the ancient tales immortalized in the great plays, the gods reserve an especially terrible punishment for those who offend them greatly."

Against all reason, fear gripped my bowels. "You can't mean the Fur—"

He held up an admonitory finger to silence me. "I mean, sometimes they release the *Friendly Ones* from the underworld to torment the sinner to his death." He used the famous euphemism because to speak the name of those horrid creatures was to attract their attention. "These spirits of divine vengeance are said to be provided with natural weapons sufficient to wreak the sort of damage we see here." He waved a hand airily. "That is, I might speculate thus were I of a superstitious turn of mind."

His little qualification was too late for some of us. At his first suggestion the thugs were backing away from the otherwise inoffensive corpse, their eyes bugging out with dread. Two of them whirled and ran toward the exits so ingeniously designed to fill and empty the theater with greatest dispatch. *Wonderful,* I thought. Before nightfall, the City would be swept by yet another rumor: the *Friendly Ones* were loose in Rome!

"And I had always thought you the most rational of men," I said.

"And so I am. I simply did not wish to leave any possibility unexplored."

"I see. Well, leaving aside for the moment the nature of the creature that attacked him and adhering as closely as possible to mundane precepts, can you tell me anything at all about how he died?"

"To begin, he was probably not killed where he was found."

"Why not?"

"He has been dead for at least two days, possibly as long as three. The cool weather has helped. In summer he would be very offensive by now."

"He isn't good company as it is, but I take your point."

"He is largely drained of blood, as is only to be expected with such extensive wounds. These marks around his wrists," he indicated livid lines encircling both joints, "indicate that he was bound at one point and struggling against his bonds."

"That means there were at least two assailants," I mused.

"Unless he cooperated in his binding, I would think that to be the case. It is not unheard of, but I would think it doubtful in this case. That, however, is your realm of expertise. And that," he said, straightening, "is as much as I can tell you at this time. I shall consult with my colleague who tends to the wounds of the *bestiarii,* and, if I learn anything of value, I shall get word to you."

"I am grateful for all your help."

He waved my thanks aside. "The entertainment alone is worth the effort. This is much more interesting than stitching up conventional lacerations. In the course of your campaigning in

Gaul, did you happen to encounter any unfamiliar weapons, anything capable of inflicting unusual wounds?"

So we talked shop for a while, and I told him about a really
hideous new weapon we had found some of the Eastern Gallic
tribes employing, called a *falx*. It had a handle long enough for
two hands and sported a blade two feet or more in length, which
was curved like a scythe and sharp on the inside curve. It could
lop off a man's leg with a single swipe. Asklepiodes showed great
interest in this and expressed his regret that he had no opportunity
to examine so impressive a wound. I promised him I would send
him back a *falx* for his extensive collection of weapons.

At length we parted, promising to get together for dinner
sometime soon. He called to his Egyptians, who seemed to be
performing a prayer over the body of Ateius, as if they, too, saw
in his sad condition some fearful manifestation of the vengeance
of the netherworld gods.

By this time it was nearly noon. Without reluctance I took
my leave of the late Ateius, who was now attended by only three
or four intrepid supporters of Clodius, men apparently unafraid of
maleficent underworld creatures.

As I walked back toward the City, head down and hands
clasped behind my back, I must have looked like one of those
Peripatetic philosophers who did their cogitating while walking.
Or maybe it was their talking that they did while walking. Something like that, anyway. Great as was my abhorrence for philosophy
and its practitioners, most of whom, in my opinion, might be better
employed doing something useful, like herding geese, I found myself trying to break down my problem by categories and subcate-
gories, as philosophers are so fond of doing while feeling very
clever about it all, too.

I had two investigations to conduct: the first was into the
source from which Ateius Capito learned the Secret Name of
Rome. The second was to find the murderer or murderers of the

same Ateius Capito. Thinking philosophically, either the two cases were connected, or they were not. This, I think, is called a syllogism. I am not certain, and I am not about to ask a philosopher.

If they were connected, might Ateius not have been murdered to conceal the identity of his informant? If so, find the murderer and I would find the betrayer of the Secret Name, and it would be all very tidy. Unfortunately, this case bore no discernible aspects of tidiness. On the contrary, it spread out in too many directions. It involved foreign war, domestic politics, the ambitions of men great and petty, and it involved the gods and spirits of the underworld.

But what if most of these elements were peripheral, and the true motivation behind all of it, the prime mover, if you will, was a single thing that they all had in common? This is what I call the nexus, and in discovering this nexus I have solved a number of investigations, although few as odd as this one. The nexus may be right out there in plain view. The trick is to ignore all the irrelevancies. That can be very difficult to do when the irrelevancies are as colorful and diverting as they were in this case. I had certainly never had to take the *Friendly Ones* into consideration before.

One thing I have learned that has never, to my knowledge, been articulated by any philosopher. It is that nobody thinks better for being hungry. Desiring to improve my mental powers, I went in search of something to eat.

It is a virtue of Rome that you never have to go far to find a wineshop. They are to be found on every corner, and almost all of them supply a few tables and benches where one may repose, ponder, and watch the passing show. I found just such an establishment a few streets off the Forum, took a table, and, with a forbearance not entirely characteristic of me, waited until the food arrived before I began making inroads upon the wine.

With the mental clarity induced by a full stomach, I sought

inspiration (Bacchus being a very inspiring god). I tried to lay out the facts as I had received them. Where had all this begun?

First, Ateius had cursed Crassus. More specifically, he had cursed Crassus's expedition, and all who took part in it. Not very helpful. Crassus was not a popular man, just a man to whom many people owed debts. His proposed war was not a popular one. But would these things inspire such hideous crimes? Would not assassinating Crassus be easier, quicker, and more to the point? And who profited from this catastrophe? First off, the king of Parthia, one Orodes by name, who had to my knowledge no adherents in Rome. Opposition in Rome had nothing to do with affection for the Parthians, who were just another pack of horse-eating barbarians. Once again, if Orodes wished to take preemptive action, why not hire a man with a dagger instead of a tribune with a curse? It would be cheaper and probably more effective.

And since Crassus was so roundly detested, why kill Ateius? Most of the men who opposed Crassus must have felt only delight at his discomfiture when his expedition was cursed. In the entire City, the only man I could think of who would kill Ateius for his actions was the younger Marcus Crassus, who keenly felt the insult to his family and had much to lose if his father's war failed. He had expressed to me a quite reasonable and laudable desire to horsewhip Ateius as soon as he stepped down from office. Had he been concealing far-more-dire intentions? I rather doubted it. He had too much of his father's unemotional, dispassionate nature. Still, I did not discount him as a possibility.

Then there was the curse, more specifically the Secret Name of Rome. Was Ateius murdered to protect the identity of the person who had divulged that name? This looked more promising. Also, it suggested a conspiracy. One thing I knew from long experience: it is easier to hide an elephant under the bed than it is to hide a conspiracy in Rome, especially one that involves not only important men, but foreigners like the sorcerers I had interviewed.

Sometimes, it seems as if conspirators are actually eager to talk, if you can just give them an excuse.

I was beginning to get impatient with Bacchus when he tapped me with one of those inspirations: I had been concentrating on the cursed man and the murdered man, but suppose these were just minor casualties of an attack aimed at Rome itself? This seemed promising and got my patriotic, republican feathers ruffled. After all, the indignation over the curse was not because of its assault on Crassus, whom nobody liked, but because it endangered Rome. Orodes again? But the business of the curse seemed incredibly subtle for some long-sleeved, trousers-wearing barbarian tyrant. Unless, of course, he had the aid of a Roman traitor.

I realized that I was trying too hard to pin the blame on a foreign enemy. I did not want to believe that, once again, Romans were engaged in fratricidal, internal warfare. A will to believe or disbelieve something is the enemy of all rational thought.

Somehow, I knew that I was overlooking something. I was sure that there was a motivating factor that I was missing, as well as a unifying center, a sort of double nexus at which all the tangled strands of this maddening business crossed. I slammed my cup on the table in frustration.

"Is something wrong, Senator?" asked a plump young serving woman.

"I am receiving insufficient inspiration," I told her.

"I thought maybe it was because your jug's empty."

I looked into the lees swirling in the bottom of the jug. "So it is. Well, that's easily rectified. Bring me another."

She took the empty and returned with a full jug. "I can't promise inspiration, but the wine's good."

It may be that I was walking a trifle unsteadily when I made my way back through the Forum. Even for the greatest gossiping spot in the world, it was in something of an uproar. Self-appointed public orators were haranguing knots of idlers from the bases of monuments; people were babbling away as if they were actually well informed about the affairs of the world; senators stood around on the court platforms and the steps of the great public buildings, arguing vehemently about one thing or another.

"Decius Caecilius!" It was Cato, standing in the portico of the Temple of Castor and Pollux. He was with Sallustius Crispus, the hairy oaf I'd met at the baths a few days before. Just what I needed. The man who had been one of my least favorite Romans for many years was friendly with my latest object of dislike. Oh, well. After shaking Clodius's hand in public the night before, I could smile my way through this.

"Any progress on the investigation?" Cato asked. He smelled like a wine cask, but then so did I. For a moment I wondered which investigation he meant, then I realized he might not know about the first.

"Things are coming along nicely," I lied. "I was looking for Milo to make my report."

"Have you heard the rumor that's sweeping the City?" Sallustius said. "People have reported seeing the Furies right here in Rome!" He grinned, apparently proud of his bravery in speaking the name right out loud. "They are described as having the heads of hags with snakes for hair and long fangs, vulture bodies, huge claws, and tails like serpents."

"I always knew they'd look just like the pictures on Greek vases," I said.

"Word has it they came to destroy Ateius Capito for his sacrilege," Sallust said.

"Asklepiodes says he's been dead at least two days," I told them. "Why are they still hanging about?"

"What I want to know is how such a rumor got started," Cato said in ill temper. "As if people weren't enough on edge already."

"I'm sure I have no idea," I told him, my second lie in as many minutes.

A lictor came up the steps and stopped in front of me, unshouldering his *fasces*. "Senator, the consul Pompey wishes to speak with you. Please come with me."

"I am summoned," I said. "Will you gentlemen excuse me?"

"Do not let us detain you," said Cato.

Perhaps I should explain our ironic tone. In these days of the First Citizen, subservience is the rule, but back then Roman senators resented being summoned like the lackeys of an Oriental despot. A consul had the right to convene a meeting of the Senate, but he had no power over individual members of that body. We all chafed at Pompey's high-handed methods, which may have resulted from his ignorance of constitutional forms. Pompey was, as I have said, a political lummox.

I followed the lictor to the temporary Grain Office established in the Temple of Concord. Here Pompey and his staff had their headquarters, and from here he amended and controlled the grain supply of Rome and all its possessions. We passed through a foyer where slaves, freedmen, and their supervisors went over the heaps of documents that arrived daily by special courier. These were sorted, reduced to manageable size, and reported to Pompey and his closest advisers. The messengers would be sent back out with orders for the many local Roman governors and purchasing agents all over the world. It was a formidably efficient organization.

We passed out onto a roofed terrace, and Pompey looked up from a broad, papyrus-strewn desk. "Ah, you found him. The rest of you, give us leave." The other men filed out of the terrace like dismissed soldiers, and the two of us were alone.

"What progress, Senator?" Pompey asked. I told him what little I'd learned so far that day, and he shook his head in exasperation. "Whatever killed the wretch, I am sure it wasn't some snaky-headed Greek harpy."

"I believe the harpies are supposed to live above ground," I said, "and while mischievous, are not so fearsome as the *Friendly*

162

Ones. Prettier, too, if we're to believe the paintings."

"I know that. I am just not interested in tales to frighten children. I need somebody to throw to that mob before they get out of hand." This was an uncommonly blunt statement, even for Pompey.

"I'll have a name for you soon," I said.

"Not unless you go easier on the wine."

"It's never interfered with my attention to duty," I said, fuming. Bad enough to be summoned like a straying slave by this jumped-up soldier, but I had to listen to him berate me as well.

"Now, what about your other investigation?"

"Other investigation?" I said innocently.

"Yes," he said impatiently, "the one that charges you to discover who betrayed the Secret Name of Rome."

"Well, so much for the Pontifical College being able to keep a secret."

"Are you serious? Three of the men at that meeting told me all about it within the hour."

I told him of my investigation and whom I had interviewed so far. "It all seems rather far-fetched, and I suspect I am pursuing the wrong people altogether," I said untruthfully. Actually, I was very sure that I was close to something, but I felt no need to tell him anything prematurely.

"Most likely. Syrian mountebanks! Cumaean scholars! Forget about them. Find me some aristocrat who's plotting against Crassus, and most likely against me and probably against Caesar, too. I know the Senate's packed with them, and your family is not backward in that regard."

"When my family has opposed you, Cnaeus Pompeius, we have never plotted behind your back. We have spoken out in public." Doubtless the wine made my tongue a little freer than it should have been.

He reddened, but quickly regained composure. "So you have.

Well, not everyone in the august body is so courageous, and no few members proclaim themselves my friends but plot my ruin and that of my colleagues. I suspect it was one or more of them who put Ateius up to it, and who probably got rid of him immediately afterward."

Like most men who rise to great power over the bodies of other men, Pompey saw plots and conspiracies everywhere. Of course, when you behave as he and Caesar and Crassus had, you *create* plots and conspiracies against yourself.

"I can't say whether this was aimed at you personally," I told him, "but I suspect you may be right in thinking he was eliminated by his confederates rather than by an enemy. I spoke with the man only once, but he struck me as unstable, not somebody a conspirator would want to keep around once he'd been used."

"And murdering a tribune got the whole City in hysterics, distracting everyone from the real business at hand, which was the curse itself."

"Very true," I admitted. This interview might not be so unproductive after all.

"Well, get back to it. Let me know the instant you've found out something substantive." He returned his attention to the papers on his desk. I resisted the urge to salute and whirl on my heel like a dismissed soldier. Instead, I strolled out, wondering if Pompey had been sharing his own musings, or if he had been sowing confusion for reasons of his own. Since I was disinclined to think any good of Pompey, I was biased toward the latter possibility.

As I went out onto the temple steps, something that had been tickling the back of my mind without result suddenly came up for my inspection. Ateius's body had been found on the Tuscan side of the river. Why there? He was wrapped in that strange robe, but he hadn't been seen since delivering his curse. Had he really fled all the way from the Capena Gate to the river and across one of the bridges without being seen while wearing that eye-catching outfit in broad daylight?

I glanced at the angle of the sun. There was still plenty of time left before nightfall. I needed a walk to clear my head, anyway. I set out for the Capena Gate.

10

At that time the Servian Wall had some sixteen gates in common use, and two or three others for ceremonial purposes. I know this does not sound very impressive for a city as important as Rome. After all, Egypt boasts "hundred-gated Thebes." Well, I have visited Thebes, and it doesn't have a hundred gates, nor anything close to that number. That is just Egyptians for you. They like to think everything they have is bigger than anyone else's. But there is no denying that Rome's walls and gates were rather humble in comparison to those of, say, Syracuse or Alexandria or Babylon. They were, furthermore, in a state of perpetual disrepair. But then, we believed that the best defense of the City consisted in keeping our enemies several hundred miles away and prostrated by defeat.

Nonetheless, we maintained a tiny guard keeping watch in a minimal state of readiness at each gate. These men were unarmed in keeping with the law forbidding armed soldiers within the City, but they wore military insignia. Real soldiers laughed at them.

I found the captain of the gate watch lounging against one of the massive, oaken gateposts, arms folded and one booted foot propped behind him, head down, apparently napping in this half-upright position. At my approach a lesser guard nudged him.

"Sorry to disturb your repose, Captain," I said, "but I must ask you some questions."

The man blinked and came to a sloppy version of attention. "Yes, sir!" He wore a red tunic and over that a harness of handsomely polished leather straps arranged in a lattice. It made him look military, although it had no discernible function, since it neither supported armor nor suspended weapons. He was clearly a freedman who had lucked into this easy job through patronage.

"Were you on duty the other morning when the consul Marcus Licinius Crassus made his memorable exit?"

"I was, sir," he nodded.

"Excellent. Doubtless you recall the activities of the late tribune Caius Ateius Capito atop this very gate?"

"Hard to forget, Senator."

"Even better. Did you by chance notice how the tribune made his exit?"

"To be honest, sir, I was rooted to the spot like everyone else, until the consul Pompey and the *virgo maxima* got things under control."

"I see. Did, may I hope, any of your stalwart companions take note of his route of escape?"

"Those buggers?" he laughed. "They took to hiding when Ateius started reciting his curse."

"I should not have bothered to ask. What about outside the gate? Is anyone out there now who was there that morning?"

"There's a whole crowd of vendors and beggars that're out there every day, Senator."

"Splendid. Might any of these be considered reliable informants?"

"Well, sir, I wouldn't bother asking Lucius the sausage-seller. He's blind. And the foreigners are all liars, so you can forget about them. The rest might've seen something, if they weren't covering up their heads from terror."

"Thank you, Captain, you've been a great help. Nice outfit, by the way."

"Thank you, Senator," he beamed. It was certainly a good thing that our legions kept everyone terrorized.

I went through the gate, which was just about wide enough for two oxcarts to pass through, if the oxen were thin. It was an amazing contrast to the magnificent road just outside, the Via Appia, first and still the greatest of our wonderful highways. Built more than two and a half centuries before by the Censor Appius Claudius, it connected Rome with Capua before being extended all the way to Brundisium. It cut through mountains, bridged valleys and swamps, tunneled through hills, and ran straight as a taut bowstring from one city to the next, perfectly usable all year in any weather because of its perfect drainage and solid construction. Where it crossed soft or marshy ground, it was more like a buried wall.

Just outside the gate, the first mile or so was lined with fine tombs, interspersed with the occasional crucified felon. It was also mobbed with beggars and with vendors who thus escaped paying the market fees. People sold all manner of goods, both sound and fraudulent. Others offered to act as guides for visitors to Rome, and it was not a bad idea to hire one. The Labyrinth of King Minos was not as confusing as Rome to a stranger. Unlike the great Greek and Roman colonial cities, which were usually laid out in a grid, Rome was an overgrown village of narrow, tangled streets and alleys. I got lost there myself, sometimes.

Very near the gate, a stout peasant woman sat beneath an awning, surrounded by straw cages holding doves, cocks, and other sacrificial birds. By law, all livestock, including sacrificial animals, were to be sold in the Forum Boarium under the supervision of the aediles. The commons assumed that the authority of City officials extended only as far as the walls. This was not true, but it is notoriously difficult to convince people that their inherited folk beliefs have no legal basis.

The woman's eyes narrowed when they caught sight of my senator's stripe. "I'm doing nothing wrong here, Senator," she protested before I said a word. "You're not an aedile, anyway."

"No, but I will be next year, so you may as well cooperate, or I'll make your life miserable."

"Well, what do you want, then?"

"Were you here when Crassus left the City a few days ago?"

"I was, and it was quite a show, too. We missed the best of it out here. Couldn't see that crazy man laying his curse on the whole City."

"I was on the other side and saw it. But then he disappeared in this direction. Did you see him?"

"Couldn't miss him. He was wearing that robe, looked like a Babylonian whore's tent at a country fair."

At last, an eyewitness. "How did he get down from the gate?"

"Had a ladder, over there." She pointed to the wall just to the west of the gate. "It's not there, now."

"Did you see him go up?"

She thought. "Maybe. The ladder was there when I got here before dawn that morning. Sometime after dawn there was two or three men using the ladder. I didn't pay much attention. I thought it was people getting a good spot to watch the show. Everybody knew Crassus was going out that morning. His horsemen were all gathered over there on the road. Made a good show."

As I had suspected, Ateius had had help. It had struck me from the first that he'd had little time to lug all his gear to the top of the gate and get a fire going. His trappings had been awaiting him when he ran there from the Forum.

"What did he do when he reached the ground?"

"Well, first thing, he skinned out of that robe, stuffed it in a sack. A man came up, looked like he was wrapping a bandage around his arm. I heard the tribune cut his arm as part of his curse."

"Where did he go after that?"

She pointed to the west, where the wall made a great curve to the south to go around the base of the Aventine before turning north again to meet the river. "They took off that way. I didn't see them after they passed those horse stables." Much of the land just outside the wall in that area was still pasture, but there were numerous houses and stables as well.

"Thank you. You've been the first real help I've had in days."

"You won't give me a hard time when you get to be aedile, will you?"

"I'll be far too busy." I asked a few more people, but most hadn't noticed anything in all the uproar, and the few who had confirmed the bird-seller's story.

So they had fled westward, two and possibly three of them. There were three more gates before the wall reached the river. They might have reentered the City at any of them, unnoticed. Or they may have gone on to the river and taken a boat across, or trudged up the embankment to cross one of the bridges. Sometime shortly after that, Ateius had been murdered and his body dumped on the western bank of the river.

As always, questions arose. Who were the other men? Were they some of his supporters, such as I had met at his house, or were they other men entirely? Why had his body been deposited on the bank, instead of in the river? Above all, who had killed him?

It did seem that he had not been immediately attacked by indignant *Friendly Ones*. And it occurred to me to think, what would have happened if his body *had* been thrown into the river?

171

To begin with, it might have floated all the way to Ostia and gone out to sea, there to feed the fish. And the woman had seen him stuff the robe into a sack, whereas the body had been wearing it. Brilliant philosophical deduction: the killers *wanted* the body to be found, and by wrapping it in the incriminating robe, they wanted to make sure that it was properly identified, despite its untidy state.

Feeling rather pleased with myself, I began to walk toward home. I was making progress. The problem was, would I progress all the way to the end of this riddle before the funeral obsequies of Ateius and the subsequent dismantling of the City by a rioting mob?

It was a long walk to my home. I came to the rounded southern end of the Circus Maximus and turned up the Triumphal Way, one of the broader of Rome's narrow streets. The day was fading; Rome was shutting down for the night. Doors were closed, shutters latched, awnings lowered. The hammering of carpenters and smiths was stilled; people were sitting down to their evening meal. Somehow, it didn't seem like a city poised on the edge of riot and destruction, but Rome is deceptive.

Where the Triumphal Way intersected the Via Sacra, I encountered Hermes.

"I thought I might catch you here. Julia's been asking about you. I've been hanging around the Forum most of the afternoon. She's worried about you."

"I can't imagine why. She knows I am on a special investigation, and I can't keep regular—"

"No, she's worried you're lying around drunk someplace." The little wretch was enjoying this.

"See what I must put up with? The woman has no faith in me." I glanced toward him, but he averted his face, hiding his expression.

We went northeast past the fine houses of the Carinae, and

then were in the crowded warren of the Subura, where I had lived most of my adult life. My head was beginning to throb from too much wine too early in the day. But I was almost home.

We were no more than two streets from my house when I saw the two men strolling very slowly ahead of us: squat brutes in coarse tunics, their massive shoulders almost spanning the narrow street, looking around idly in every direction except toward us. Their steps kept slowing so that we drew unavoidably closer. No way past them without getting within touching distance. Dusk was drawing on, but I could see them clearly.

"Uh, Master—" Hermes rarely used that address in private unless he had something important to say.

"I see them," I told him. "Right ahead. Well, we'll just have to—"

"Actually," he said, "I was going to tell you about the two coming up behind us."

"Thank all the gods I'm not wearing one of my good togas. Got your stick?"

"Right here."

"Then we're about to find out if I've wasted my money sending you to the *ludus*." My hands dipped into my tunic, and the left came out with fingers slipped through my *caestus*, the right gripping my dagger. Hermes took out his stick—a hardwood club a little longer than his forearm, the same length and weight as the practice sword used for training in the *ludus*.

"Take the two in back," I said. The *caestus* allows limited use of the hand it adorns, and with that hand I whipped off my everyday toga. It had lead pellets stitched into its corners, which improved the drape, kept it from flapping in the wind, and allowed for more-imaginative uses.

The two in front whirled, crouching, daggers in their fists. I was not interested in talk or negotiation, not at two-against-one odds. The man on the left caught the lead weights in the face before he had properly gotten himself set. I let the toga go, its loose folds enveloping his head as I attacked. I have always found that there is little use in fencing when outnumbered and in conditions of uncertain light. An immediate, unrelenting attack is the best tactic then, unless you have a good escape route, which was distinctly lacking in this instance.

The man to the right was a veteran street fighter and came in fast, undistracted by the other's plight. He feinted high with his short, curved knife, then came in low, sending a gutting stroke at my belly below the ribs. I blocked with my left forearm, felt the very tip of his blade nick the skin over my left hip, sent my dagger into his chest as the fingers of his left hand clawed at my eyes. We smashed together, and I brought my knee up into his groin as his knife hand sought weakly to carve me and I drew out my dagger and stabbed upward beneath his chin.

The other man bowled into me even as the first fell away, mortally wounded. He had my toga still draped across his shoulders and chest, but his eyes were clear and he had the advantage. I dived for the pavement rather than try to come to grips with him, always a mistake if you don't have some sort of control over your opponent's knife hand. He slashed but only nicked the top of my ear, then he kicked at my side and connected solidly. The wind went out of me, and I thought I felt a rib or two give way, but I got onto my back, my legs doubled up and ready to kick as he dived toward me.

He jerked and grunted as something struck him. I thought it was Hermes, but from my new vantage point I could see him dealing with the others. A man howled, clutching a smashed elbow, the cry cut off abruptly as Hermes brought up the blunt tip of the stick hard into the spot an inch below where the ribs join the breastbone. That is a killing blow even with a stick.

In the instant my knife man staggered from the invisible blow, I kicked out, catching him in the belly and sending him backward. In a moment I had my feet beneath me and charged in, catching him in the jaw with my *caestus,* hearing the bone snap even as I jammed my dagger into his side. He went down with a grunt, and I saw Hermes circling the last man, who was armed with a short sword, grinning as they shuffled their feet on the treacherous footing. I heard shutters banging and voices shouting and things crashing all around. I reached out and grabbed the back of the sword-wielder's tunic, jerking hard. In the instant that he was off balance, Hermes darted in and fetched him two blows, forehand and backhand, alongside the temples. With a faint crunch of soft bone, the man dropped like a sacrificial ox. The boy really was coming along nicely.

Something hit me between the shoulder blades, accompanied by a screaming, feminine imprecation, and a flowerpot narrowly missed Hermes. Then I knew what had staggered my second knifer: the neighbors were throwing things. It is the almost automatic response of Romans to sounds of riot in the street outside. They throw objects from the windows or go out on the roof and cast down roofing tiles. It is their way of telling the offenders to take their argument somewhere else.

"Come on!" I said to Hermes. I stooped to grab my toga, and we took to our heels, getting out of missile range as quickly as we could. I had seen veteran brawlers killed by flowerpots and roofing tiles.

"Are you hurt?" I asked Hermes when we were safely out of range.

"Me? Hurt? There were only four of them."

"Getting cocky, aren't you? I must be getting old, then. One of them nicked me at least twice."

"Some of that blood's yours? Let me see."

"Your concern is touching, but we're almost home. Let someone else fuss over me."

"Are you going to report this?"

I paused for thought. "No, best not. There's too much chance that whoever hired those louts is someone I'd have to report to. Let's keep them guessing, whoever they are."

We were almost to my door by this time. I had been ambushed many times in my life, and it was usually near my house. In a city as chaotic as Rome, the easiest way to assassinate someone was to lurk near his house and wait for him to come to you.

Julia was there as the door swung open, glaring. "I hope that's not wine all over you."

"No, my dear, just blood."

"Oh, Decius! When are you going to listen to me and hire bodyguards? Cassandra! Cypria! Bring water!" All this while hustling me into the house, an arm over my shoulders as If I were about to collapse.

"Bodyguards?" Hermes said, offended. "I was with him!"

"Oh, be silent, boy! Decius, where are you hurt? Sit down here." She pushed me onto a stool and peeled the clothes from my upper body. The slave women appeared with basins and cloths. Cypria was excited, but old Cassandra had done this so many times she was just resentful of the extra work.

"Cypria," Julia said, "take this toga and soak it in cold water before the blood dries." The girl carried it out at arm's length, her nose wrinkling in disgust. Julia dabbed at my cut ear and side. The damp cloth was pleasantly cool. "I'm afraid this tunic is beyond salvage," she sighed.

"Whereas my hide is self-repairing?" I said.

"Quit complaining. These things wouldn't happen if you had the slightest foresight. You've been making enemies again, haven't you?"

"Not personal ones," I informed her. "I'm investigating something certain parties would just as soon did not come to light. You heard about last night's doings in the Forum?"

"I went to the baths this morning as soon as I returned to

the City. I heard about it from the wives of most of the men who were on the basilica steps with you."

"Then you heard I've been appointed *iudex,* on top of the other investigation for the Pontifical College?"

"And Milo gave you full praetorian authority, which means you should have an escort of lictors, at the very least. You just like to run around snooping on your own." She rubbed my side with a stinging ointment and covered the slight wound with a pad while Cassandra wrapped it in place with a bandage around my body.

"Anyway," Julia said, "it's really just a single investigation, isn't it?"

"I am certain of it."

"Cassandra, bring a clean tunic and tear this one up for rags." She dabbed at the top of my left ear, which was now fractionally shorter than my right. "This is going to make you look lopsided," she said.

"Next time I'll have to get into a fight with a left-hander. Maybe I can get them evened out."

Cassandra arrived with the clean tunic, and Julia drew it down over my poor, bruised old body. She took me by the hand. "Come have something to eat and tell me everything."

After dinner, we lingered over fruit, cheese, and wine, which Julia diluted with far too much water. She had listened with great attention as I described the events of the momentous night before and the day just then drawing to its mercifully tranquil close.

"How utterly strange," she said when I was done. "Not the murder—those are certainly common enough these days—but his body mangled by wild beasts, you say? What are we to make of that?"

"I think you may have hit on an important point."

"How so?"

"That murders are common. True, this one involves a tribune, but that is just a legal complication; it has nothing to do with motive. Earlier today, I was lamenting that there were so many distractions in this case, and this strange method of eliminating a tribune is a distraction. What do you say, for the moment, we just get rid of the distractions? Forget the forbidden name and the curse and the involvement of gods. Let's forget wild animals and Friendly Ones or whatever it may have been. What have we left?"

"A murder."

"Exactly. A powerful politician named Ateius tried to thwart another powerful politician named Crassus and got killed for his pains. What is at stake here?"

She thought for a moment, then came back, just like a Caesar: "Political power at home and the wealth of Parthia abroad."

"Precisely. You see, Julia, nobody fights and kills over matters of religion anymore, if they ever did. Sometimes they do it for reasons of revenge, or of jealousy; but here we are dealing with important men, and among this class, in Rome these days, all fighting and killing are done for purposes of wealth and power."

"To gain wealth and power?" she said.

"Or else to prevent an enemy from attaining them. A long time ago, Cicero taught me a very important political principle: *Cui bono?* Who profits from this? Let's examine the problem from that perspective."

Julia smiled delightedly. She loved philosophy. "Let's do that. Who profits if Crassus conquers Parthia?"

"Crassus does. His sons will. Almost nobody else. Even his soldiers won't do well out of it, Crassus being such a tight-fisted skinflint."

"So who profits if he is defeated?"

"His political enemies, who are legion. The people who owe him money, who are likewise numerous. Pompey, who wants all the military glory in the world for himself. Even your uncle, Caius

Julius Caesar, who grows increasingly embarrassed by Crassus. This last year Pompey has been of more help to him than Crassus. And, of course, Orodes of Parthia profits, by keeping his country and his throne."

"But does Orodes really profit in the long run?"

"What do you mean?"

"I mean, if he defeats Crassus, then someone else will be sent out to avenge Roman honor. He will just have to face a far more competent Roman general."

"You are right," I said. "This bears thinking about."

She smiled complacently. "I am not Julius Caesar's niece for nothing."

"And," I went on, "there are other nations involved. Crassus goes out to take over Syria from Gabinius, who's been fighting and negotiating there for years. By extension there's Egypt. Gabinius put Ptolemy back on the throne. There's no love lost between Ptolemy and Crassus. Crassus opposed using Roman arms to support the Egyptian king." Something tickled the back of my mind. "Just a minute. Wasn't there something about a consultation of the Sibyllene Books involved in that?"

"I thought we were setting aside the religious implications as unnecessary distractions," she said.

"So we were. Now, where were we?"

"I was going over the political implications of the murder, but you were going cross-eyed from fatigue and wine. Come along, my dear, time for you to go to bed." She took my hand, and I followed meekly.

Tired though I was, I found it difficult to get to sleep. Having spent the better part of three years fighting in Gaul, I was not kept awake by the little battle out in the street, despite a few new pains. Rather, it was the nagging, unrelenting sensation that I was being misdirected. Despite the illuminating conversation with Julia, I felt

179

that, somehow, the sacrilege investigation was the more important of the two. I just couldn't imagine why. It was enough to make me wish that I was back in Gaul.

Well, almost.

11

A NATIVE-BORN ROMAN KNOWS THE moods of the Forum far better than he knows the moods of wife, children, and close relatives. After all, from childhood he has spent a considerable part of nearly every day there. That is why, when we must be away on foreign service, or even while we are escaping the heat and crowding of the City in a country villa, there is something in us that longs for the Forum. Despite our imperial posturing we are still a village people. Our ancestors lived their entire lives within hailing distance of the Forum. In those days, it was not only the assembly place. It was also the only market in Rome as well as the place where most religious ceremonies were performed. It is impossible to exaggerate the centrality of the Forum in the life of every Roman.

These thoughts passed through my head as I walked toward it the next morning, nursing my almost unprecedented number of cuts and bruises. My problem, I decided, was that I had been away too long. I had lost that ineffable sense of what the Forum was feeling and thinking. Nearly three years of the City's experience had escaped me, and letters from friends had given me only the barest idea of what had been going on.

Conducting an investigation in Rome was largely a matter of discovering correspondences and linkages. Ordinarily, my sense of these things was extremely acute, but now everything was off: my timing, my judgment, my ability to sense the life and experience of the City. I was sure that, had I been in the City continuously these last three years, I would have arrived at the common point shared by all these events long before.

Amid such ponderings I reached the Forum itself, and I knew that its mood was ugly. That much of my sensitivity was functioning. The day before the mood had been vehement. Today it was dark and brooding. People weren't shouting; they were muttering. The senators on the steps weren't arguing so much as hissing at one another like a nest of disturbed vipers.

In front of the *curia* I saw a very distinctive conveyance: a huge litter draped with colorful curtains, its poles of polished ebony tipped with golden lions' heads with jewels for eyes. Over its roof a golden vulture spread sheltering wings. It was the litter of the Egyptian ambassador, Lisas. A dozen magnificently clad bearers stood by the poles, patient as oxen.

As usual, a number of senators stood around on the steps of the *curia*. These were men with committee meetings to attend or juries to organize or, often as not, just senators with nothing else to do. I walked into the midst of one such group and jerked my head toward the litter.

"What's going on?" I asked.

"Old Lisas showed up about an hour ago," said a man named Sulpicius. "He looked like a man under death sentence. Demanded to see Pompey at once. The two of them are in there now."

"Must be bad news out of Egypt to get that fat pervert up this early," said another.

"When is there ever any good news out of Egypt?" Sulpicius snorted.

Then a praetor named Gutta spoke up. "Plenty of good news for Gabinius."

"What do you mean?" I asked him.

"Haven't you heard? Word has it old Ptolemy paid him ten thousand talents to reinstall his fat backside on the throne. Took three battles to do it, but the Flute-Player's king now, and Gabinius comes home a rich man."

"I knew Gabinius had restored Ptolemy," I said. "I heard that as soon as I returned to Rome. I thought it was all rather bloodless. Who was he fighting?"

"It was one of the princesses who raised a rebellion. Had a lot of the Alexandrians on her side, too. Which one was it?" Gutta scratched his head, suffering from the usual Roman difficulty in keeping Egyptian dynastic politics sorted out.

"Cleopatra?" I asked. "She's awfully young, but she's the only one in the whole family with any brains."

"No, it was one of the others," Sulpicius said. "Berenice, that's the one."

"Berenice?" I said. "I know her. The woman can't plot her next party, much less a rebellion."

"She married a fellow named Archelaus," Sulpicius said, "a Macedonian whose father was one of Mithridates' generals. A real soldier, so they say."

I thought I remembered him: one of the hard-faced professionals who kept the degenerate Macedonian dynasty on the throne of Egypt, supporting whichever of the claimants treated them best.

"Here comes Lisas now," Gutta said.

I looked up toward the entrance of the *curia* and saw Pompey coming out with Lisas on his arm. He was patting the ambassador's shoulder as if to reassure him. Lisas parted from the consul and descended the steps, mopping at his face. His makeup was running in streaks, even though the morning was chilly.

I went up the steps to meet him. "Lisas, what's happened?"

"Ah, my friend Decius! In the middle of the night, a terribly disturbing dispatch arrived from Alexandria."

"Old Ptolemy's croaked, eh?" I said, unable to imagine that anything else would upset Lisas so deeply. "Well, it happens to them all, and there are plenty of——"

"No, no, no!" He waved his purple-dyed scarf in agitation. "It is not that at all! My master, King Ptolemy Dionysus, is in excellent health. But, it became necessary for him to put Princess Berenice to death to punish her for her unfilial rebellion."

"That's sad news," I commiserated. "The woman was just a pawn. What happened to Archelaus?"

Now he waved the scarf dismissively. "Oh, the usurper died in the last battle with Gabinius. He was of no account."

"I see. But, sad though this news may be, surely it is nothing unusual. Anyone who tries to seize a throne must expect death as the price of failure."

"Even so, even so," he said, wringing his hands, covered as they were with perfumed oil and inflamed lesions. "Great as was my affection for the princess, I understand that His Majesty had no choice in the matter. No, there were—more severe consequences."

"Ah." Now we were getting to the real news. "What manner of consequences, if this is not a matter of diplomatic secrecy?"

"On, no. I thought it best to come at once and inform the consul Pompey. I believe he will address the assembled Senate on the matter soon, although there is little to be done about it now."

"Lisas," I prodded gently, "what's happened?"

"As you may have learned, Berenice had some degree of support from the people of Alexandria, including some of the leading citizens."

"I've been out of touch," I told him. "Did these Alexandrians take it ill that Ptolemy killed his daughter?"

"I am afraid so. There was rioting."

"We have that here in Rome from time to time. And was King Ptolemy forced to execute some of these Alexandrian supporters of Princess Berenice and the usurper?"

"Only the ringleaders," he said hastily, "and the closest and most immoderate of their adherents."

"How many?"

"Oh, some three or four, perhaps as many as five thousand." He blotted again at his runny face. He did not look well at all. Seeing him in full daylight for the first time in years, I realized that poor Lisas was not going to be with us much longer. Even his heavy makeup could no longer disguise his ghastly color and the sores that covered his skin. "It happened more than a month ago. Contrary winds kept all the vessels in port until just a few days ago."

"Well," I said, "this is going to be difficult." Like Pompey, I patted him on the shoulder. "We'll work something out, but perhaps you'd better prepare yourself to serve a new king."

"I thank you for your support," he said, "but I am too old for that now. I will not outlast King Ptolemy."

"Don't be such a pessimist," I advised. I wanted to speak with him some more, but senators began to crowd around, eager to know what was going on, and I had to leave him there and get on with my day.

Egypt had been a problem for us for a hundred years. With its docile, priest-ridden peasant population and its absurd Macedonian royal family, we could have annexed it at any time, but we didn't want to. Egypt was just too rich. Put a Roman governor there with an army, and he'd make himself king and raise a rebellion, as had Sertorius in Spain. No Roman trusted another with that much wealth and power. So we propped up one idiotic weakling after another, as the Ptolemaic dynasty grew more degenerate with each passing generation.

And now this rebellion and its aftermath. I would have liked to believe that it meant the old drunk was showing some steel in his spine at last, but it sounded more like the vicious, peevish gesture of a frightened tyrant who feels his throne crumbling beneath him.

And if Lisas said five thousand had been executed, ten thousand was a more likely number. And he'd said leading citizens, which meant men with close business ties to Rome. This was going to be serious.

"Way for the praetor!" somebody shouted. I saw a file of lictors clearing a path for Milo, and I pushed my way over to him.

"Decius!" He smiled, but perfunctorily. He, too, had caught the mood of the Forum. "Anything to report?"

"Several things. Do you have a little time?"

"Not much, but Pompey's given the murder first priority, so go ahead." In his usual fashion, he kept walking as we talked. I gave him a quick rundown of the previous day's work.

"I knew that business about the Furies was too good to be true. But where did that bastard go after he came down from the wall?"

"That's what I must find out."

"Work on it. For the moment, we'll just keep this business about the men who jumped you to ourselves. A couple of bodies were found by the fire watch this morning. They weren't mine or Clodius's. Maybe the other two lived. It's not important. Who hired them is." Killings were not a major concern in Rome in those days, as long as arson was not involved.

"That's another matter I intend to find out about."

"What's going on over at the *curia?*" He asked. "Why is old Lisas in town so early?"

I gave him a quick rundown of the situation, and he shook his head.

"That's it for the Flute-Player, then. We've all grown heartily sick of him and his whole disgusting family."

"I always found him rather entertaining," I said.

"That's right, you missed the big show, didn't you? It was the first year you spent in Gaul, when Gabinius and Calpurnius Piso were consuls. For years, Ptolemy had been passing around bribes, trying to get the Senate to ratify him as king of Egypt. Finally got it the year before when Caesar was consul, but he'd squeezed the Alexandrians a little hard for bribe money, and they kicked him out, so he came here to get support for his return. The aristocrats were for it; the commons were against. Are you following this?"

"It's simple enough. What happened?"

"Well, the Alexandrians sent a delegation to ask the Senate to renounce Ptolemy and put Berenice in his place."

"How did they fare? I hope they brought plenty of bribe money."

"They never even got here. Ptolemy got wind of the mission and hired a pack of outlaws down in the South. They ambushed the delegation right outside Brundisium and massacred the lot."

This was shocking even to my jaded sensibilities. "That's brazen behavior even for a Ptolemy!"

"The tribunes were in an uproar over it—denounced the aristocrats as a bunch of corrupt money-grubbers supporting a vile barbarian tyrant and murderer—all very true, by the way. After that, support for Ptolemy faded."

"He obviously struck a deal with the consul Gabinius," I said. "Ten thousand talents, so I hear."

"It took him awhile to get all that silver together, but it was well spent. Clodius got a piece of it, too."

"Clodius? How?"

"He was tribune that year, remember?"

"How could I forget? It was the main reason my family wanted me out of Rome."

"Calpurnius got Macedonia for his proconsular province. Gabinius was to have Cilicia, but Clodius rammed through a law giving him Syria instead, putting him in a position to help Ptolemy as soon as he could get the bribe money together."

"And people wonder how we've conquered half the world," I said. "With politics like ours, who stands a chance against us?"

"It's what makes us unique," he agreed.

Something struck me. "Crassus could make use of this. He might pass up his war with Parthia and use this as an excuse to take Egypt instead!"

"Possible," Milo said, "but not likely. For one thing, to do that without permission from the Senate would be tantamount to declaring war against Rome. For another, he's not quite sane these days, as I'm sure you noticed. Taking Parthia is not just a fixed goal with him; it's an obsession. He's talked about nothing else for years. A saner man might have a go at Egypt, but not Crassus. Pompey would love to do it, but he lacks the courage to defy the Senate. Caesar would do it and make it look as if the Senate *had* given him permission."

"I hope you're right. The last thing we need just now is war over Egypt."

By this time we had reached the basilica where Milo was holding court. Pompey had cleared his docket for the murder investigation, but that was just a gesture to calm the crowd. Milo had less than two months left in office and much business to tie up. There was already a crowd assembled there waiting for him to sort out their problems.

"Get back to me as soon as you have a credible suspect for Ateius's murder. Time is getting short."

"You're not the first to remind me," I said. I took my leave of him and wandered around the Forum for a little while, soaking in the feel of the place. By eavesdropping discreetly, I determined that the murder of the tribune was still the prime subject of conversation. The news from Egypt hadn't spread and probably would not. It was a matter of great interest to the Senate, but foreign affairs occupied little of the attention of the average Roman, unless there was a war in which we were involved.

Three years ago. That, I thought, had certainly been a busy year. Gabinius had been consul. So had Calpurnius Piso, who had ordered the suppression of the foreign cults. Aemilius Scaurus had been aedile, defraying the costs of his office by letting some of those foreigners off for a consideration and putting on his extravagant Games. In fact, far too many of the events of that year seemed to have led to the fateful happenings of this year.

I pondered my next move. Whatever I was going to do, it seemed to me that I had better get it done before nightfall. The streets were getting dangerous for me.

I had always found the Capitol a good place to think, so I climbed the winding road to its summit. Before the Temple of Jupiter, the ashes of the morning sacrifice still smoldered. I went into the temple and studied the serene face of the god for a while, not trying to concentrate, just letting my thoughts wander. The smell of smoke recalled to my mind the destruction of the temple almost thirty years before in a fire caused by lightning. The augurs determined that Jupiter had destroyed the temple because he had been displeased with it, so it was rebuilt with even greater magnificence. Many of its treasures had been destroyed, though, including the Sibylline Books.

Once again I felt that featherlike tickling somewhere in the rear of my mind. I did not force things, but let my memory bring up such facts as I knew concerning the famous books of prophecy.

The sibyls were Greek in origin—that I remembered. There used to be many of them; now only a few remained. They were somehow connected with Apollo, and were given to ecstatic utterance that sounded like gibberish to most people, but which, supposedly, could be interpreted by qualified priests as the will of the gods. The sayings of some of these sibyls had been written down in nine books that, somehow, made their way to Italy.

Legend had it that, during the reign of the last king of Rome, Tarquinius Superbus, the celebrated books were brought to Rome and offered to him for sale. He considered the price exorbitant and refused, whereupon the sibyl had burned the books one by one, each time offering him the remaining books at the same price. Tarquinius, as poor a businessman as he was a king, agreed when there were three books left. These he deposited in a vault below the temple, where they were consulted from time to time. They were popularly believed to contain prophecies of the whole future history of Rome.

I considered this to be among the silliest of all our ancient beliefs, but many believed in the books implicitly. It had been these books that Lisas had told me Crassus used as an excuse to prevent the Senate from sending Ptolemy back to Egypt with a Roman army to support him.

And who was the sibyl who had sold the books, on such favorable terms, to Tarquin the Proud? Why, Italy's most famous prophetess, of course, the Sibyl of Cumae. I whirled and strode from the temple. I was bound for the burying fields east of the City and the house of that expert on all things mystical, Ariston of Cumae.

I KNEW BEFORE I REACHED THE door that I had arrived too late. There is something about a house in which nobody lives that makes it indefinably different from an inhabited place. I walked between the cypresses, oppressed by the smell of death that permeated the air of the whole district, wondering if I would find more death within the modest house. Out here no dogs barked; no chickens squawked or crowed; there were no friendly, familiar sounds.

For the sake of form I rapped on the door and waited a reasonable interval. Then I tugged on the door, and it opened easily.

"Ariston!" I called. Nothing. I went within. All was quiet, and the place showed signs of having been vacated hastily. The modest furnishings were still there, but these consisted of only a table or two and some crude beds—nothing worth carrying off on a journey.

I came to an upper room with a large window facing south. This was Ariston's study, for it received the best reading light and it contained a cabinet with honeycomb cells that must have held Ariston's books, but they were gone. Of course, he would not have left those. The kitchen contained no food, just a large water jar, half-full, and some melon rinds.

Ariston and his slaves had left without ceremony and in haste. Had he left in fear? And, if so, of whom was he afraid? Did he fear that I would return with more questions to discern his guilty secret? Or was he afraid of the same violence that had been visited upon his erstwhile student, Ateius Capito? I suspected that it was the latter. If so, I could scarcely blame him. Being caught up in the power games of the great Romans was like being trapped between the stones of a great mill.

I could find nothing of any interest within, so I went back outside, closing the door behind me. Another promising lead had been eliminated. There were not even any neighbors I could question. It would have been of some use to know whether he had started packing the moment I left his house, or when he got the news of Ateius's death.

All the way back through the gate and into the City, I pondered this turn of events. Crassus, a *pontifex* and an augur, but

191

not one of the Board of Fifteen charged with authority over the Sibylline Books, had taken it upon himself to consult them on the question of Rome supporting Ptolemy. To do so he would have needed some sort of interpreter, and who better to perform that service than the famous authority Ariston of Cumae, a man who hailed from the home of the sibyl herself?

So Crassus had suborned the interpretation he wanted from Ariston. There was the possibility that the Books really *had* said that we should not back Ptolemy with an army, but somehow I doubted it. Crassus had a way of getting what he wanted. Ariston had responded to bribery or threats. He lived simply in Rome, but for all I knew, he had been buying a fine estate for his retirement down in Cumae. Or perhaps he had just wanted to stay alive—a perfectly understandable motive. It was unlikely that I would learn anytime soon. I had neither time nor resources to scour Italy for a fleeing magician.

I turned my steps southward, wending my way toward the Via Sacra. There remained one site I had not yet visited in my double investigation.

The house of Ateius Capito was even more thronged than it had been on my previous visit. This time, instead of petitioners, the street outside was crowded with the sort of idlers who continually haunt the nightmares of those who must administer the City: the perpetual malcontents who seem to do no work, but are available at all hours to shout, argue, and riot. A couple of the remaining tribunes were there to keep them in a state of spirited outrage.

True to a unique tradition of Rome, all the nearby walls had been slathered with that unique institution of the Latin race: graffiti. Daubed in paint of every color were slogans such as *Death to the aristocrats!* and *The shade of Tribune Ateius calls out for blood!* and *May the curse of Ateius fall on Crassus and all his friends!* All of this was scrawled wretchedly and spelled worse. Rome has an extremely high rate of literacy, mostly so that the citizens can practice this particular art form.

Men nudged one another as I approached, casting one another significant glances, as such men are wont to do. I have no idea what it is that they hope to convey by these gestures, but they seem to enjoy the exercise. Perhaps it gives them a feeling of importance.

"You are not welcome here, Senator," said a tribune I recognized as Gallus, the cohort of Ateius in his strenuous efforts to deny Crassus the Syrian command.

"Why do I need to be welcome?" I demanded. "I have been appointed *iudex* with praetorian authority. That calls for no welcome."

"You're one of *them!*" yelled a meager-faced villain.

"One of what?" I said. "One of the citizens?"

"You're an aristocrat!" the man shouted back.

"Oh, shut up, the lot of you!" I shouted. "I wasn't appointed by just any praetor! I was appointed by Titus Annius Milo! I imagine that name is known to you." Now their growling died down. They may not have been among Milo's adherents, but like most of Rome's street toughs, they feared him.

"No need for a riot," Gallus said reluctantly. "What do you want here, Senator?"

"I want to speak with Ateius's Marsian friend, Sextus Silvius."

The men nearest the door looked at one another. "He's not here," one of them said.

"Is that so? Where might he be?"

"We—we don't know. Some of the tribune's closest friends have left the City. When a tribune can be murdered, who is safe?" The man looked to the others for agreement and support. I realized that they were at a loss how to act. The leaders of Ateius's little *factio* had disappeared.

"They were probably murdered as well!" said another of the door crowd. The grumbling rose.

I turned around. "Tribune Gallus! I wish to speak with you in privacy. Come with me."

"You have no authority to order me, Senator," he blustered, for the sake of his audience. "But, unlike the *factio* of Crassus and Pompey and the rest of the aristocrats, I respect the institutions of Rome." He addressed the crowd. "My friends, I will return as soon as I have straightened this man out."

We walked down the street, out of sight and hearing. A few streets away there was a little park surrounding a shrine to the *genius loci* of the district, here represented in the traditional fashion as a sculpted snake climbing a stubby column. Withered garlands draped its base, and pigeons pecked at the offerings of bread and fruit left by the people of the neighborhood. I took a seat on a stone bench, and Gallus sat beside me.

"Tribune, in the emergency meeting called by Pompey after the departure of Crassus, you said that you had no foreknowledge of the outrageous behavior of Ateius that day."

"And I spoke nothing but the truth," he insisted. Here, away from his crowd, he spoke reasonably, as one public servant to another. "After the *lustrum* I went to the Temple of Vesta with Pompey and my fellow tribunes, and we all swore this before her fire."

"Very well. I need to know certain things about the tribune Ateius."

"I knew him only in our shared public functions," he said, apparently anxious to distance himself from the man.

"That is, principally, what I need to know. On what matters did the two of you cooperate?"

"Why, on denying Crassus the Syrian command, of course. Everyone knows the harm that will be done to Rome if he—"

"What other business?" I pressed.

"There was no other business. Not for Ateius Capito!"

"Do you mean to say that the two of you spent almost an entire year in office doing nothing but opposing Crassus?"

"Nothing of the sort! Why, I worked with Peducaeus on getting the river wharfs rebuilt, and petitioning the *pontifex maximus* to extend Saturnalia for an extra day and reform the calendar, which has gotten into dreadful shape, and there's the whole business of the agrarian laws and the land commissioners to be sorted out—"

I held up a hand to stanch the flow of words. Everybody was complaining about overwork these days.

"I can see that you've exhausted yourself in service to the People, as every tribune should. Did Ateius Capito concern himself with none of these pressing matters?"

He shifted uncomfortably. "Well, no. It was only Crassus, as far as Ateius was concerned."

"What about all the petitioners who mobbed his home? How did he keep their support?"

"The vast bulk of those people do nothing but take up a tribune's time. Often as not, they just want an important ear to hear their complaints. If they do have real problems, they are usually so petty that they can be solved by a freedman with a few coins to pass around. Ateius's staff handled those. The few with substantial grievances to address, Ateius passed on to the other tribunes. He wasn't very popular among us."

"Didn't that strike anyone as odd? The office of tribune is just one step on a man's political career. Any man of sense uses it to make contacts, do favors that will profit him later on, even, perhaps, enrich himself a bit, within legal limits. How was Ateius supporting his rather expensive office if all he did was alienate the richest man in the world?"

"Ateius came of a substantial equestrian family; you've seen his house."

"Oh, come now, none of that! You know as well as I that if he wasn't doing profitable political favors for important people, he had to be buying the support he needed. That requires a great deal more than the fortune of a substantial equestrian family. Whose money was he spending, if not his own?"

"He was passing out the silver rather freely," Gallus said. "But I was not about to ask. The possible sources are rather limited, you know." The last words were mumbled, as if he was reluctant to say even this much.

I knew exactly what he meant. Crassus certainly wasn't financing his own opposition. That left the two men with the most to gain from the elimination of Crassus: Pompey and Caesar. The conference at Luca the previous year had supposedly patched up their differences, but nobody mistook it for anything but a temporary political expedient, to keep things at home quiet while two of the Big Three were engaged in foreign service and the third was occupied with the all-important grain supply.

"Is there anything else you can tell me about Capito? Any unusual visitors he may have had, foreigners who may have been seen with him, any other odd behavior?"

"Senator, I rarely saw him except in the Forum when we dealt with that single issue. I was far too busy to socialize with him. His enthusiasm for foreign religions and sorcery was well-known, but public life in Rome is ridden with crackpots."

"All too true. Well, Tribune, I thank you for your cooperation." We both stood.

"This is a vicious business," Gallus said. "I hope you find who murdered him. He was a tribune and shouldn't have been touched while he was still in office." He adjusted the drape of his toga. "Aside from that, I'm glad the bastard's dead."

I went back to the Forum, stopping on the way to snack at the stands of some street vendors. With commendable moderation, I washed it down with nothing stronger than water.

I hailed a few friends as I crossed the Forum, but I did not stop, instead climbing the lower slope of the Capitol to the Tabularium, the main archive of the Roman State. There I located the freedman in charge of the Censor's records.

"How may I help you, Senator?" he asked. He was surrounded by slaves who actually looked busy for a change, that year being one in which the Census was taken.

"I need the records pertaining to the late tribune Caius Ateius Capito's qualifications for office." The fitness of candidates to stand for office coming under the purview of the Censors, Capito would have deposited a statement of his age, property, and military and political service with them. The man went off, shaking his head at this unreasonable imposition on the time of a busy, busy official. It was getting to be an old story.

I waited for him amid the rustlings and cracklings of papyrus, the rattlings of wooden binders containing wax tablets, the thumpings of lead seals as the slaves and freedmen went through the motions of the most notoriously tedious job required by the constitution. It was a good thing we only had to do it every five years.

"Here you are, Senator," the archivist said, handing me a small roll of papyrus. I unrolled it and read.

There was not much to it. Ateius stated that he possessed the minimum property required for equestrian status, that he had been enrolled in the equestrian order by the Censors Cornelius Lentulus and Gellius Publicola, fifteen years before. He had served with the legions for the required number of campaigns, under Lucullus, Metellus Creticus, Pompey, and Philippus, he of the famous fishponds. Most of his service had been in the East, I noticed—Macedonia and the wars with Mithridates and Tigranes and their heirs, for the most part, plus the bandit-chasing that inevitably takes up so much of an army's time in that part of the world, even when it is nominally at peace. Perhaps, I thought, it was during these years that Ateius acquired his taste for strange, foreign religions and magic. The Eastern world is rank with sorcery.

Of previous electoral offices he had none, but then none are required to hold the office of tribune. He had, however, served on the staffs of several serving officials, in the purely informal fashion that prevailed in those days. There was no need for him to list them in his declaration to the Censors, but, like so many of our lesser political lights, he seemed to feel compelled to boast of his associations with the mighty. One of these jumped out at me immediately: three years previously, he had served as assistant to the aedile Marcus Aemilius Scaurus, provider of wonderful Games and scourge of all vile cultists who could not pony up his price.

I returned the scroll to the surly freedman and went out onto the portico atop the broad steps of the Tabularium. The view of the Forum was a good one that day, the clear light of winter bringing out the whitened togas of the candidates, who were doing what I should have been doing. The next year's praetors and consuls, the aediles and tribunes and quaestors, were out there—hardly an honest man among them, to my way of thinking. Always excepting Cato, of course, who was standing for praetor. He was the one incorruptibly honest man in public life. Unfortunately, I couldn't stand Cato.

I descended the steps. I had lost my most promising lead, but the absence of Ariston made my thoughts drift back to that other suspect foreigner, Elagabal. Elagabal was from Syria. Ateius Capito had served in Syria under more than one proconsul. The connection was tenuous, but it was there. Roman men with ambitions for public office had to serve in a specified number of campaigns, and that meant going wherever there was a war. I had served in Spain and Gaul, but had the timing been different, I might have served in Syria instead. But now I remembered something Elagabal had said just as I left his house that I realized I should have followed up on, only I had failed to understand its implications.

THE HOUSE WAS UNCHANGED, and I hoped that I would not find it deserted, as I had the house of Ariston. Over its door brooded the serpent swallowing its own tail, and I now remembered that I had seen a ring in that shape on the finger of Ateius the one time I had spoken with him. At my knock, the hulking guard opened the door.

"Bessas, fetch your master." The man glared for a moment, then disappeared within.

"Why, Senator Metellus, I was not expecting to see you again so soon. Please, come in." He smiled, but the smile showed a certain strain. I followed him up the stairs to the roof garden. "May I inquire what brings you back?"

"The other day, after I spoke to you, I visited with Eschmoun and Ariston, and I found them both to be much as you described them: Eschmoun a relatively harmless fraud and Ariston a scholar of high reputation."

He gave a self-deprecating little bow. "As you see, I am no liar."

"Today, I went back to the house of Ariston, and he had fled without a trace."

His eyes went wide. "Can it be that the man has a guilty conscience?"

"That or a wholesome fear of death. Above your door there is a symbol painted—a serpent in the act of swallowing its tail. What does this signify?"

He looked puzzled but did not hesitate. "It is a very common symbol in many parts of the world. It means creation and eternity. I have seen examples in the art of Egypt and Greece, as well as in the East."

"I see. Ateius Capito wore a ring in that shape. Might he have received this from you?"

"By no means. As a dabbler in mystical things, such a trinket might have caught his eye almost anyplace, even in the jewelers' stalls here in Rome."

"That may be it. Now, Elagabal, just before I left here on the occasion of my last visit, you said something: you said that soon I would be an important official—"

"And so you shall be," he assured me, looking relieved. He thought we were back to negotiating a bribe.

"And you said that you had found that previous acquaintance made such an official more approachable. Had you previous acquaintance of the aedile Marcus Aemilius Scaurus, who was charged with expelling the foreign cults?"

"Why, yes, long before he held that office."

"Now we're getting somewhere. When was it?"

"It was about ten years ago, when Aemilius served as proquaestor in Syria under Proconsul Pompey."

"I see," I said, hearing one of the names I most feared. "How did you happen to meet him?"

"You must understand, General Pompey was much occupied with affairs in the northern part of his province and with the final stages of the war with Mithridates. The southern part of his dominions he therefore left in the charge of his subordinates. Aemilius Scaurus was charged with settling the dynastic disputes of the princes of Judea. It was said, later, that Aemilius Scaurus—how shall I say—that he allowed certain of these princes to be excessively generous toward him."

"Took bribes, eh? Well, no surprises there. What was your part in all this?"

"When the proquaestor was in Damascus on his way to Judea, he consulted with me on the very peculiar religion of that part of the world. I had great difficulty in explaining to him the concept of monotheism."

"I have problems with that one myself. Doesn't seem natural. Was Ateius Capito with him?"

"That I could not say. He had a number of wellborn young men on his staff. And at that time, if you will forgive me, Roman names sounded much alike to my untrained ear."

"That's odd. They sound very distinctive and individual to us. So, was this the extent of your acquaintance with Aemilius Scaurus?"

He nodded vigorously. "Yes, yes, until I moved to Rome. In the year of his aedileship, when I was unjustly accused of practicing forbidden rites, I went to him and reminded him of how I had aided him when we were in Syria." Elagabal nodded again. "He was most accommodating."

"I can well imagine." I rose to leave. "I have other places to go now. Elagabal, if you have told me the truth, you may expect to find me a friend when I am in office. But this investigation is by no means over. Do not take it into your head to imitate Ariston and leave Rome. He dwelled without the gates, and for him, escaping was easy. I have left word with the gate guards to allow no foreign residents to leave until I am finished." What a laugh. As if those louts could bestir themselves to stop a blind donkey from wandering out. Besides, they could be bribed with the smallest coins. I suspected that Elagabal was aware of this, but he had the good manners not to smile.

"I wish only to serve you," he protested, "and to spend the rest of my days in the greatest city in the world, under benevolent administrators."

I left him with some more important facts in my possession, but they were facts I would almost have preferred not to know. Too many of the wrong people had too much in common: Aemilius Scaurus, Ateius Capito, and Pompey, and all of them were tied together by Syria, the province just assigned to Crassus. Crassus, who, if he failed, would leave the East wide open to Pompey, who had been there before. Once again, he would have military glory, wealth, and a great army behind him. Caesar would have Gaul and the West, with immense armies of his own. The two of them would be the last players on the big game board, poised for a final, catastrophic civil war. And smack between them: Rome.

I didn't even want to think about it.

12

I T WASN'T AS IF IT WAS THE FIRST time I had suspected Pompey of murder. In fact, I had personal knowledge of his summary disposal of more than one inconvenient person. Men like Pompey and Caesar and their ilk were not the sort to balk at the odd bit of homicide from time to time. Of course, they made their reputations by slaughtering people by the townful, but those weren't citizens.

But somehow the strange sequence of events seemed unlike Pompey. To put Ateius up to cursing Crassus's expedition, then kill the man to silence him and divert suspicion at the same time, was ruthless, and Pompey was sufficiently ruthless. But it was also brilliant and subtle, and these were qualities I would never have attributed to Pompey. I had to admit to myself that I had underestimated people before: I would never have guessed what a fine writer Caesar was.

Complex murder plots are more serious than an excellent prose style, though. Caesar was eminently capable of such a scheme, but he was far away and perfectly happy with conquering Gaul.

Would Pompey have sent the four killers after me? Killing a tribune was a major political crime. Eliminating a minor senator was not a serious matter, given the violent nature of the times. Pompey and I had been at odds before, and my family had resisted his ambitions for years. We had cooperated with Caesar and mended fences with Crassus, but Pompey and the Metelli had never become reconciled. He would kill me without blinking, if it seemed to be to his advantage.

The four killers were a little crude. There were plenty of Pompey's veterans in the City. A little hint dropped in the right ears, and I would be dead on the cobbles. But his veterans were, naturally, soldiers. The men who attacked me were *sica*-wielding street thugs of a sort that thronged the gangs of Clodius and Milo and lesser gang leaders, but they were men with no interest in serving in the legions.

That, too, could be a way of diverting suspicion from himself, making it look like a common street killing. He would never have contacted the cutthroats personally, of course. He had nail-hard former centurions in his following who would take care of any such chores for him and keep their mouths shut. Every powerful man has such useful henchmen.

These were not comfortable thoughts. Gaul was looking better to me with each passing hour. Maybe I should quietly leave town and go rejoin Caesar. The office of aedile was even more objectionable if I didn't live to exercise it.

But, no. I had been charged with an investigation, and I would see it through. I was a Roman official, and I had been given this assignment by the Senate, the consul, and the *praetor urbanus*, not to mention the whole Pontifical College and the *virgo maxima*. I would get to the bottom of the matter whatever the cost. It is with foolish thoughts like these that men frequently deceive themselves into great personal disasters.

The afternoon was drawing to a close, and almost without conscious thought my steps had taken me back to the Forum. I stood amid the monuments of past glory and wondered if I was seeing the end of it. Scipio Aemilianus, it is said, having destroyed Carthage, stood amid its ruins and wept. Not because he had destroyed that magnificent city, but because, surveying the ruin he had wrought, he understood that someday Rome, too, would look like this.

I tried to picture the Forum as a weed-grown field of deserted, roofless hulks, shattered columns, and limbless statues. The very thought was painful, and I tried to shake off the mood. If this was Rome's eventual destiny, it was the duty of men like me to forestall it as long as possible.

On the steps of the Temple of Vesta, I saw a large group of ladies who carried themselves with unmistakably patrician bearing. I went to the old, round temple and located Julia.

"Practicing for the Vestalia?" I asked her.

She caught my mournful expression. "Yes. You've found out something bad, haven't you?"

"I may have. Come walk with me."

She took her leave of the other ladies and came down the steps with Cypria close behind. "We are going to excite gossip," Julia said, not entirely serious.

"Let people talk," I said scornfully. Of course, I had my hands clasped behind my back. At the time it was considered the absolute depth of bad taste for a husband and wife to display affection in public. Just walking together like this, without a flock of friends and clients, was slightly scandalous.

"Maybe Cato will show up," I said. "If he does, I'll kiss you, and we can watch him die of apoplexy."

"You're in a wonderful mood," she said. "What's happened?"

I told her of the day's events and what I had found out from the records in the Tabularium. She considered these things for a while as we sauntered northwestward, toward the huge basilicas that dominated that end of the Forum. She did not seem terribly upset, but then Julia rarely got upset. I could see the signs that she was thinking hard, which was something she did well. When she spoke, she did not seem to be addressing the problem at hand.

"It was terrible news out of Egypt this morning."

"Yes, I believe old Ptolemy's finally stepped over the line, massacring the Alexandrians like that. This is going to bring us years of trouble."

"Well, yes, but I was thinking of poor Berenice. I can't say that I admired the woman, but she was kind to Fausta and me while we were at her court. How can a man put his own daughter to death like that?"

"Dynastic politics is a murderous business," I told her. "But then, so is republican politics. Tyrants are always afraid, and close family members are the nearest rivals."

"I don't think Pompey would try to have you killed," she said, making what seemed to me an illogical leap.

"Why not?"

"He can't afford to alienate Caesar just now. Forget about Crassus for the moment. I loathe the man, but I don't think he's as stupid as you seem to believe."

"He wouldn't alienate your uncle Caius Julius if Caesar never knew about it."

She looked at me. "Surely you know Caesar better than that. He keeps track of what goes on in Rome. He maintains a huge correspondence with friends and family members, and he has the subtlest mind in the world. He's as brilliant as Cicero, and unlike Cicero he isn't blinded by his own importance. He would put together all the little details and come up with the true answer."

"I suppose you are right," I said. More than once, Caesar

206

had sent me off to investigate some matter to which he already knew the answer, just to see if I would arrive at the same solution by different means. But I did not tell her that, if Caesar needed an alliance with Pompey, he would consider my life a minor price to pay for it.

"What bothers me more," I told her, "was how the"—I lowered my voice to a whisper lest Cypria or some passerby hear "—Secret Name got into it. I mean, Pompey intends to be virtual king of Rome. He's not especially superstitious, but even he would hesitate to perform an act that would endanger the City itself."

"Why didn't Ateius hesitate?" she shot back instantly.

"Why, he—" I paused, realizing that I hadn't thought about this. When you assume someone to be mad, there is always a tendency to look no further for motive or intention, still less for signs of future plans. "I see what you're getting at. Pompey said he intended to prosecute Ateius for *perduellio* and *maiestas* and sacrilege. Even if he was bluffing to cover his own complicity, someone else would have done it. There are at least a hundred senators with the legal expertise to bring those multiple charges against him. Any of them would have jumped at the chance."

"And Ateius must have known it. Before he went up on that gate, he knew that death or exile would be his inevitable reward."

"So he must have been planning for it. He knew that he would never be able to return to Rome. Julia, this gives me a great deal to think about."

"It should," she said complacently. "Think about this: for a Roman politician, what is the ultimate dread?"

"Exile," I said. "Everyone dies, but to live in exile is unthinkable." I shuddered at the thought. Even when I was away from Rome for years at a time, I always knew I would return. Everyone knew of the fate of the supporters of Marius, exiled twenty years before by Sulla and never allowed to return. They sought refuge with foreign rulers or joined rebellions like that of

Sertorius. They lived on sufferance, always having to move on as Roman territory expanded, growing ever older. No wonder so many of them chose suicide instead.

"Ateius Capito," Julia went on, "had been in public service, in one capacity or another, for most of his adult life, you say?"

"It's a matter of public record, right over there." I nodded toward the Tabularium, which was visible above the roofs of the Basilica Opimia and the Temple of Saturn, the three structures ascending rather like three uneven steps up the slope of the Capitol.

"So he toiled for fifteen years, serving in the legions and on the staffs of more important men. Finally, he achieved the tribuneship, a truly important office. With a successful tribuneship behind him, he was poised for high office, military command, and prestige. He gave it all up to put a curse on Crassus. Does this make sense to you, Decius?"

"Someone must have offered him a truly Titanic bribe!" I said.

"Which was not paid," she said. "Instead, he was killed."

"Well, naturally. I mean, would you reward a man that unscrupulous?"

"You need to find someone who could make such a bribe credible," Julia said. "And you had better find him soon. Time is getting short."

SHE DIDN'T HAVE TO REMIND ME of that, I thought that evening as I went to the Grain Office. Julia and I had gone home, and I had eaten dinner hastily, with little appetite. Then, accompanied by Hermes, I left the house to make my report before the streets got too dark to negotiate.

I found Pompey and Milo together, along with Clodius, Cato, and even the *rex sacrorum*.

"I do hope you have someone for us, Decius," Pompey said grimly.

"I've made great progress," I assured him.

"That means nothing!" Pompey said, slamming his palm on the table. "I need more than your 'great progress'! I need someone to try, publicly, for the murder of that wretched tribune! I was not in a good mood to begin with, and this incredible mess in Egypt has made me even less tolerant of your prevarication!"

"And," said Claudius, the *rex sacrorum*, "since it seems that this terribly delicate matter cannot be kept secret, I must know who gave him the Secret Name."

"It seems you've taken on a large task, Decius," Clodius said. He was getting immense satisfaction out of my discomfiture.

"Let's hear what he has to say," Milo put in.

"You see, it's like this." I launched into a carefully edited version of my findings. I didn't think it would be terribly wise to mention that I strongly suspected Pompey himself. In fact, there were few men in the room whom I exempted from suspicion. Cato was too upright, and the *rex sacrorum* was too unworldly. I was always ready to suspect Clodius in connection with any villainy. Milo was my friend, but I knew all too well that he would balk at nothing in his ambition to control the City.

"This man Ariston—" Claudius put in, "you believe that he gave Ateius the Secret Name?"

"His behavior certainly warrants the suspicion. I would like very much to question him further. If even Cicero has consulted him on the ancient cult practices of Italy, then of all non-Romans he must be the most likely to know the Name."

"And he is from Cumae," Claudius said. "The sibyl there is said to know all things concerning Italy and the gods, although she usually keeps these things to herself. He might have learned it from the sibyl herself."

There had always been a sibyl at Cumae. The succession

was supposed to be adoptive. Some of them were famous proph-
etesses, but many were obscure. I had never paid much attention.

"I'll have the whole peninsula scoured for him," Pompey
said. "If the bugger's still alive, I'll have him brought back to
Rome for interrogation."

Or, I thought, *he'll be murdered upon apprehension, if he's
another of your tools.* I was careful not to say this aloud.

"Consul," I said, "ten years ago, Ateius served on the staff
of your proquaestor, Marcus Aemilius Scaurus, in Syria. Might
they have had any contact with the Parthians?"

He rubbed his chin, thinking. He did not seem to me to be
apprehensive that this was getting a little too close to him. I certainly hoped not.

"Let me see—I negotiated a boundary dispute that year, between Armenia and Parthia. Phraates was king of Parthia back
then, the father of the present king. I don't remember whether I'd
sent Aemilius south by that time or not. In any case, the princes
weren't present. There were two of them at the time. They killed
the old man, and the elder seized the throne; then he was kicked
out by the council of nobles, and the younger took over. That's
Orodes."

"Aemilius stopped in Damascus on his way to Judea," I said.
"That's where he consulted with Elagabal. Is it possible that Orodes was in Damascus at that time?"

"Anything's possible," Pompey said impatiently. "Do you
think Orodes could be behind this? He certainly has plenty of
reason to lay a curse on Crassus."

"I don't want to discount the possibility," I said.

Pompey barked a humorless laugh. "I hope he isn't. I bear
no love for him, but it's a little difficult to go out and arrest a
foreign king. The only way to bring him back is in chains behind
a *triumphator*'s chariot."

"Crassus may do just that," said Clodius with his usual consummate lack of tact. Pompey gave him a poisonous look. It was good to have his wrath directed elsewhere.

"We need something better than this," Cato said. "Decius, you have one more day to get some results; then we can all prepare to see the City go up in flames."

"I'll have him by tomorrow evening," I promised. It was as empty a promise as I had ever made, but by that time my options were severely limited.

There was a little more talk, most of it commentary upon the inadequacy of my investigation; then it broke up. I went out of the building with Milo. As we went down the steps, rough shapes detached themselves from the deepening shadows and formed a barrier around us. They were Milo's closest thugs.

"Now give me the real story," Milo said.

I knew better than to prevaricate with Titus Milo. I laid out my findings and my suspicions. As usual he was perfectly silent, absorbing everything. Then he was silent for a while longer, thinking about it all.

"Pompey definitely has the most to gain from this," he said at last. "And Julia is right: Pompey is far more intelligent than most people give him credit for being. It is subtle for him, but he's learned to be subtle in the years he's been separated from his legions."

"But would he kill a tribune, knowing that it would cause a riot?"

Milo shrugged. "Rome's burned before. It always gets rebuilt. The City doesn't mean much to Pompey. He only cares about the army. He's complaining about this crisis in Egypt, but it's like a gift from the gods for him. All day the senators have been talking about a special command for him to go to Egypt and sort out the mess."

"To do it he'd have to have next year's tribunes behind him," I said.

"Pompey always has enough tribunes bought up to get his commands pushed through the Popular Assemblies. I don't see him setting himself up as the first Roman pharaoh, but he might well install a puppet who would act as his personal client."

I shook my head. "It could be Pompey, but I can't get rid of the feeling that I'm letting my dislike of him cause me to overlook something obvious."

"You'd better get it figured out soon," he advised.

"Everybody seems determined to remind me of that," I told him.

13

I AWOKE IN A STATE OF ANXIETY. This would be my last day to find the killer or killers. I had to stop a riot. I had to satisfy the gods. I had to save Rome. Needless to say, my wife was very annoyed with my behavior.

"Decius," she said as we sat down to breakfast, "stop acting as if the fate of the world hinged upon your actions. If there is trouble in the City, Pompey and Milo and the rest can handle it. That is the job of public officials. We have priests to act as our intermediaries with the gods. Settle down, eat, and plan out what you have to do."

So, in obedience to this very sensible advice, I managed to get down some bread with honey and a few slices of melon. It was far from my usual very substantial breakfast, but Julia was trying to wean me away from what she considered a barbaric and un-Roman practice.

"Now," she said, "where do you propose to start?"

I thought about it. "At the Sublician Bridge."

"Why there?"

"Because Ateius and probably his friends almost certainly crossed the river there. He was probably killed shortly after that somewhere in the Trans-Tiber district. His body was discovered on the western bank, and if you're going to dispose of a body in the river, you dump it in from the nearer bank. You don't carry it across a bridge and leave it on the other side."

"Your mind seems to be functioning clearly again. That's a good sign. The Trans-Tiber is nowhere near the size of the City proper, but it's still a sizable district. How will you conduct your search?"

"To begin with, there are always beggars at bridges. They like to catch people in narrow spots where they can't get away. What's more, the same beggars are always in the same spot every day, because they defend a good begging spot against the competition. I'll find out if anybody remembers seeing them."

"The bridge is heavily used," she said doubtfully. "Was there any distinctive mark that would have made Ateius stand out?"

"Unfortunately, no," I said. "He was a fairly ordinary-looking man. So was Silvius, the one I am pretty sure was with him. He stuffed the famous robe into a sack."

"I suppose it's worth a try," she said.

"It's not just information I'll be looking for there," I said.

"What do you mean?"

"It's more—I want to get into his mind. Maybe, by retracing some of his steps, I can get a feel for him, for the way he was thinking and where he would go from there."

"Well, I've always known your mind doesn't work like those of normal people."

"I knew you'd understand." I stood. "I'd better be going. If I don't come up with something, maybe I can line up a fast horse. With luck, I can reach Transalpine Gaul before the passes get snowed in."

"Don't be ridiculous," she said, giving me a warm embrace. "If you can't live with disgrace, you have no business in Roman politics. All of the great men have far worse things to live down than a failed murder investigation."

"At least I always know where I can come for comfort."

"Will you be home for lunch?" she asked.

"Don't count on it. If I sniff out the very faintest trail, I will pursue it until I drop."

"Be careful, Decius."

"Am I not always careful?" She rolled her eyes upward, and I made my escape.

"Come along, Hermes," I said. "We're going to the Trans-Tiber."

"I was headed that way anyway," he said. "It's time for my morning lesson." As if he had any choice in the matter. I never knew a slave more determined to make it look as if my orders to him were just what he would have done on his own. Insolence takes many forms.

I avoided passing through the Forum. There I would inevitably encounter many friends and acquaintances and be forced to talk to them and lose time thereby. Instead, we took the narrow streets through the neighborhoods to the east of the Forum, pushing past the heavy morning traffic and avoiding as best we could the things being dumped from the balconies overhead.

The facades of the towering, firetrap tenements were covered with graffiti as high as the human arm could reach. Most of them were election notices, some of them very well lettered by professionals, many of whom would append brief advertisements at the bottom of the message. One such, for instance, read: *Vote for Lucius Domitius Ahenobarbus for consul. He will see that Pomptinus gets to celebrate his triumph. Domitius will oppose the greedy generals and save the Republic. Vote for Lucius Domitius Ahenobarbus.* Below this, in smaller letters: *Echion wrote this by moonlight. Hire*

Echion, and he will work for you day and night. I deduced from this that the neighborhood contained many clients of Pomptinus. Seven years before he had put down a rebellion of the Allobroges and had been pestering the Senate ever since for permission to celebrate a triumph. Seven years was a long time to spend outside the walls waiting for permission, but that was how important a triumph was to a Roman politician.

I saw more ominous wall-scrawlings calling for vengeance for the dead tribune. A few of these even attacked me personally for the ineffectiveness of my investigation. Most of these, luckily, had already been painted over by the men I had hired to paint my own election notices.

When we reached the river, I noticed that the river wall just shoreward of the wharves was badly in need of repair, and I made a mental note to do something about it as soon as I took office. Now that I knew there was a flood coming, it would have to be given priority. I wondered if anybody during the last ten years had been paying attention to the upkeep of the City. Probably not. The great men just built grandiose theaters and put on shows, leaving all the real work to drudges like me.

The Sublician is the oldest of our bridges, although it has been destroyed and rebuilt several times. The very name refers to the heavy timbers of which it was once built, but the present bridge is of stone. For many generations it was the only bridge over the Tiber at Rome, because the Etruscans lived on the other bank, and Rome was strong enough to defend only one bridge at a time.

The most famous story concerning the bridge is the one about Horatius Cocles, who is said to have held off the army of Lars Porsena single-handed while the Romans dismantled the bridge behind him. There are several versions of this celebrated tale. In one of them, Horatius is simply the point man of a wedge of Romans. In another, he held the bridge with two companions, who fell at his side before the bridge was destroyed. In a third, Horatius held the bridge alone right from the first.

Personally, I think only the first version has any truth to it. I have been in many battles and skirmishes and played a heroic part in none of them. But I have seen last-ditch stands and delaying actions in plenty, and I have never seen a place, however narrow, that could be defended against an army by a single man for more than a minute or so. No matter how strong and skillful you are, while one man engages you, somebody else can always thrust a spear over the rim of your shield. And then there are the arrows and sling-stones that always fly about in such profusion when men thirst for one another's blood.

Supposedly, when the bridge was destroyed, Horatius somehow found leisure to address a prayer to Tiberinus, god of the river, and leaped in fully armed and swam across to great applause, to be rewarded richly by the citizenry. Another version has him drowning, which is what usually happens when a man in armor finds himself in deep water.

Whatever really happened, it makes a good story.

The day-fishers were already there with their poles, spaced along the stone parapet as evenly as gulls on a ship's rail. The flocks of beggars were at work, too. At my approach, the ones who had eyes immediately recognized the quality of my toga. As one man, they came toward me with palms outstretched, except for the ones who had no hands.

I used a palm of my own to warn them back. "I am the *iudex* Metellus. Which of you is the head beggar?"

A truly pitiable specimen came forward. "I am, Senator." Some nameless disease had rotted away the left side of his face, although he spoke clearly enough considering he had what seemed to be only half a mouth. He wore verminous rags and hobbled on a crutch, his left leg being gone below the knee. He managed the crutch with his left hand and held out a wooden bowl with the three remaining fingers of the right.

"You're Mallius, aren't you? You used to beg at the Quirinal Gate."

"That's me," he agreed.

"How did you end up here at the bridge?"

"The guild promoted me."

"Really?" I said, intrigued. "You mean, like in the legions? How do you get promoted? Are you a better beggar than the others?"

"It's more a matter of seniority, Senator," he said.

"Amazing." There are facets of Roman life that even lifelong residents never dream of. "Well, the reason I am here is to determine the whereabouts of some fleeing felons. Were all of you here on the morning that Crassus departed the City?"

"Most of us. A few had permission to beg at the Capena Gate, on account of the big crowd that was to be there that morning. But most of us stayed here. We didn't figure that crowd would be feeling very generous, what with Crassus and his war being so unpopular. People in a nasty mood would rather kick beggars than give them coins."

"I see that you know your trade. Anyway, on that morning, does anyone remember a man, possibly two or three men, crossing the bridge from the City side in great haste? One of them was carrying a sack."

Mallius frowned, a truly alarming sight on that face. "That's not much to go on, Senator. Hundreds of people use this bridge every morning. Most of them are carrying something, and a lot of them are in a rush."

I was afraid of that. Then I remembered something. "One of them had a freshly bandaged arm. And he may have had some paint on his face."

"I remember that one!" An emaciated, one-armed man

pushed forward. "There was three of them, two men in good clothes, another one behind them, looked like a slave, carried a sack over his shoulder."

This seemed promising. "Go on."

"Reason I remember, I went up to the one in front, he snarled like a dog, pushed me back, and I almost went over the parapet there into the river. Arm he pushed me with was wrapped in a white bandage with fresh blood showing through. And he had streaks of paint in front of his ears and down the sides of his neck. Now that I remember, the whole front of his tunic was wet, like he'd just washed off the paint."

"What color was the paint?"

"Red and white."

Others claimed that they, too, remembered the trio, but this confirmation was unnecessary. I now knew that Ateius had crossed the bridge under his own power. He hadn't been killed in the City and carried across. Two citizens, Ateius and, almost certainly, Silvius. The third a probable slave brought along to carry the magical paraphernalia, help with the ladder, and so forth. Ateius was keeping his circle of conspirators as limited as possible—always a good idea when conspiring.

"Can you give me a physical description of the men?"

The one-armed beggar thought for a while. "Man that pushed me was shorter than you, pretty thin, dark hair and eyes. I think the second was taller, but I don't remember what his face was like, or his hair. He wore some pretty expensive-looking rings. Third was just a slave, maybe the same height and color as the man with the bandages; a few years younger, maybe." Like most beggars, he was used to sizing people up by the quality of their clothes and jewelry. As it was, I was delighted to get so much information from this source.

"Did you see which way they went when they were off the bridge?" I asked him.

"Up that way," he said, pointing up the hill along the ruinous old wall of Ancus Marcius, which led to the equally ruinous old fort atop the Janiculum, where the red banner flapped listlessly in the morning breeze, waiting to be lowered in warning of an approaching enemy.

I distributed some money, took my leave of the beggars, and crossed the bridge into the Trans-Tiber. At that time, the district was mainly devoted to businesses involving the river trade, as well as those that could not be practiced within the walls of the City.

"Where will you go now?" Hermes asked.

I thought for a moment. "I'll come along with you."

"To the *ludus?*" he said, surprised.

"I want to speak with Asklepiodes."

The *ludus* of Statilius Taurus was one of those activities forbidden within Rome proper. It had been sited on the Campus Martius, but the building of Pompey's theater complex had forced it to move. The Senate had been trying to forbid *ludi* near Rome ever since the rebellion of Spartacus. Back in the days when most of the gladiators were volunteers, nobody had worried much about them. But the increasing use of slaves and barbarian prisoners for this purpose made people nervous, and with good reason.

The familiar clatter of arms came from within as we passed beneath the entrance portal, its lintel carved with trophies of arms, the doorposts engraved with the names of famous champions of the school. Inside, about a hundred men practiced against one another and strove with the various ingenious pieces of training equipment while others stood around awaiting their turn, all under the watchful eyes of the trainers. Hermes went off to get into his practice armor while I went to the infirmary.

I found Asklepiodes there, splinting the fingers of a careless trainee. He smiled as he looked up. "Ah, Decius! How good of you to visit me." He turned to his Egyptians and said something.

One of them took over the task, carefully wrapping the mangled finger of the stoically unflinching combatant.

"Come up to my study," Asklepiodes said. We went up the stairs into the spacious, airy room with its racks of books and its profusion of weapons hanging on the walls, each carefully labeled as to origin and effects.

"I made enquiries," he said, "but I was unable to locate any *bestiarii*. There are no schools for them nearer than Capua."

"I was afraid of that. Even if I'd summoned one the minute I was appointed *iudex*, I doubt he'd have reached Rome before Ateius's body, along with half the buildings on the Campus Martius, went up in flames."

"It is unfortunate," he said complacently. He lived safely on the other side of the river. "May I offer you refreshment?"

"I'm afraid not, thank you. I have a lot to accomplish today."

He quirked an ironic eyebrow. "You must be truly concerned. Have you learned nothing of any help in this matter?"

I told him of the facts I had been able to glean, leaving aside much of the religious accretion that so occluded the demonstrable facts. Asklepiodes nodded wisely as I spoke, but then, physicians always do that.

"You say he was enrolled in the equestrian order some fifteen years ago?" he said when I was finished.

"Why, yes. It's done every five years when there's a Censorship. The Censors conduct the Census of the citizens, assess their property holdings, and assign them to classes. An equestrian or candidate for that status has to demonstrate that he possesses at least the minimum wealth required. If he can't, he's reduced in status. It comes from the days when the Roman cavalry was made up of men who could afford to maintain their own horses. Now it's just a property class."

"I see. I must confess that I am not terribly knowledgeable

concerning your political institutions. You allow children into this class?"

"What?" I was utterly mystified at his words. "What do you mean? Candidates for equestrian status are still of military age, just like in the old days."

"The man I examined at the Theater of Pompey was badly mangled, but not so badly that I was unable to estimate his age. Fifteen years ago, he was no more than seven or eight years old."

I felt like a man struck on the head with a padded club. "Are you sure?"

"Please," he said, offended. "I am an expert on wounds caused by weapons, not the mauling of beasts, but I can still judge age as well as any physician."

"Of course, I mean, it's just—"

"Perhaps some refreshment is in order after all. You look rather pale." He said something in a foreign tongue, and one of his Egyptians came into the study, then dashed out. I sat at a table with my mind working like an overturned beehive as the implications swarmed all around. I was looking for two men now; one of them was Ateius. Silvius might be alive as well. Out of the picture was the slave who carried the sack, the one the beggar had described as being about the same size and coloration with the man in front, but a few years younger. The slave lay, unknowingly, in state in the Theater of Pompey. The Egyptian came back in with a pitcher and cup. He filled the cup and placed it in my half-numb fingers.

"I met Ateius Capito," I said, "and he was a man about my age. The bastard's still alive, hiding someplace."

"The same thought just occurred to me," Asklepiodes said. "What a pity neither of us thought to consult on the age question at the time. I thought then that the unfortunate fellow seemed young to have held an office as important as the tribuneship, but

222

I have no vote here and never paid attention to the various age qualifications."

"There's no age requirement for tribune," I told him. "It isn't one of the offices you have to hold to climb the political ladder. But I never knew a tribune to be much younger than thirty. It takes time and long service to build up a political following."

"I fear I have failed you," he said.

"Not at all. I just haven't been asking the necessary questions." I sipped at the wine, trying to remember any other questions I might have failed to ask. I glanced up at the man who held the pitcher so attentively.

"Asklepiodes," I said, "back at the theater, just before we parted company, your Egyptians went through some sort of ceremony or prayer over the body. I thought it was just one of those superstitious rituals people always perform in the presence of death. What was it about?"

"Oh, yes. They spoke to me about it on the way back here. They are from a Nile village near the First Cataract. It is still rather savage and wild country. Their prayer was a propitiation of the god Sobek."

I knew that god. My scalp prickled. "Why Sobek?"

"They thought that the dead man looked just like one who has been savaged by crocodiles, and Sobek is the crocodile god. Those killed by crocodile attack are considered his sacrifices." The Greek smiled indulgently. "Of course, I told them that there are no crocodiles in Rome."

I jumped to my feet. "Asklepiodes, you have come through for me again, if somewhat belatedly. I must be off!"

"I am always overjoyed to be of aid to a servant of the Senate and People," he said bemusedly. The last words were addressed to my back as I dashed down the stairs.

All the way back into the City, I had to force myself not to run. It would display a terrible lack of *gravitas* to dart into the

223

City with my toga flapping around my legs. Luckily, from the City end of the bridge to the Temple of Ceres was but a short walk.

I went into the headquarters beneath the portico. The aedile Paetus was nowhere in evidence, but I didn't need him. "Demetrius!" I bellowed.

The clerk came from in back, his eyes wide with astonishment. "Sir?"

"Demetrius, I want you and your staff to drop everything you are doing. I want *all* the records pertaining to the aedileship of Marcus Aemilius Scaurus, and I want them *now!* Bring everything out onto the terrace outside, where we'll have decent light. I order this as an official *iudex* with full praetorian authority. Jump!"

He scurried back inside, and I went out into the fine light of late morning, studying the facade of the Circus Maximus, thinking while the temple slaves brought out folding tables, then emerged with armloads of scrolls and tablets.

Of all things to stumble over, I thought as they got things in order. Asklepiodes had helped me in so many investigations, and this time he had the answers but didn't know it. He was unaccustomed to injuries of animal origin, but his slaves weren't. He was ignorant of our political institutions and had no experience of the diplomatic life of Rome. He could have solved this for me days ago at the Theater of Pompey.

But I knew I was foolish to rebuke him, even mentally. This was my investigation, and I had been misled by all the mystical mummery. I should have asked him the right questions.

"What are we looking for, sir?" Demetrius asked. In an amazingly short time they had arranged the records in neat piles. There were five slaves besides Demetrius, including Hylas, the boy who had assisted me on my previous visit.

"I want anything that may involve Egypt, either foreign correspondence or contact with Egyptians here in Rome, most especially with King Ptolemy, who was here in Rome for much of the time Scaurus was in office. I also want anything concerning the Games he put on—particularly, who contributed money toward his financing of them. I want anything that bears the name of his assistant, Ateius Capito. Get to work!"

It was not an easy task, and it did not go swiftly. An aedile generates an awesome amount of documentation in the course of his year in office. Much of what I really wanted probably never made it into the official record, anyway, especially those things involving gifts of money. But there was hope. Powerful, arrogant men can be amazingly maladroit when it comes to leaving evidence of their malfeasance. They assume that nobody will ever investigate them, and that they are immune from attack anyway.

"Did any of you attend these Games?" I asked as I went over a huge bill for animal fodder for such exotic beasts as lions, bears, zebras, even ostriches.

"Most of us went to the races," Demetrius said. "Some watched the plays. As slaves we couldn't attend the *munera* and the animal fights."

"That's a law seldom observed," I noted. Women weren't supposed to attend them, either. That didn't stop them from going.

"It was enforced this time," Demetrius said. "So many people came in from the countryside to see them that everyone had to get entry passes months in advance and show proof of citizenship."

"I suppose it makes sense," I said. "If the whole purpose of an aedile's *munera* is to win votes, why waste them on people who can't vote in the first place?"

While we were going over the accounts, the aedile Paetus showed up.

"Back again, Metellus? What's all this?" I told him, and he pulled up a bench. "I'll give you a hand. Do you plan to prosecute him next year for the Sardinians? It'll make your reputation if you can pull it off." He picked up a tablet with an elaborate seal and opened it, then let out a low whistle. "Rather generous contribution from Ptolemy, here. The old drunk was really spreading the money around that year. I wish I'd been in a position to have some come my way."

"Let me see!" I snatched it from him. "Hah! Two talents toward the expenses of his Games, as a loving token from the king of Egypt, Friend and Ally of Rome."

"Nothing illegal about it," Paetus reminded me. "He put it in the public record."

"But it's evidence. Anyway, while I'm sure Scaurus deserves flogging and exile, he's not really the one I'm after. Keep looking," I told the others.

Paetus shook his head. "What shows that man put on. The first hippos ever seen in Rome. Do you have any idea of the expense involved in bringing hippos to Rome? Took a whole ship converted into a big fish tank for each beast. Crocodiles, too. First ever shown in public.

"Crocodiles, eh?" I said. Today, everyone was dropping these little tidbits in my lap. "You don't get hippos and crocodiles from Gaul, now, do you?"

"No, but his timing was right," Paetus went on. "That year and the next, if you were a man of influence and there was any favor old Ptolemy could do for you, it was done. The Alexandrians kicked him out, but he could get anything he wanted from his upriver estates: gazelles, lions, leopards, elephants. All he wanted was your vote and your influence. If he hadn't been so strapped for ready cash, he would have bought the whole Senate. Lucky for Aemilius Scaurus he was able to tap Ptolemy that first year, when he still had some of his treasure."

By midafternoon we had reduced the heap of documentation to enough scrolls and tablets to fill a bushel basket. I borrowed a temple slave to carry the basket, and with the slave following me I went to the Grain Office to make my report.

door with the butt of his *fasces,* and when the doorkeeper opened it, we went inside without waiting for permission. The hairless, eunuch majordomo came into the atrium, all indignation, but I cut him off before he could speak a word.

"Get Lisas!" I barked. Squawking and wringing his hands, the eunuch hustled off. Minutes later, Lisas appeared.

"Why, Senator Metellus! and Praetor Milo! What an unexpected pleasure!" He was trying hard, but even his skills could not hide the deathly gray of his face. It was not entirely attributable to his progressive diseases, either. "What brings you—"

I brushed past him. "We will speak with you presently." With Milo and his lictors behind me, I went out into one of the side courtyards. At the crocodile pond I surveyed the torpid animals, which didn't seem to have moved since I had last seen them, the night the supposed body of Ateius Capito was discovered. I walked around the periphery until I found the animal Julia had pointed to that night. It still had the bit of gold wire wrapped around a fang in its upper jaw. "Here's the one," I said.

Milo took off his purple-bordered toga and tossed it to a lictor. Then he fearlessly vaulted the railing into the ankle-deep water on the border of the pool.

"Praetor!" Lisas squawked, beside himself with anxiety. "Those are wild creatures! They will—"

Milo ignored him. He clamped one hand over the creature's muzzle and wrapped his other arm around its body just behind its front legs. Then, with no more effort than most men would display in lifting a large dog, he hauled it upright. The monster thrashed a bit, but the cool November weather seemed to have sapped its energy.

Milo hauled the thing over to the edge of the pool, and I

reached out for the golden glint. I managed to get the wire between my fingernails and slowly worked it loose from the tooth. When it came out, I saw that a tuft of purple-and-black threads was twisted into the end of the wire that had been in the animal's mouth. With a surge of his whole body, Milo flung the great beast into the water, and it disappeared beneath the water with a lazy wave of its tail.

Lisas did not try to bluster as Milo climbed out and resumed his toga. "Let's go back inside," I said.

In the great audience room Lisas sat. "How may we resolve this?" he said wearily.

"My fat old friend," I said sadly. "You had better speak swiftly and to our great satisfaction, if you value your life."

"Oh," he said, almost managing a smile, "I don't value my life very highly these days." He sighed deeply, almost buried his face in his hands, then stiffened his spine and sat upright. "But I must still serve my king. What would you have of me?"

"The men you hide in this villa," Milo said, "Ateius and Silvius. They must go back with me to Rome to stand trial."

"My friends," Lisas said, "this is an embassy. By treaty, I am not bound to surrender anyone to you. This is Egypt."

"Matters have moved beyond the stage of public embarrassment, Lisas," I told him. "You have been in collusion with Ateius Capito for at least three years, from the time he agreed to become King Ptolemy's agent in Rome." Lisas said nothing, and I went on. "On behalf of Aemilius Scaurus, he approached Ptolemy for bribe money, found out just how much money Ptolemy had to spread around, and let it be known that he would be Ptolemy's servant, for a price. What did Ptolemy buy him with? A villa near Alexandria? A big estate in the Delta with hundreds of peasants to work it for him?" Still, Lisas said nothing.

"There was one service Ptolemy needed more than any other. He wanted to prevent Crassus from getting the Syrian command. When Ptolemy was here in Rome, Crassus publicly humiliated him by coming up with that patently fake reading of the Sibylline Books. He knew that Crassus was greedy beyond all other Romans. Ptolemy could deal with Pompey; he could deal with Caesar. He could not and would not deal with Crassus."

Still Lisas held his silence.

"But even the most heroic efforts of Ateius Capito and his confederates were in vain. However many votes he could buy with Ptolemy's money, Crassus could buy more. If Ptolemy hadn't had to pay Gabinius so much to put him back on the throne, maybe he could have managed it, but that was not to be. I must admit, though, that the curse was an amazingly clever device. It robbed Crassus of whatever Roman support he had left. And who knows? It might even be a perfectly good curse. If anything ever got the gods' attention, that ceremony did."

Lisas sighed deeply once more. "It seemed so fitting. Crassus thwarted His Majesty with a false reading of the prophetic books, and His Majesty revenged himself with the curse of a suborned tribune."

"Was it Ateius's idea?" Milo asked him.

Lisas nodded. "He was very enthusiastic about it. He had always wanted to produce a truly potent curse, and now he would have the—the resources to do it."

"Because he knew that Ariston of Cumae was corruptible. He knew because Crassus himself had bought the man to advise him on his fraudulent reading of the Sibylline Books. With Ptolemy back in power in Alexandria, he had the money to buy a really unique curse from Ariston, one that contained the ultimate name of power."

There was a commotion at the door, and twelve lictors came into the audience chamber. Behind them came Pompey.

"Cnaeus Pompeius Magnus, Consul of Rome," Lisas said, wearily. "How you honor me."

me. We both nodded, and I held up the bit of gold wire with its colorful threads. He turned to Lisas. "Produce them, Egyptian."

"This is Egyptian territory, Consul," Lisas said. "Greatly as I esteem you, and the Senate and People of Rome, I must insist that the treaty obligations pertaining between our nations be observed."

"Lisas," Pompey said, "I have lost patience with King Ptolemy. Rome has lost patience. Do you know what I am going to do if you do not produce those men, Lisas? Now, I know you are familiar with the Temple of Bellona, out on the Campus Martius near my theater. The Senate always meets there to deal with foreign ambassadors."

"I have been there many times, Consul," Lisas affirmed.

"Excellent. Are you aware of the special priesthood called the *fetiales?* In the old days, they used to accompany the army to the enemy's border and hurl a spear dedicated to Mars into enemy land to declare war before the gods. That was practical when our enemies were no more than a day or two from here, but now they are too far away. Instead, there is a patch of bare earth before the temple, with a column in the middle of it. That patch is designated enemy territory, and when we go to war, a *fetial* hurls a spear of Mars into it."

"I am familiar with your custom," Lisas said.

"Good. Because tomorrow I am going to go to the Temple of Bellona and declare that patch of land to be Egypt. A *fetial* will hurl a spear of Mars into it. I will demand that the Senate declare war on Egypt, and it will do it. The tribunes will get the Assemblies to vote me the command, and I will go collect Ptolemy's head. After that I may put one of his children on the throne, or I may not. If I want to, I will make Decius Metellus here pharaoh.

I will be able to do anything I feel like doing because I will be absolute master of Egypt. Do you understand me, Egyptian?" This last sentence was roared out in Pompey's parade-ground voice, a phenomenon dangerous to any delicate objects in the vicinity.

Lisas wilted, the last defiance gone from him. He spoke to the majordomo, and the man beckoned to Milo's lictors. They passed into the rear of the estate.

"That's better," Pompey said. "Perhaps something may still be worked out. Ptolemy has offended us greatly, both with the massacre of the Alexandrians and with this unprecedented tampering with the internal administration of Rome. But we are long accustomed to dealing with degenerate drunks, and forgiveness follows repentance. And reparations, of course."

"I wish only to serve my king," Lisas said.

Minutes later the lictors returned holding two men by the scruff of the neck. With the efficiency of long practice, they cast them down to sprawl on the polished, marble floor at our feet.

"You've furnished us with some extraordinary entertainment, Ateius Capito," Pompey said. "What have you to say for yourself?"

Ateius struggled to his knees. Silvius remained prone, despairing. Ateius glared at us madly. "I say that I am in an embassy and may not be touched!"

"Lisas has seen fit to waive that ambassadorial privilege," Pompey told him.

Ateius whirled on Lisas. "You Egyptian pig!"

"Such language," I said, "to address a man who has stood by you faithfully, until we brought pressure against his king."

"You still may not touch me!" he shouted. "I am a Tribune of the People, and my person is inviolable by ancient law."

"Ateius," I said, "by the same ancient law that grants the Tribunes of the People their inviolability, they are forbidden to be absent from Rome for as long as a single day. You have forfeited your office and all its privileges." I saw with some satisfaction the

231

curtain of fear descend over him as the mad defiance left his eyes. "You were unlucky in the time of year," I said. "In summer you could have ridden to the coast and caught a ship for Egypt. You were hiding out here until the sailing weather got better, weren't you?" I shook my head. "You should have chanced it anyway."

"Ateius," Pompey said, "you are to have a rare experience. You are going to attend your own funeral tomorrow in my theater, where you will have a chance to explain to your assembled supporters why it is not you on the pyre, but some unfortunate slave who resembled you in size and build." He signaled his lictors. "Take them away. Keep them under close watch. I want them alive tomorrow."

The lictors dragged the two out, both of them too paralyzed by terror to use their own feet.

"Lisas," Pompey said, "I will not lay hands upon you, but you are no longer welcome in Rome. Tell Ptolemy to send us another ambassador, one with a long list of favors Ptolemy is eager to perform for us." With that, Pompey and his lictors swept out.

Milo looked at me. "Are you ready to go?"

"I'll be along shortly."

Milo left with his lictors. Lisas and I were alone, Lisas looking more like a corpse than a man.

"Lisas, you didn't send those thugs to kill me, did you?"

He shook his head. "It was Silvius; he slipped out after we heard that you had been appointed *iudex*. No one was looking for Silvius at that time. You are too famous for your specialty. I rejoice that they failed."

"Why the crocodile?"

He shrugged. "They came in that morning, and I concealed them as we had agreed. Ateius told me he intended to kill the slave and disfigure him so that the populace would think their tribune was murdered. This would make him safe and throw Rome into turmoil at the same time. I thought, *I have been accused of throwing men to my crocodiles for so long, might it not be amusing to try it?"*

"What will you do now?"

"I must go and compose a letter to my king."

"Why not deliver your message personally?"

He shook his head. "It was such poor timing that you reached the climax of your investigation at the same time the news came from Alexandria. Pompey and the Senate might have been inclined to smooth things over otherwise. Now, as the intermediary, I must take the full blame for how things have fallen out. I am too old for that, and I am tired of life, anyway."

"I shall miss you," I said. He was a strange man, but I couldn't help liking him.

"Leave me now. I hope the balance of your life will be prosperous." He knew better than to hope it would be peaceful.

So I took my leave of Lisas. Word came to us later that he retired to his chambers, wrote out his letter to Ptolemy, and took poison.

THE NEXT DAY, ROME WAS treated to a rare spectacle. The surly crowd assembled for the funeral and riot; then Pompey appeared and exposed Ateius and Silvius to them and explained, with great sarcasm, how they had all been duped. Derisively, he put a torch to the pyre, giving the nameless slave a fine send-off. Then he led the whole mob back to the Forum, where a court was convened and the two men were condemned on all three counts. I gave a summary of my investigation, and Pompey addressed the jury. There was no need for rhetorical flourishes. As Cicero used to say, the facts spoke for themselves.

The men were taken up to the top of the Capitol and hurled from the Tarpeian Rock; then their shattered but still-living bodies were impaled on bronze hooks and dragged down to the Sublician Bridge, where they were cast into the river.

After these odd events Rome settled down like a man trying to wait out a bad hangover. A few weeks later I was elected aedile, and new scandals occupied the attentions of the people. The gods accepted their sacrifices again, and Rome, at least, seemed to be out from under the curse. Not Crassus, though.

For my part, I knew I was going to miss Lisas. He was an amusing companion, he served his king loyally, and he threw the best parties ever seen in Rome.

These things happened in the year 699 of the City of Rome, in the second consulship of Cnaeus Pompeius Magnus and Marcus Licinius Crassus Dives.

GLOSSARY

(Definitions apply to the year 695 of the Republic.)

Arms Like everything else in Roman society, weapons were strictly regulated by class. The straight, double-edged sword and dagger of the legions were classed as "honorable."

The *gladius* was a short, broad, double-edged sword borne by Roman soldiers. It was designed primarily for stabbing.

The *caestus* was a boxing glove, made of leather straps and reinforced by bands, plates, or spikes of bronze. The curved, single-edged sword or knife called a *sica* was "infamous." *Sicas* were used in the arena by Thracian gladiators and were carried by street thugs. One ancient writer says that its curved shape made it convenient to carry sheathed beneath the armpit, showing that gangsters and shoulder holsters go back a long way.

Carrying of arms within the *pomerium* (the ancient city boundary marked out by Romulus) was forbidden, but the law was ignored in troubled times. Slaves were forbidden to carry weapons within the City, but those used as bodyguards could carry staves or clubs. When street fighting or assassinations were common, even senators went heavily armed and even Cicero wore armor beneath his toga from time to time.

Shields were not common in the city except as gladiatorial equipment. The large shield *(scutum)* of the legions was unwieldy in Rome's narrow streets but bodyguards might carry the small shield *(parma)* of the light-armed auxiliary troops. These came in handy when the opposition took to throwing rocks and roof tiles.

Balnea   Roman bathhouses were public and were favored meeting places for all classes. Customs differed with time and locale. In some places there were separate bathhouses for men and women. Pompeii had a bathhouse with a dividing wall between men's and women's sides. At some times women used the baths in the mornings, men in the afternoon. At others, mixed bathing was permitted. The *balnea* of the republican era were far more modest than the tremendous structures of the later empire, but some imposing facilities were built during the last years of the Republic.

Arval Brotherhood   One of Rome's many priestly colleges, the Arvals were twelve men chosen from distiguished senatorial families. Their rituals were obscure, but were concerned with nature and agriculture. Their most important annual ceremony was in honor of Dea Dia, a goddess of fields and crops.

Basilica   A meeting place of merchants and for the administration of justice.

Campus Martius   A field outside the old city wall, formerly the assembly area and drill field for the army, named after its altar to Mars. It was where the popular assemblies met during the days of the Republic.

Centuries   Literally, "one hundred men." From greatest antiquity, Rome's citizens had been organized into centuries for military purposes. They assembled by their centuries for the yearly muster to be assigned to their legions. Since this was a convenient time to hold elections and vote upon important issues, they voted by centuries as well. Each man could cast a vote, but the century voted as a whole. By the late Republic, it was strictly a voting distinction. The legions had centuries as well, though they usually numbered sixty to eighty men.

Chthonian From a Greek word meaning "underworld," the chthonian gods and demons were those of the underworld. Their services were held in the evenings and animals sacrified to them were black. In praying to them, the hands were held out with palms downward.

Circus The Roman racecourse and the stadium that enclosed it. The original, and always the largest, was the Circus Maximus. A later, smaller circus, the Circus Flaminius, lay outside the walls on the Campus Martius.

Compluvium An opening in the roof of a Roman house through which rain fell to be gathered in a basin called the impluvium. Eventually, it became a courtyard with a pool.

Conscript Fathers A form of address used when speaking to the Senate. Cicero used it almost exclusively.

Curule A curule office conferred magisterial dignity. Those holding it were priviledged to sit in a curule chair—a folding camp chair that became a symbol of Roman officials sitting in judgment.

Curia The meetinghouse of the Senate, located in the Forum, also applied to a meeting place in general. Hence Curia Hostilia, Curia Pompey, and Curia Julia. By tradition they were prominently located with position to the sky to observe omens.

Cursus Honorem "Course of Honor": The ladder of office ascended by Romans in public life. The Cursus officer were quaestor, praetor, and consul. Technically, the office of aedile was not part of the Cursus Honorem, but by the late Republic it was futile to stand for praetor without having served as aedile. The other public offices not on the cursus were Censor and Dictator.

Equestrian *Eques* (pl. *equites*) literally meant "horseman." In the early days of the military muster soldiers supplied all their own equipment. Every five years the Censors made a property assessment of all citizens and each man served according to his ability to pay for arms, equipment, rations, etc. Those above a certain minimum assessment became equites because they could afford to supply and feed their own horses and were assigned to the cavalry. By the late Republic, it was purely a property class. Almost all senators were equites by property assessment, but the dictator Sulla made senators a separate class. After his day, the equites were the wealthy merchants, moneylenders, and tax farmers of Rome. Collectively, they were an enormously powerful group, equal to the senators in all except prestige and control of foreign policy.

Families and Names Roman citizens usually had three names. The given name (praenomen) was individual, but there were only about eighteen of them: Marcus, Lucius, etc. Certain praenomens were used only in a single family: Appius was used only by the Claudians, Mamercus only by the Aemilians, and so forth. Only males had praenomens. Daughters were given the feminine form of the father's name: Aemilia for Aemilius, Julia for Julius, Valeria for Valerius, etc.

Next came the nomen. This was the name of the clan (*gens*). All members of a *gens* traced their descent from a common ancestor, whose name they bore: Julius, Furius, Licinius, Junius, Tullius, to name a few. Patrician names always ended in *ius*. Plebeian names often had different endings.

Stirps A subfamily of a *gens*. The cognomen gave the name of the stirps, i.e., Caius Julius Caesar. Caius of the stirps; Caesar of *gens* Julia.

Then came the name of the family branch (cognomen). This name was frequently anatomical: Naso (nose), Ahenobarbus (bronzebeard), Sulla (splotchy), Niger (dark), Rufus (red), Caesar (curly), and many others. Some families did not use cognomens. Mark Antony was just Marcus Antonius, no cognomen.

Other names were honorifics conferred by the Senate for outstanding service or virtue: Germanicus (conqueror of the Germans), Africanus (conqueror of the Africans), Pius (extraordinary filial piety).

Freed slaves became citizens and took the family name of their master. Thus the vast majority of Romans named, for instance, Cornelius would not be patricians of that name, but the descendants of that family's freed slaves. There was no stigma attached to slave ancestry.

Adoption was frequent among noble families. An adopted son took the name of his adoptive father and added the genetive form of his former nomen. Thus when Caius Julius Caesar adopted his great-nephew Caius Octavius, the latter became Caius Julius Caesar Octavianus.

All these names were used for formal purposes such as official documents and monuments. In practice, nearly every Roman went by a nickname, usually descriptive and rarely complimentary. Usually it was the Latin equivalent of Gimpy, Humpy, Lefty, Squint-eye, Big Ears, Baldy, or something of the sort. Romans were merciless when it came to physical peculiarities.

Fasces A bundle of rods bound around with an ax projecting from the middle. They symbolized a Roman magistrate's power of corporal and capital punishment and were carried by the lictors who accompanied the curule magistrates, the *Flamen Dialis*, and the proconsuls and propraetors who governed provinces.

Fetiales A priestly college whose most important duties concerned treaties and war. The Fetiales declared war at a special ceremony, at which one of their number cast a spear into enemy territory. In later years, when enemies were too far away, a piece of ground near their temple was designated enemy territory and the spear was cast into it.

First Citizen In Latin: *Princeps*. Originally the most prestigious senator, permitted to speak first on all important issues and set the order of debate. Augustus, the first emperor, usurped the title in perpetuity. Decius detests him so much that he will not use either his name (by the time of the writing it was Caius Julius Caesar) or the honorific Augustus, voted by the toadying Senate. Instead he will refer to him only as the First Citizen. Princeps is the origin of the modern word "prince."

Floralia A springtime festival in honor of the goddess Flora, in which her protection was invoked on behalf of fruit blossoms. It involved a number of unusual practices. Upper-class women and prostitutes sounded trumpets at one point, and actresses performed nude on stage.

Forum An open meeting and market area. The premier forum was the Forum Romanum, located on the low ground surrounded by the Capitoline, Palatine, and Caelian Hills. It was surrounded by the most important temples and public buildings. Roman citizens spent much of their day there. The courts met outdoors in the Forum when the weather was good. When it was paved and devoted solely to public business, the Forum Romanum's market functions were transferred to the Forum Boarium, the Cattle Market near the Circus Maximus. Small shops and stalls remained along the northern and southern peripheries, however.

Freedman A manumitted slave. Formal emancipation conferred full rights of citizenship except for the right to hold office. Informal emancipation conferred freedom without voting rights. In the second or at least third generation, a freedman's descendants became full citizens.

Friendly Ones "Eumenides." These were the Furies. They were so frightening that it was deemed the worst of luck to pronounce their true name: Erinyes, "Terrible Ones," because speaking their name could attract their attention. Several euphemisms were employed, of which *Friendly Ones* was the most common. The names are Greek, but the Romans used Greek terms in religion the way we use Latin.

Haruspex (pl. Haruspices)   A member of a college of Etruscan professionals who examined the entrails of sacrificial animals for omens.

Imperium   The ancient power of kings to summon and lead armies, to order and forbid and to inflict corporal and capital punishment. Under the Republic, the *imperium* was divided among the consuls and praetors, but they were subject to appeal and intervention by the tribunes in their civil decisions and were answerable for their acts after leaving office. Only a Dictator had unlimited *imperium*.

Impluvium   See compluvium.

Insula   Literally, "island." A detached house or block of flats let out to poor families.

Iudex   An investigating official appointed by a praetor.

Janitor   A slave-doorkeeper, so called for Janus, god of gateways.

Legion   They formed the fighting force of the Roman army. Through its soldiers, the Empire was able to control vast stretches of territory and people. They were known for their discipline, training, ability, and military process.

Lictor   Bodyguards, usually freedmen, who accompanied magistrates and the *Flamen Dialis,* bearing the *fasces*. They summoned assemblies, attended public sacrifices, and carried out sentences of punishment.

Ludus (pl. ludi).   The official public games, races, theatricals, etc. Also training schools for gladiators, although the gladiatorial exhibitions were not *ludi*.

Maiestas   A type of treason, defined as an offence against the majesty of the Roman people. An extremely loose category of crime, *maiestas* was a favorite charge to bring against one's political enemies.

Matronalia A festival celebrated by Roman matrons in honor of Juno.

Munera Special Games, not part of the official calendar, at which gladiators were exhibited. They were originally funeral Games and were always dedicated to the dead.

Mundus An opening into the underworld. there were serveral located around the Mediterranean. They were used for rituals in volving the chthonic deities and to convey messages to the dead.

Municipia Towns originally with varying degrees of Roman citizenship. A citizen from a *municipium* was qualified to hold any public office. An example is Cicero, who was not from Rome but from the *municipium* of Arpinum.

Offices A tribune was a representative of the plebeians with power to introduce laws and to veto actions of the Senate. Only plebeians could hold the office, which carried no *imperium*. Military tribunes were elected from among the young men of senatorial or equestrian rank to be assistants to generals. Usually it was the first step of a man's political career.

A Roman embarked on a political career had to rise through a regular chain of offices. The lowest elective office was quaestor: bookkeeper and paymaster for the Treasury, the Grain Office, and the provincial governors. These men did the scut work of the Empire.

Next were the aediles. They were more or less city managers who saw to the upkeep of public buildings, streets, sewers, markets, and the like. There were two types: the plebeian aediles, and the curule aediles. The curule aediles could sit in judgment on civil cases involving markets and currency, while the plebeian aediles could only levy fines. Otherwise, their duties were the same. They also put on the public Games. The government allowance for these things was laughably small, so they had to pay for them out of their own pockets. It was a horrendously expensive office but it gained the holder popularity like no other, especially if his Games were spectacular. Only a popular aedile could hope for election to higher office.

Third was praetor, an office with real power. Praetors were judges, but they could command armies and after a year in office they could go out to govern provinces, where real wealth could be won, earned, or stolen. In the late Republic there were eight praetors. Senior was the *praetor urbanus,* who heard civil cases between citizens of Rome. The *praetor peregrinus* heard cases involving foreigners. The others presided over criminal courts. After leaving office, the ex-praetors became propraetors and went to govern propraetorian provinces with full *imperium.*

The highest office was consul, supreme office of power during the Roman Republic. Two were elected each year. For four years they fulfilled the political role of royal authority, bringing all other magistrates into the service of the people and the City of Rome. The office carried full *imperium.* On the expiration of his year in office, the ex-consul was usually assigned a district outside Rome to rule as proconsul. As proconsul, he had the same insignia and the same number of lictors. His power was absolute within his province. The most important commands always went to proconsuls.

Censors were elected every five years. It was the capstone to a political career, but it did not carry *imperium* and there was no foreign command afterward. Censors conducted the Census, purged the Senate of unworthy members, and doled out the public contracts. They could forbid certain religious practices or luxuries deemed bad for public morals or generally "un-Roman." There were two Censors, and each could overrule the other. They were usually elected from among the ex-consuls, and the Censorship was regarded as the capstone of a political career.

Under the Sullan Constitution, the quaestorship was the minimum requirement for membership in the Senate. The majority of senators had held that office and never held another. Membership in the Senate was for life unless expelled by the Censors.

No Roman official could be prosecuted while in office, but he could be after he stepped down. Malfeasance in office was one of the most common court charges.

The most extraordinary office was Dictator. In times of emergency, the Senate could instruct the consuls to appoint a Dictator, who could wield absolute power for six months. Unlike all other officials, a Dictator was unaccountable: He could not be prosecuted for his acts in office. The last true Dictator was appointed in the third century B.C. The dictatorships of Sulla and Julius Caesar were unconstitutional.

Patrician   The noble class of Rome.

Perduellio   A serious crime against the state. The difference between *perduellio* and *maiestas* is not always clear.

Plebeian   All citizens not of patrician status; the lower classes, also called "plebs."

Pomerium   The ancient boundary of Rome, marked out by Romulus with his plow. Though by the late Republic Rome had spread far beyond this boundary, it was retained and nothing could be built upon it. The dead could not be buried within the *pomerium*, not could citizens bear arms within it.

Pontifical College   The pontifexes were a college of priests not of a specific god (see Priesthoods) but whose task was to advise the Senate on matters of religion. The chief of the college was the *Pontifex Maximus*, who ruled on all matters of religious practice and had charge of the calendar. Julius Caesar was elected *Pontifex Maximus* and Augustus made it an office held permanently by the emperors. The title is currently held by the Pope.

Popular Assemblies   There were three: the Centuriate Assembly (comitia centuriata) and the two tribal assemblies: *comitia tributa* and *consilium plebis, q.v.*

Populares   The party of the common people.

Princeps: First Citizen   An especially distinguished senator chosen by the Censors. His name was the first called on the roll of the Senate and he was first to speak on any issue. Later the title was usurped by Augustus and is the origin of the word "prince."

Priesthoods In Rome, the priesthoods were offices of state. There were two major classes: *pontifexes* and *flamines*. Pontifexes were members of the highest priestly college of Rome. They had superintendence over all sacred observances, state and private, and over the calendar. Head of their college was the *Pontifex Maximus*, a title held to this day by the Pope. The *flamines* were the high priests of the state gods: the *flamen martialis* for Mars, the *flamen quirinalis* for the deified Romulus, and, highest of all, the *Flamen Dialis,* high priest of Jupiter. The *Flamen Dialis* celebrated the Ides of each month and could not take part in politics, although he could attend meetings of the Senate, attended by a single lictor. Each had charge of the daily sacrifices, wore distinctive headgear, and were surrounded by many ritual taboos.

Another very ancient priesthood was the *rex sacrorum,* "King of Sacrifices." This priest had to be a patrician and had to observe even more taboos than the *Flamen Dialis*. This position was so onerous that it became difficult to find a patrician willing to take it.

Technically, *pontifexes* and *flamines* did not take part in public business except to solemnize oaths and treaties, give the god's stamp of approval to declarations of war, etc. But since they were all senators anyway, the ban had little meaning. Julius Caesar was *pontifex maximus* while he was out conquering Gaul, even though the *pontifex maximus* wasn't supposed to look upon human blood.

Rostra (sing. rostrum) A monument in the Forum commemorating the sea battle of Antium in 338 B.C., decorated with the rams, *rostra*, of enemy ships. Its base was used as an orator's platform.

Sacerdotes A term for priests and priestesses.

Senate Rome's chief deliberative body. It consisted of three hundred to six hundred men, all of whom had won elective office at least once. It was a leading element in the emergence of the Republic, but later suffered degradation at the hands of Sulla.

Sibylline Books   These mysterious books of prophecies were brought to Rome in legendary times and were kept by a college of priests called, in pedantic Roman fashion, the *quinquidecemviri* (the Fifteen Men). In times of extraordinary calamity the Senate could order a consultation of the Sibylline Books. The language was obscure and subject to eccentric interpretation. The prophecies were usually interpreted to mean that the gods wanted a foreign deity brought to Rome. Thus Rome built a temple to Ceres, a goddess of Asia Minor, and others. When the deity was Greek, the rites remained in the Greek rather than the Roman fashion.

Soothsayers   The Roman government used two types: First were the augurs. These were actual officials who belonged to a college and it was a great honor for a Roman to be adopted into the College of Augurs. They interpreted omens involving heavenly signs: lightning and thunder, the flight and other behavior of birds, etc. There were strict guidelines for this, and personal inspiration was not involved. An augur could call a halt to all public business while he watched for omens. The augur wore a special, striped robe called a *toga trabaea* and carried a crook-topped staff called a *lituus,* which survives to this day as a part of the Roman Catholic bishop's regalia.

The second type was the *haruspex* (pl. *haruspices*). These were not officials but professional soothsayers and most were Etruscans. They took omens by examining the livers and other organs of sacrificial animals. Highly educated Romans considered them fraudulent, but the plebs insisted on taking the *haruspices* (the term also referred to the omens themselves) before embarking on any important public project.

Official Roman soothsayers did *not* predict the future, a practice that was, in fact, forbidden by law. Omens were taken to determine the will of the gods *at that time*. They had to be taken repeatedly because the gods could always change their minds.

SPQR Senatus Populusque Romanus.   The Senate and people of Rome. The formula embodying the sovereignty of Rome. It was used on official correspondence, documents, and public works.

Tarpeian Rock   A cliff beneath the Capitol from which traitors were hurled. It was named for the Roman maiden Tarpeia who, according to legend, betrayed the Capitol to the Sabines.

Temple of Saturn   The state Treasury was located in a crypt beneath this temple. It was also the repository for military standards.

Temple of Vesta   Site of the sacred fire tended by the Vestal virgins and dedicated to the goddess of the hearth. Documents, especially wills, were deposited there for safekeeping.

Toga   The outer robe of the Roman citizen. It was white for the upper class, darker for the poor and for people in mourning. The *toga praetexta*, bordered with a purple stripe, was worn by curule magistrates, by state priests when performing their functions, and by boys prior to manhood. The *toga picta*, purple and embroidered with golden stars, was worn by a general when celebrating a triumph, also by a magistrate when giving public games.

Trans-Tiber   A newer district on the left or western bank of the Tiber. It lay beyond the old city walls.

Trebonian law   The *lex Trebonia*, proposed by the Tribune Caius Trebonius, that gave Spain to Pompey, Syria to Crassus, and Gaul and Illyricum to Caesar. One of the more fateful pieces of Roma legislation.

Triumvir   A member of a triumvirate known as the Three Men— a board or college, most famously, the three-man rule of Caesar, Pompey, and Crassus. Later, the triumvirate of Antonius, Octavian, and Lepidus.

Witches   The Romans recognized three types. Most common were *saga*, "wise women" who were simply herbalists and specialists in traditional cures for disease and injury. More ominous were *striga*, true witches ("strega" still means witch in modern Italian). These could cast spells, and had the power of the evil eye, could lay curses, and so forth. Most feared were *venefica* "poisoners." Ancient peoples had a supernatural dread of poison and lumped its use together with sorcery rather than pharmacology. The punishments for poisoning were dreadful even by Roman standards. The Romans associated all forms of witchcraft and magic with the Marsians, a neighbor people who spoke the Oscan dialect.